# Shining Knight

### Gentlemen of Knights
### Book Five

# Elizabeth Johns

DRAGONBLADE
PUBLISHING, INC.

## ARE YOU SIGNED UP FOR DRAGONBLADE'S BLOG?

You'll get the latest news and information on exclusive giveaways, exclusive excerpts, coming releases, sales, free books, cover reveals and more.

Check out our complete list of authors, too!

No spam, no junk. That's a promise!

### Sign Up Here

www.dragonbladepublishing.com

*Dearest Reader;*

*Thank you for your support of a small press. At Dragonblade Publishing, we strive to bring you the highest quality Historical Romance from the some of the best authors in the business. Without your support, there is no 'us', so we sincerely hope you adore these stories and find some new favorite authors along the way.*

*Happy Reading!*

*CEO, Dragonblade Publishing*

# Additional Dragonblade books by Author Elizabeth Johns

## Gentlemen of Knights Series

Duke of Knight (Book 1)
Black Knight (Book 2)
Knight and Day (Book 3)
Dark of Knight (Book 4)
Shining Knight (Book 5)

# PROLOGUE

*Autumn 1811*

O NCE UPON A time, there was a girl.

Not only was she the youngest of five, she was the only girl at that. Eugenia Knight was already different from most ladies of her station. However, being raised by four brothers, without a mother, put her into an entirely different realm. If you counted their neighbor, Graham Tinsley, then she had five brothers. She lovingly referred to them as *the herd*. Having nothing better to do with her, they allowed her to tag along on their adventures, and frankly, treated her like one of the boys.

Eugenia was a hoyden, a minx. But the thing was, she did not have a malicious bone in her body. She was a devilish good sport. She had been a part of Graham's life since…forever. She had always been there when he played with the other Knight siblings, and even though she was by far the smallest, she always kept up. When Graham had left for the diplomatic service, after Oxford, Eugenia had still been a skinny stick with unkempt hair and always a smudge of dirt somewhere.

Graham had been gone for six years. Seeing her now across the ballroom, after returning from Vienna, he had to look twice. Gone was the skinny child, all arms and legs. Now she was beautiful, and the thought made him feel dirty, as if it was incestuous. Eugenia Knight was more like a sister to him than his own, who spent most of her time in Marseille with their mother. What was she now, sixteen? Seventeen? He could not remember. Had she changed so much? Or was the hoyden still wrapped up in this pretty picture?

"You remember Mr. Tinsley, Eugenia?" the Duke of Knighton asked.

"Of course I do, silly," she replied.

The hoyden was definitely still there, Graham thought, trying to repress his laughter. But then she looked up at him and smiled and a warm, uncomfortable tingling rushed through his body—one he instantly recognized as attraction. He was going to hell.

"Would you care to dance, pet?"

She smiled up at him again with those big, blue eyes that she had finally grown into as she leaned forward and whispered, "I hope you've got steel in the toes of your boots."

"Still ungraceful, Genie?"

She jabbed him with her elbow. "Only on the dance floor. Have you ever tried to dance in skirts? Yards and yards and layers and layers of fabric swirling in and out of your legs and under your slippers while you try to remember all the steps and keep rhythm?" She snorted. "If I remain upright, I feel I have succeeded."

Graham could not help but be enchanted. Truly, after years away charming kings and queens, princes and every beauty on the continent, he felt jaded by the callousness of it all. Eugenia was a breath of fresh air. How refreshing it was to be with one so innocent who spoke her mind without artifice.

"Are you returned for good?" Eugenia was asking him. He turned his attention back to her face which was also not quite as it ought to be for a Society miss. It was sun bronzed, with a dusting of freckles beneath her eyes and across her nose.

"I am. Father's health is failing and he asked me to return to help manage the estate."

"Thank goodness," she said in all seriousness, then realized how it must have sounded. The emotions flitted across her face like an open book. "I mean not good that your father's health is failing, but if you are here, then it means I always have someone to dance with!"

He could feel the side of his mouth rise in a smile. "I will always save a dance for you, pet."

She nodded as though there was never any doubt. They were separated by the movements of the dance, and he noticed that a couple of young lieutenants were eyeing her hungrily.

When they rejoined, she was smiling wistfully. Oh, dear. He would have to warn Rowley. For all of the duke's managing ways, he tended not to pay enough attention to Eugenia as a female. He had engaged a governess for her, but Graham feared Eugenia was so comfortable with men that she would not see the sharks in the water.

"I cannot wait to go to London!" Her voice was filled with dreaminess.

"Knighton is taking you for the Season?" Everyone knew Rowley hated London.

"Emma is trying to convince him. He does not believe I will behave myself," she added ruefully.

Graham did his best to keep his face straight, but he must not have succeeded.

"You don't believe it either!" She looked crestfallen.

"I think you can do anything you put your mind to, Genie."

"Thank you. I do not mean to misbehave, truly. It is just that there are so many rules for girls. It is quite unfair!"

Allowing her to run wild in Devonshire was going to haunt Rowley, Graham thought sympathetically. Yet the child was a force of nature and she might have been just as unbroken had her mother lived. A part of Graham hated to see her go to London, where the gardens were perfectly manicured and anything that grew beyond its boundary was immediately plucked. Eugenia was never going to be able to be herself and thrive under those strictures. She needed to be wild and free, growing with nature.

"I agree with you. There are certainly many restrictions on females and particularly for young, unmarried ones."

"Well, I am very glad you are home."

Graham was a bit afraid of what she meant by that, but he was very glad he was not Eugenia's brother in truth. He suspected she would have an overabundance of suitors, if the gleam in those soldiers' eyes was anything to go by. "Just be careful, minx. I should not wish anything to happen to you," he warned as the dance drew to a close.

"Why, Graham, I think that is the nicest thing you have ever said to me!" She laughed musically, but as always, just a little too loudly.

Her smiling candor was like a bright light amongst the cynicism of Society, and he hoped no one would ever snuff it out. As their dance finished and he began the next with Lady Sybil, he watched one of the young lieutenants lead Eugenia from the ballroom. If the governess, and then Rowley, had not gone after her, Graham would have done. Responsibility for Lady Eugenia Knight was not something that could be achieved alone. He was a part of her herd, and he had a feeling it would take every one of them to save her from herself.

# CHAPTER ONE

*Autumn 1813*

EUGENIA GROANED AS she tried to keep her attention on the news-sheet in front of her. She was not feeling quite the thing after consuming a wee bit too much champagne—and perhaps other unknown beverages—at her best friend's wedding breakfast. To be precise, her only friend.

"That is a horrid likeness," Eugenia muttered to herself in the dining room which was quiet and empty now that Sybil had married. Aunt Hambridge always took a tray in her room.

Eugenia forced down a bite of toast to quell her stomach; it threatened to erupt at any moment as the drawing of herself tripping over Sybil's veil mocked her. Sybil had not been looking at her in horror, nor had Lord Darling stared at her thus disdainfully. They had been all solicitousness for her safety. Really, she was only clumsy when she danced...or drank champagne, apparently.

Indeed, the entire day had been most provoking. Eugenia did not know what she was going to do. The only reason she had survived the *ton* thus far without catastrophe was because of Lady Sybil being by her side. Well, and perhaps the small matters of her name and fortune.

Three of her brothers had married and now lived on opposite sides of England, while Felix was soldiering in Spain. Aunt Hambridge was no chaperone at all and Eugenia knew she would be bored out of her mind without Sybil to bear her company. To be sure, Graham would take her riding and driving on occasion, but what was she to do in between? She supposed she would have to grow accustomed to making calls with all of the dowagers and attending boring card parties. Why could she not make lady friends more easily? Now she had no one.

Everything was changing. Her world was collapsing beneath her feet. She snorted as she eyed her ungraceful caricature. Literally, it seemed.

She loved the adventures to be had in London, especially after all those years alone in Devonshire. If only London loved her more. At first, she had relished the excitement—dancing every night, new gowns, attention from gentlemen and ladies alike. Yet, frequently, she was the source of ridicule in the news-sheets. She could not understand why. She was not dashing or glamorous like her brothers or sisters-in-law.

She had attracted loads of attention and hordes of suitors, yes, but not the kind that came up to scratch. She put her head down on her arms on the table, in hope that the room would stop spinning.

"Not feeling too well, this morning, pet?"

Eugenia groaned again. "I did not hear you come in, Graham."

"Of course not. You were too busy wallowing in self-pity and nursing your sore head," he said cheerfully.

"Why are you here?" she snapped, her head still down on the table.

"I thought you might need some company after yesterday."

There was one thing she and Graham had in common and that was the news-sheets' seeming fascination with them. On the one hand, they lived for her mistakes and never missed one, while on the other, he was their darling. Perhaps racing her brother's curricle had not been the wisest choice, but climbing the tree to save a kitten had been necessary. Graham was always portrayed in a good light. She would wager half her dowry that the person drawing the caricatures was a female. There she went again, she reflected, being unladylike and gambling even in her thoughts.

"Why the sour face, Genie?"

She lifted a one-eyed gaze enough to scowl at him. Winfred, the old butler, entered the room and handed a glass to Graham, which he then proceeded to shove under her nose.

"Drink this. Trust me, it will help."

"What is it?" she asked as she eyed it distastefully.

"Do not ask, just drink it. It will help your impaired head."

"Ladies do not get foxed," she muttered, as yet another thing to add to her list of unladylike sins.

"Pinch your nose and down it," he advised.

She did as he said, then gasped at the horror of the taste and burn as the potion went down her throat.

"Now, eat some eggs and bacon and you will be as right as rain in no time," he said as he placed a plate in front of her.

Of one thing she was fairly certain, and that was that what she just drunk was likely to reappear at any moment.

"Eat up, we must not keep the horses waiting," he urged.

"You expect me to ride this morning?"

"We ride every morning, Genie."

"I suppose we do," she acknowledged, after taking a mouthful of coddled eggs. She had not thought he would continue doing so after Sybil was wed, but she was grateful for the company. She managed to swallow down the breakfast and, surprisingly, felt better.

"You already look improved," Graham said, as though reading her mind. "Go and change into your habit. I will meet you at the front entrance."

Eugenia dressed and returned downstairs in less than ten minutes. One thing she had learned, whilst being raised by four brothers, was that they would not wait for her. If she could not be presentable in fifteen minutes or less, it was not worth doing. Now, being in Town and having to wear the latest fashions did not quite fit that mantra, but she still did not fuss over her appearance like most ladies. There were times when she longed for trousers to go riding, but she did like feeling feminine and wearing bright colors.

She smiled at Winfred, who handed her her gloves and riding crop, then opened the door.

"Well, you are very…bright, are you not?" Graham said carefully.

"You do not approve," she answered, trying not to feel disappointed. She loved her new jonquil riding habit with the green trim. Her brothers teased her mercilessly over her dress, but Graham was considered to be the height of fashion amongst the *ton* and it smarted somewhat to know he disapproved. She looked up into his bright green eyes that were much too beautiful to be a man's along with his perfectly chiseled face, golden locks and easy smile. No, she certainly was not envious of his looks or the way that every female in the room stopped to look at him or fall over themselves flirting with him.

"Not at all," he said, lifting her chin with his finger. "You look like a ray of sunshine."

She did not meet his eyes. "You do not have to lie to me, Graham."

"That is one thing I would never do, but this self-pity does not become you."

She looked up at him quickly, with suspicion, ready to argue.

"That's better," he said. His smile told her he had deliberately goaded her.

She turned away, towards her sleek black mare, Cleo, short for Cleopatra. He boosted Eugenia into the saddle as he always did. They walked their horses while they negotiated the morning rush of wagons, carts, and carriages. Really, she was unusually maudlin and she did not like it one bit, and it was too bad of Graham to mention it.

As soon as they crossed into the park near Rotten Row, Eugenia was spoiling for a gallop. Sybil was afraid of horses and they always had to keep to a walk when she was with them. Eugenia glanced over at Graham with a mischievous smile before she let her mare have its head. She heard Graham shout her name, but she only laughed as she leaned over Cleo's mane. Galloping was so exhilarating and the speed made her feel freer than she had in months. From the corner of her eye, she vaguely registered people staring at her and a small warning bell began to jingle in her head.

Was this one of those rules she had forgotten about? She had always lived by the premise that it was better to ask forgiveness later, but Society was extremely unforgiving. It was still not enough for her to slow down before she reached the end ahead of Graham, someone would see and admonish her. She reined in and waited for him, which was not long.

"I assume, by the look on your face, that I did something wrong again. Are you very angry with me?" she asked, as one of the bright flowers from her bonnet flopped down into her face to mock her.

He let out a big sigh. "It is difficult to be angry with you, Genie, and you know I think the rules are ridiculous for gently bred females, but Society is not kind if you flaunt its dictums in its face over and over and over."

"I concede your point. It was an innocent mistake. I truly had forgotten about the rule until I noticed everyone staring at me. We have been riding with Lady Sybil, of course, and it slipped my mind."

"It will not stop the gossip columns from mentioning it."

She groaned for the third time at least that day. It was becoming too much of a habit lately, and she hated to have Graham scold her like a small child. "That means Rowley will hear of it."

"He has eyes and ears everywhere, regardless," Graham muttered. Then he swore as a group of gentleman riders came towards them.

She recognized several of them as friends of Graham and her brother Heath. Lord Perth was one of Emma, the Duchess's, cousins.

"Capital seat there, Lady Eugenia," Sir Martin Hardy said appreciatively.

"Do not encourage her."

"I am right here, thank you," Eugenia said, tired of being treated like a petulant child. So what if she had the memory of a wigeon. She was not hurting anyone else!

"Are any of your brothers coming back to Town soon?" Perth asked.

"They are not," she answered curtly, turning to Tinsley. "And I absolve you of playing my nursemaid, Graham." She turned her mare around and galloped back from whence she came, leaving the group of them behind.

⟫⟫⟪⟪

PETERSHAM WHISTLED. "I do not think she appreciated you speaking of her like a child."

"She is certainly not a child," Hardy remarked—rather too warmly for Graham's liking.

"She needs to stop behaving like one if she does not wish to be treated like one," he snapped.

"It is hardly an irredeemable quality to gallop," Petersham argued.

"Does she deliberately flout the rules?" Perth asked.

"That is the devil of it. She seems to forget them. Thankfully, she has the beauty, connections and name to keep her from complete censure. Knighton will still hold me responsible, however, if anything happens to her. He asked me to look after her."

"She is not your kin," Sir Martin pointed out unhelpfully.

"She might as well be," Graham retorted.

"Is that the way the wind blows?" Perth asked. "I was thinking about courting her myself."

"Not at all. She might as well be my sister."

"Then to whom do we apply for permission to address her? You or

Knighton?"

Much though Graham hated to admit it, Perth was an excellent choice for Eugenia. He was of an age with Knighton and was cousin to the duchess. Knighton would very likely welcome the match. Graham would be delighted to have her off his hands too, would he not? He turned his horse about to follow after Eugenia. "If you are serious, I would write to Knighton. I have no objection."

"I will call on her this afternoon, then," the earl remarked.

Graham doffed his hat and took off after his wayward charge. Why did he suddenly feel so unsettled?

He dismounted in front of his town residence, which was only two houses away from that belonging to Lady Hambridge. He handed his mount to a groom and then walked up to Hambridge House to have a word with Eugenia.

"My lord," Winfred greeted him as he opened the door.

"I wish for a word with Lady Eugenia."

"Unfortunately, my lord, she requested that she be left undisturbed." The butler looked most uncomfortable. Graham could press the issue—he had been charged with protecting Eugenia as much as Lady Hambridge, who was chaperone in name only. However, he did not feel like arguing with her just now. Her feelings were hurt and much though he was aware she did not wish to hear it, she needed to live within certain boundaries whilst in Town.

"Very well, Winfred, I will abide by her wishes...on this occasion." He had little doubt that Eugenia could hear his words. He left and walked back to his own house.

Perhaps he should write to Rowley and encourage a match with Perth. For the entire previous Season, he had discouraged every fortune hunter who came sniffing at Eugenia's skirts. But Perth was an earl with a vast fortune and also a bit of a dull dog. Perhaps that was exactly what Eugenia needed.

He sighed heavily. It was not yet noon and he was already exhausted. He supposed he should write to Knighton before he received the news-sheets and read of more of Eugenia's antics. During her come-out Season, having Lady Sybil by Eugenia's side had mediated most of the chit's impulses to do things before properly considering, but this morning was a perfect example of her needing someone to watch over her. Graham had not minded doing so from a distance, but he could hardly sit in her pocket all the time without causing a great deal of remark or even ruining her reputation. The Knight brothers considered him one of the family, but Society would talk, and much though it pained him to admit it, it was time he found his own wife. He did not know of many gently-bred females who would want him tagging along like a puppy behind another eligible lady whilst he was trying to woo them.

And for all of Eugenia's mischievousness, she was still extremely eligible. He had overheard more conversations and betting about the youngest Knight sibling than he would care to recall. Many of the men believed they could tame her once she was leg-shackled and many did not care about her eccentric behavior so long as they had her dowry and connections.

He ran his hand over his face. He hated the thought of Eugenia being forced to conform into a stuffy Society lady, but what could he do? Unless the duke and duchess or one of the sisters-in-law were willing to come to London to take her in hand, it was all that was left. For the past year, he and the brothers had deflected more than a dozen offers from unsuitable gentlemen, yet they had done nothing to facilitate a proper match.

He sat down at his desk, pulled out a sheet of paper and dipped his quill in the standish, but the words were difficult in taking form on the page.

*Dear Knighton,*

*I believe the time has come. I further believe Perth will be applying to you shortly and I can see no objections.*

*Your servant,*
*Tinsley*

There was no need to be verbose. Knighton would know exactly what he meant. This week's worth of news-sheets would arrive at approximately the same time as this letter. He expected the duke to arrive post haste. Eugenia would not be delighted with the news, but she had had a year to make a proper choice and had proven she needed a little push.

He sanded the letter and folded it, stamping his seal down into the hot wax. He sat staring at the window that overlooked the park for some time, feeling morose and somewhat guilty, as if he were betraying Eugenia. But it was what he would have to do for his own sister one day, he supposed.

A flash of a colorful bonnet flew by his window with a maid trailing behind.

He cursed and then scurried from his study to the front door, barely grasping his hat as Wallace held it out to him. Where the devil was she going now, trying to hurry in front of his window? Eugenia was tall enough that she had to be bending down in order to pass as she had. She knew very well it was his house.

Had he not been in his study, writing to her brother, it was unlikely he would have seen her. Now he was obligated to follow her. At least she had had the forethought to take her maid along.

She crossed the street into the park, walking with long strides like a man. He followed discreetly behind, but if she bothered to look at her surroundings, she would see him.

Graham wondered if Knighton completely understood that their Aunt Hambridge was too old, too lazy or too tired—or, whatever the reason, was hardly fit to properly chaperone a young lady with so much energy. He lingered in the shadows and hid behind trees until he watched Eugenia sit down on a bench near the lake and begin to toss crumbs of bread to some eager ducks.

He relaxed and wondered why she had felt the need to slip by his house as though she were going to a clandestine meeting.

She began muttering to herself, which made him smile. He went as close as he dared and tried to eavesdrop but it appeared she did have the ability to speak somewhat quietly. Perhaps he was not being fair. Eugenia had made strides in being a lady, he thought, as he watched the serene beauty of her innocently tossing bread. But when she did have a lapse, it was always on a grand scale. Rowley had paid off several of the news-sheets during the past Season, in order to prevent some things from being printed, but Eugenia could not continue to escape—as witnessed by the cartoon that morning.

Two little boys and their nurse came close to where Eugenia sat on the bench. One was flying a kite, and the other was very interested in the ducks. Eugenia smiled at the child and handed some of her bread to him.

The nurse, seeing that one of her charges was safe enough for the moment, went off after the boy with the kite. Of course, that was when the other boy took alarm as the ducks begin giving chase… straight into the water.

Graham immediately ran after the boy, who seemed to sink straight down, but he need not have bothered. Eugenia was already in the water. The lake was not deep, but deep enough to cover the boy's head, and it was covered with a disgusting layer of effluent, besides frigid.

Having been raised with brothers, of course she knew how to swim, and she emerged with the boy in her arms choking and spluttering water while crying for his nurse.

Waiting on the bank, Graham took the boy from her arms and walked to the bench with him. A crowd had gathered as if from nowhere. He looked about for the nurse, who finally seemed to realize something had gone amiss and ran back to comfort her charge.

He looked around for Eugenia, who was…why the devil was she

still in the filthy water?

He hurried back over to her. "What are you doing in there? You will catch your death!" he scolded. Teeth chattering, she had her arms wrapped about her huddled and shivering body.

"Go away, you are drawing attention to me," she snapped.

"Not until I help you out."

"I am waiting for the crowd to leave," she replied with an exasperated look that indicated he was lacking understanding.

"Oh. Oh." At least she had had the wherewithal to realize she might be indecent. He began removing his coat. "Where is your maid?"

Eugenia had the ability to look guilty even while she was soaked through and shaking from cold. "She is visiting her beau."

"Your maid will be lucky if she is alive when Rowley is finished with her." He wrapped his coat around her and then pulled her from the water as onlookers gaped.

"How brave you were, rescuing that little boy," he said, loudly enough for everyone to hear, while praying that no one of their acquaintance was nearby.

# Chapter Two

EUGENIA WAS STILL shaken from her ordeal—a child could have drowned—and decided to use this as an excuse to stay at home and not attend the Everleigh ball that night. She huddled into a blanket near the fire while her hair dried and tried to warm from the inside out.

The worst part was, Graham had not even said anything to her. He had helped her home without troubling to find her aunt, and had directed the servants to prepare her a warm bath. Besides the fact that misfortune seemed to plague her no matter her best intentions, how had Graham been at the same place at the same time? He always seemed to be there when trouble found her. Yet what else could she have done?

A soft knock on her door broke her trance-like musings. The door opened and her aunt Hambridge looked inside wearing a puce gossamer satin. "May I come in?"

"Of course," she answered, still feeling a bit nervy on the inside.

Her aunt came inside and took the chair near her by the fire. She was dressed for the ball that Eugenia had decided not to attend.

"Would you care to tell me what happened?"

That surprised Eugenia. "You have not heard?"

"Only a disjointed version from the servants."

Eugenia put her forehead on her knees; she had drawn them up before her. "Trying to be someone I am not is exhausting. I shared some bread with a little boy to feed the ducks. They all went after him and he became frightened and fell into the water. I went in after him when it was apparent he could not swim. That is all."

Her aunt stared into the fire. "Perhaps it is time you sought a husband."

Eugenia's head popped up and her jaw snapped open. "That is all you have to say? Not, are you unharmed? How lovely that you saved a child from drowning."

Aunt Hambridge waved her hand. "Yes, all of those things, my dear, but you must see that you will be portrayed somehow as having caused the incident, not to mention looking indecent, with your gown clinging to you. I fear you must find a husband soon before you acquire a reputation for notoriety."

"I cannot believe we are having this conversation," Eugenia muttered.

"I agree it is not fair, but once you are married and start begetting babies, all of this will go away."

"My pension for accidents?" she asked doubtfully.

"That and your restlessness. You are bored and lonely with Sybil now gone."

Well, that was true. "But there is no one I wish to marry," she argued. "I will simply return to the country if my presence is so embarrassing."

"Sulking does not become you. Now, hasten and dress for the Everleigh ball."

Had she not heard that more than once today? She wanted to sulk. "I do not feel like going."

"Neither do I, my dear, but we will go and if there is any talk of this afternoon's mishap in a negative light then we can correct the story."

"I am chilled and wish to sleep. One night away from parties will not make a difference."

"It will make all the difference. I will have some tea sent to you while you dress. And Lord Perth called while you were out. He wished you to save him the first waltz."

"I imagine Emma instigated this."

"Even so, it will do good to be seen dancing with him," Aunt Hambridge replied.

Perth was nice, Eugenia supposed, but she always felt a little uncomfortable with him. He was too perfect.

Her aunt stood and left the room while Eugenia threw her head back and moaned. If only there was a suitor her family would approve of, or who would accept her as she was. Unfortunately, outspoken and outlandish was not à la mode, but it was who she was.

Her maid entered the room bearing a tea tray and looking repentant. She was a pretty ginger-haired girl, much of an age with Eugenia.

"I beg your pardon, my lady. I did not mean to abandon you this afternoon."

"Nonsense, Stevens. Trouble seems to find me. Spending a few minutes with your beau is not criminal when I gave permission."

She let out a snort. "Mr. Tinsley seemed to think so, but at least he did not dismiss me."

"He does not have that authority," Eugenia snapped, just refraining from stamping her foot.

She accepted a cup of tea from the maid, who then went to pull out some gowns from the dressing room. "This is the only one I have pressed except for the violet one, but that is not suitable." She held out a white gown bedecked with lace and ruffles.

Eugenia was sick of white and ruffles and looking like a doll. Really, did the maid not know better than to bait her? Bold was precisely what she wanted. She scowled and waved it away.

Stevens shook her head. "As you will, my lady," she said politely, although the look on her face said she thought Eugenia was overstepping yet again.

"I am sick of wearing white, Stevens."

"Yes, miss."

It was just a dress and it was her favorite color. Besides, it was her birth date – not that anyone had bothered to remember. This was her favorite dress, and she had been saving it for a special occasion. If she had to go to a ball when she would rather stay at home, then at least she could comfort herself by wearing something she liked for once.

Stevens dressed her hair and then slipped the purple silk gown over Eugenia's head. She actually felt feminine and pretty in the gown, despite the *ton* thinking her an ungraceful tomboy. Tonight she would prove them wrong.

She descended the staircase and heard her aunt gasp. "You look beautiful, niece, but are you certain you wish to be so bold?"

"Is that a rhetorical question?" she answered.

Aunt Hambridge shook her head. "We are too late to change." They started out of the door and her aunt stopped. She returned to her sitting room and brought out a few wrapped parcels. "These are for your birthday, my dear. I forgot to give them to you earlier, but I think you will wish to have them now."

Eugenia's heart warmed at being remembered. She quickly opened the note attached to a slender package.

*Genie,*

*These were Mother's. I think it time for you to have them. I hope your day was all that you hoped. Your loving brother,*

*Rowley*

If he only knew. With a huff, she opened the gift to find a beautiful diamond necklace and matching earrings.

Rowley had not thought her mature enough for such a gift before. Her eyes filled with tears as Aunt Hambridge helped her put them on. Perhaps, if her brother was beginning to believe in her, then maybe

Society would too.

GRAHAM DID NOT mind balls and dancing like some of his acquaintances. He did not even mind dancing with the young maidens. He only had one rule – he only waltzed with married ladies, widows, or family. Eugenia was considered family. He had always been good at charming people – hence his natural abilities as a diplomat. Besides, he had made that unspoken promise to Eugenia before her come out that he would always dance with her.

Tonight was the Everleigh ball – one of the largest of the Season. It would be a crush, yet still it would be noted if one did not attend. Part of him wondered if Eugenia would be there after the afternoon's incident. He could tell it had shaken her. Yet, she was a good sport and generally did not seem to let things upset her. He wondered if she simply forgot things she did not think mattered, ergo, her gallop along Rotten Row. Had that truly been this morning? It had been quite a day and it was not yet over. He closed his eyes as his valet tied his neckcloth, hoping the ball would be uneventful. He had not realized what a calming influence Lady Sybil had been on Eugenia until it was left solely to himself to rescue her and put out the ensuing fires.

By the time he arrived at the ball, it was as crowded as he had suspected. After greeting the hosts, he looked around the room, glittering in the candlelight, and breathed in the fresh fragrance of hothouse flowers mixed with the odor of warm bodies. The terrace doors were open, but it did little to mitigate the heat. His gaze strayed past acquaintances and the rainbow of brightly colored gowns twirling about on the floor. It was already the second set. Where were Lady Hambridge and Eugenia? Graham frowned inwardly. Perhaps Eugenia had taken a chill, but he could not remember her ever before being sickly or catching any complaint.

He would call on her tomorrow. Perth, Sir Martin Hardy and Petersham were chatting near the terrace doors, and Graham made his way towards them.

"Evening, Tinsley," Perth said cordially. "Is Lady Eugenia to be here tonight? I had thought to begin my courtship in earnest."

"I have not yet seen her. I assumed she would be here." He toyed with mentioning the incident at the park, but thought better of it. Perth was high in the instep, and he might take the situation out of context. Graham secretly hoped the story remained quiet. He had not been able to discover anyone of their acquaintance who had witnessed it.

"Look at that, by Jove," Sir Martin Hardy said appreciatively, looking over Graham's shoulder. It was probably just the dashing widow Winslow, who was fond of grand entrances, but Graham turned anyway.

He glanced over and then immediately had to take a second look. "Eugenia?" he asked, as a whisper mostly to himself. She looked different...lovely.

"That is Lady Eugenia," Perth remarked. "Excuse me, gentlemen. I mean to have a dance before there are none left to have."

Graham heard him, but was rather slow to follow as he tried to comprehend the image before him. He had known she was beautiful, in the same way that all the Knights were beautiful with their dark coloring, but he had never seen her look so exquisite. She wore a gown that was both bold in color and the cut. If he had had doubts about her womanhood before, they were all gone. As he walked towards her and Lady Hambridge, who had immediately escorted her niece towards the dowager's circle, Eugenia was already surrounded by gentlemen. That was nothing new, but the way she was being ogled was.

He waited patiently in line, though there were a few young bucks he would be happy to send on their merry way. When at last he reached her side, she did not have her usual welcoming smile.

"What is the matter, pet?"

She looked sideways at him, like she did when she was annoyed. The strains of a waltz began in the background and he held out his arm to her. "Shall we have our dance?"

"I believe this is my waltz, my lady?" Perth said from behind him simultaneously.

For some reason, Graham felt betrayed and gave her an arch look. "This is always my dance."

"I told you this morning I absolved you of your obligations," she said as she placed her hand in Perth's.

Graham stood there for a moment in disbelief and watched as she smiled up at Perth while he drew her close for the dance.

Unaccountable anger swept through him and he was glad he had not yet asked anyone else to dance, for he escaped the ballroom, no longer in the mood for company. Let Lady Hambridge do her duty, for how much trouble could Eugenia get into at a ball? This was Eugenia, he reminded himself. She could get into trouble anywhere. He had done his fair share of watching over her. He did not wish to stay there and watch men pine after her, looking the way she did that night.

Thankfully, the hosts were no longer at the door, so his hasty retreat would not be remarked upon.

He stopped at the door, no doubt confusing the butler. What he should do, Graham mused, was go inside and start looking for his own bride. He smiled at the majordomo—who kept his face impassive— then made an about face and slipped back into the room.

The sound of Eugenia's laughter rose to his ears. Turning his back on the tinkling notes, he looked over to the wallflowers, who were lining the wall, and marched straight towards them. He found the most frumpy, spotted one and begged a dance. Thankfully, he remembered her name. He led her to the floor. Perhaps she would have a surprising wit and he could find a bride amongst the over-looked.

"Are you enjoying yourself, Miss Crittenden?"

She looked at his neckcloth, a crease between her brows. He realized she was counting. He stopped asking questions. At least it was easier that way.

He caught Eugenia's look of surprise when she saw him waltzing with someone else and he smiled his grandest smile, truly enjoying himself. It was hard not to laugh when Eugenia tripped over Perth's feet, but he was amused nevertheless.

When the waltz ended, he delivered Miss Crittenden to her chaperone and selected the next neglected young lady for a quadrille, then the next for a cotillion.

He stopped short of dancing the supper dance, having his own limits. He rejoined his friends and noticed Farnsworth leading Eugenia in for the meal.

"It looks like Lady Eugenia will finish this Season wed," Petersham said, patting Graham on the back. "She has led you a merry dance. Do you think Knighton knows how much he owes you?"

Perth was watching Farnsworth with Eugenia, to all appearances not paying their conversation any mind.

"Do you think you have a chance?" Sir Martin asked Perth.

"He could almost be her grandfather," Perth scoffed.

Graham coughed into his hand. "You could almost be her father."

"But he is a duke. Ladies go crack-brained to be a duchess," Sir Martin argued.

"I do not think Eugenia gives a fig for a title," Graham interjected. "She is the least pretentious person I have ever met."

"At least one would never grow bored being married to her. It would almost be like marrying one of the fellows. She can ride, shoot and play billiards," Sir Martin said wistfully. "'Tis too bad she wouldn't look at the likes of me, come to think of it... but I won't poach your territory, Perth."

Perth frowned at that. Good. "She is not my territory—yet, any-way—but I am glad to hear it," he said dryly.

"May the best man win." Petersham held up his glass and took a drink. "I imagine the betting books will be in a frenzy after tonight."

Graham chewed on his lobster patty but it tasted like dust. Eugen-ia's name being in the betting books was nothing new, of course, but this was the first time she had had any suitors he would take seriously.

They finished their meal and began to make their way back to the ballroom. Petersham and Martin made their excuses, since they were leaving for their club. No doubt to start the betting, Graham reflected dourly.

Perth went off to dance again and Graham thought he might just go home. He toyed with speaking to Eugenia, but he had little doubt she had given all her dances away by then if she had not bothered to save their usual dance. She could not have forgotten, since they had danced the first waltz since she came to Town two years ago.

"I think she might take, after all," a lady's voice said beside him. He looked down to see Lady Hambridge watching Eugenia proudly.

"I never doubted she would take. I only hope he is worthy of her."

Graham bowed before the lady and took his leave. It did not seem Eugenia needed him after all.

# CHAPTER THREE

S OME THINGS FELT different this Season. Eugenia felt different. Surely it could not be simply a matter of changing her wardrobe? Bolder colors and a little more daring cut were all it took to bring on more serious suitors? Were men really so shallow or visual that they could not see beyond the color white? Apparently so. Suddenly, gentleman who she knew her brothers would approve of were calling on her and asking for dances. In a way, she missed the younger, more frivolous bucks because their expectations were low. With those of the stature of Lord Perth and the Duke of Farnsworth, it seemed as though her every word and action were to be scrutinized. Did they not know her reputation?

She had danced Graham's normal waltz with Perth, and she had been surprised by the hurt she'd seen on Graham's face. She would have expected him to be relieved. Perth was of an age with Rowley—around ten years her senior. He was certainly handsome, but seemed a bit fastidious. She feared she would constantly disappoint him, but perhaps he could guide her better in the ways of the ton. That was a ridiculous notion, and she knew it inside. However, she would give the earl more time in order to know him better. He was Emma's cousin and had stood by the duchess when scandal had threatened to ruin her.

The Duke of Farnsworth was approaching, presumably to claim

the second waltz of the evening, which was also the supper dance. There was something about him that was comforting in a paternal sort of way. If she remembered correctly, he had been married twice and had daughters who were older than her. What would he want with her? Perhaps he was simply dancing with her as a friend of her family. He had been friends with her father and had visited The Grange when she was but a babe.

"Lady Eugenia." He bowed low over her hand.

"Your Grace." She curtsied low.

He led her to the dance floor and immediately she felt at ease. His scent of sandalwood made her think of her father. Farnsworth was still quite handsome and fit, for a man of his age, but surely he did not wish to court her?

"You have grown into a beautiful young woman, Eugenia," he said, interrupting her thoughts.

*Oh, dear.*

"I will be frank with you, as you must wonder why I have sought you out."

She held her tongue, for once.

"You probably know that I have been married twice and have failed to produce any sons. There are few ladies of a childbearing age who I consider eligible. I realize I am quite old for you, but it would be an amicable arrangement."

*For who?* Was he proposing? "I do not know what to say, Your Grace."

"You do not need to say anything yet. Allow me to court you for a few weeks and consider whether or not you could be happy with me. Why the frown? Have I surprised you, my dear?"

She met his kind gaze. "You are not the first man to say that to-night."

"Have you already someone in mind? Your brother indicated you were unattached."

"Knighton did?"

"Indeed. I went to Devonshire to ask his permission."

"Gracious heavens," she whispered breathlessly, quite at a loss. Why had Rowley said nothing to her about this? He had always led her to believe she could choose her spouse, yet he had never given his permission to any of the other gentleman who had asked.

Thankfully, the dance ended, although she still had to endure supper with this man. He left her at a table while he went to fill her a plate. She reminded herself that she had felt comfortable with him before he had begun speaking of marriage. She tried to put aside her misgivings and determined to be cordial. Unfortunately, her thoughts were in a muddle and it felt as though the walls were closing in on her. Perhaps she was just too tired after the day's adventures.

"Have I shocked you?" the duke asked kindly when he brought a plate of food full of lobster patties, ham, cheeses and fruits back for her.

"A little," she confessed honestly.

"You will have to forgive my boldness, then. As the daughter and sister of a duke, I am certain you understand we act with decisiveness. When we see something we want, we take measures to acquire it."

At this moment, she felt like an object instead of a person. Nonetheless, she did understand and she was not certain that was how she wished to live her life. "I do appreciate, sir, and I am not at all convinced I am suited to be a duchess. If you were not aware, I have a tendency to get into scrapes."

"Knighton warned me of your tendencies, but I do not think there is any harm in you. It will be good for our children to have a spirited mother."

Eugenia felt sick. What could she say to that? It was the truth, and it seemed they were being honest with each other.

Eugenia's glanced across the room and met Tinsley's gaze. The lot of his friends were looking over at her. Were they discussing her? Did they know Farnsworth's intentions? Eugenia's heart squeezed at the thoughts of Graham being privy to this with her brother. No, squeezed was too mild a term. It felt more like a stab of betrayal. She caught herself glaring and forced herself to turn and smile at Farnsworth.

"Do I take it some of those gentlemen are courting you? At least two of them have been shooting daggers at me since we entered the supper hall."

She opened her mouth to deny it, but then thought better of it. "Yes."

"Then I shall endeavor to win your favor. Please know that my offer stands until you tell me nay. Shall I lead you back to Lady Hambridge?"

"Yes, thank you."

"I shall call on you tomorrow. If you would like to go on a drive or to one of the museums, I will be at your service."

She forced a smile she did not feel and curtsied to him.

"Well, my dear, you are making some rather grand conquests," her aunt said, beaming.

"Is that what it was?" For some reason Eugenia did not feel very grand. "Is Tinsley leaving?" Her eyes followed Graham as he left the ballroom.

"Yes, I believe so. Perth is one of the catches of the Season now that he is looking for a wife. I had not thought Farnsworth intended to marry again, but I had thought there were nephews," her aunt continued.

Eugenia could not bear to say the words that he had offered for her, because it made them feel more real. "Rowley gave his permission to the duke," she managed to admit, knowing her aunt would understand.

"Did he, now?" She knew as well as Eugenia that Rowley had not approved of anyone previously. "I wonder why, but I am sure he has his reasons. Perth has also applied to him. At least you will have good choices, my dear. Both men are of impeccable lineage and reputation."

*Unlike me,* she thought. "May we go home? I do not feel much like dancing anymore."

Her aunt looked keenly at her. "Perhaps the afternoon's events took more of a toll than I realized. You have certainly met your obligations tonight. Is there any partner you need to make an excuse to?"

Eugenia shook her head. "No. I saved the last just in case."

Why had she said that out loud? That she had hoped Graham would apologize and ask her to dance?

Mayhap it was only the fact she felt at odds with him that was affecting her spirits. He had always been there to talk to; to give advice in a non-prosy way and laugh with her at her mishaps. She shook her head as they climbed into the waiting carriage. There was a hollow feeling in her chest, left by his absence, even as his scolding words from that morning came back to her. He needed to realize she was no longer a child and, hopefully, that did not mean they could no longer be friends.

A tear escaped and rolled down her cheek. She was grateful for the darkness. Growing up was a cursed business. Besides being allowed to behave independently, it seemed she was going to have to make some difficult choices. What she would not give to go back to that morning and start again! Now was when she needed his advice more than ever. Graham had always been easier to talk to than her brothers, except Edmund. And now she was facing one of the biggest decisions of her life.

THE NEXT MORNING, Graham could not decide if he should call on Eugenia to go riding or not. He had known her since the cradle and this enmity really disturbed him.

She had made it clear she did not wish for him to protect her like a brother, but could they not still be friends? That decided him. He would go on as though nothing had changed between them. That is what he would do for his own sister, would he not?

He gathered his whip and hat and stopped at Lady Hambridge's mansion before sending a groom for the horses. He was not completely certain of how Eugenia would behave that morning. Winfred let him into the house.

"Good morning, sir."

"Good morning, Winfred." Graham began walking to the breakfast room, as he had every day for almost two years.

"Lady Eugenia is not here, sir."

Graham spun about. "She is not here?" He refrained from pulling out his pocket watch. He knew very well how early it was.

"She has gone riding with Lord Perth this morning."

That was the second time in less than four-and-twenty hours that Perth had taken away what had always been his. He tried not to examine his anger while in front of the old butler.

"Very good. She must have forgotten to send word."

Graham left and headed for the mews. He was perfectly capable of riding by himself and there was every chance his friends were already in the park as well. Certainly, he was not going to see Eugenia and Perth flirting. The thought made him ill—just as it would if someone were flirting with his sister, of course.

Thinking of siblings, he reflected, it would be another week before Knighton could reach London. One more week and then Graham would be free. He would not take up this obligation again for thousands of pounds.

As he mounted Xerxes and headed for the park, he realized he had not even thought to check the news-sheets that morning. Although he assumed Perth would know if Eugenia had been credited with something scandalous and in that case would have cried off from the ride. Graham was hopeful as he crossed the street and headed for the riding path. As he urged Xerxes to a healthy canter, he did feel somewhat guilty about the contretemps with Eugenia yesterday. He could take off on his mount as hard as he wanted to go and no one would say a word. As he rode, he nodded to a few acquaintances, but he did not see Perth or Eugenia anywhere.

Petersham and Sir Martin would doubtless arrive shortly, so Graham continued a circuit around the park, keeping an eye out. There were not many places in London to ride, and Perth was a high stickler, so Graham had no idea where they could be.

He made a full circle of the park before he ran into Petersham and Hardy. "Good morning, gentlemen. Have you seen Lady Eugenia and Perth?"

They cast glances at each other.

"What is it?"

"He is... ah... letting her drive his phaeton."

"Eugenia is quite handy with the ribbons. Why the look?" Suddenly, images of her racing her brothers across the open spaces at The Grange flashed into his mind, but surely Perth would not allow her to go tooling through Hyde Park in such a fashion. There had been that curricle race when she had very first come to London, but Graham had been able to join her so that it did not appear so scandalous. Perth was a member of the Four-Horse Club, however, and perhaps he would approve of a wife who was a notable whip. There had been a few ladies who had driven phaetons around the park, but usually they were not young, fresh-faced debutantes.

"Are you going to tell me?"

Petersham inclined his head. "You can see for yourself."

A sick feeling in the pit of Graham's stomach preceded the visual assault on his eyes. There she was, high in the phaeton... except there were two of them and she wasn't driving. Thank God.

"The devil, you say! I do believe they are racing!" Hardy exclaimed.

It appeared that the Duke of Farnsworth and Perth were racing through Hyde Park.

"Hell has frozen over," Petersham muttered.

Perth was their friend, but he was very upstanding.

"Is this about winning Eugenia's hand?" Graham looked at Petersham and Hardy for answers because he was utterly dumbfounded. He received a blank stare and a Gallic shrug for answers.

As they passed, Eugenia gave a smile and a wave.

"They are going to kill someone," he remarked.

"I never, ever would have bet on the chances of that happening. Should we see who won?" Hardy asked, already leading his horse in that direction to follow. "Fifty on Perth?" Hardy called to Petersham.

"Why not?" he returned and followed Hardy.

As they made their way in the trail of dust behind the two racing vehicles, Graham could only shake his head. If there was any consolation to be had, at least Eugenia had not been driving.

When the little party caught up with the carriages, Graham could hear a great deal of laughter, so at least it seemed to be amicable.

"Who won?" Sir Martin asked.

"Farnsworth, by a hair," Perth said, half grudgingly. "Only because the fair lady distracted me."

"That is a most ungentlemanly thing to say," she said, giving him a teasing nudge on the arm.

"That was an easy fifty," Petersham goaded Sir Martin.

Farnsworth chuckled. "I do declare I have not done anything like that in ages. Perhaps not since your father and I raced to Brighton," he said to Eugenia.

And this was how he thought to woo her? "What was the inspiration for such a display in the park, may I ask?" Graham sounded like a prude even to his own ears.

"Why, for the honor of escorting Lady Eugenia to the Oglesby garden party tomorrow."

They had all lost their minds. Graham was the last person to preach propriety, but such a caper was just not done and he could not believe a duke and an earl would risk her reputation like this. He at last met Eugenia's gaze, which she seemed to have been avoiding. The defiant glare she shot at him was as though she were daring him to scold her. There would be no satisfaction from that quarter today. Knighton was the one who had given Farnsworth permission to court her, and Perth was a relation.

Graham no longer felt in the mood to be riding. He tipped his hat without a word and turned his horse to leave. He rode to his club and decided he had also lost his mind. However, when he arrived, the news had already reached the hallowed doors of White's.

Bets were being placed left and right over which man would win her hand. Graham could not shut his ears. Perth had a slight edge because he was younger, but Farnsworth was not far behind because being a duchess apparently outweighed almost everything else.

"What would she think of a mere viscount?" he drawled to himself.

"What's that, Tinsley?" Hardy asked, apparently having followed him there in order to place his own bets. "If you have any private information, help a friend out. I just lost fifty quid to Petersham, after all."

Graham could point out that he could abstain from wagering all together, but it would be a waste of breath.

"Your name is falling to the bottom, Tinsley," someone called out from amongst the crowd around the famous book.

"My name?"

"Did you not know you were in the lead until the ball last night?" Lord Ravenhill asked, also appearing from out of nowhere.

"That is appalling."

"I could think of a thousand worse things than being shackled to such a tasty morsel," Ravenhill baited him unmercifully.

"You are about to taste my fist instead," Graham growled.

The weasel held up his hands and backed away. "I think he doth protest too much. Perhaps I will put my money back on Tinsley," he shouted over the din, but fortunately for him, far enough away from Graham's fist.

Graham sat down with a groan and ran his hands through his hair. Petersham placed a glass in his hand as he gave him a look laced with amusement.

"*Et tu?*"

Petersham gave a casual shrug. "You do seem a bit out of sorts about Perth and Farnsworth."

"Only because I want her to be happy."

"And they cannot make her so?"

"It is not logical, I know," Graham admitted as he tossed back the brandy. "Perhaps it is just too sudden."

"For her or for you?"

Graham smiled. "That is not amusing."

"I think Ravenhill might be correct. You protest too much. You did mention you would need to find a wife soon. Perhaps the one you seek is right in front of you."

Graham did not bother to reply. The thought of he and Eugenia married was preposterous. She was as good as a sister to him, and he'd as good as sworn to protect her...not claim her as his own.

# CHAPTER FOUR

THE NEXT MORNING, when Eugenia came down for breakfast, the day's papers were on the table, spread out before her seat. Yesterday had been glorious. Two respectable gentlemen were vying for her attention, and neither was nearly as boring, stuffy or insipid as she had thought.

Perth had let her drive a little, if sedately, until Farnsworth had appeared. How it had turned into a race to win her favor, she could not even recall. If she had raced, it would have resulted in a scandal. No one would dare reprimand Farnsworth or Perth. She filled her plate and taking her seat, began to turn through the pages, beginning, as always, with the gossip columns and then reading the rest. She spread plum jam on her toast, took a bite and then nearly choked. There was a caricature of her, standing with one foot on each phaeton as they raced through the park. She was holding a hand out to both. It was grossly unfair! It was as though she were dividing her favors between the two and a race could decide who won her hand! She bit off another mouthful of toast, then searched through another paper, looking to see how they had depicted the race, for clearly it was public knowledge already.

This one had another drawing altogether, however. They were at the theatre and Perth was on one side and Farnsworth on the other. Both gentlemen were on bended knee, looking up at her while offering her gifts of jewels and flowers, with drawings of large estates and bags of money behind the men.

She slammed the paper down on the table. "As if I could be bought!"

She drank her tea and stared at the wall. Her brother—brothers—would think this was her fault. She had done nothing wrong. Well, nothing *truly* wrong, such as being caught in an alcove with a man like Lettie Bancroft had or running around the park in her unmentionables like Heath had done. She snorted at the mental picture the latter presented. Of course, she *ought* to be shocked. However, the stakes were higher now that Perth and Farnsworth were openly courting her. She liked both gentlemen in a friendly way and did not wish for this to become a ridiculous contest, nor did she wish to choose a husband in the public's eye.

She had four brothers and knew that competitiveness was in their blood. Today was the Oglesby garden party and Farnsworth had won the right to escort her.

Things had changed a great deal in a few short days. She had no one she could truly talk this over with. Sybil was on her way to Italy with her new husband on their holiday, and Graham… she sighed heavily. What had happened? He was angry with her, and she with him—but she wasn't truly angry, just annoyed. If she had quarreled with one of her brothers, they would have talked it over and found a solution. So why did she feel she could not speak with him?

It made her unaccountably sad. It felt as though she had suffered a loss when he was perfectly well only two houses away. What could she do? She had made it abundantly clear she did not wish to be his obligation, but from his reactions, it seemed she had hurt him.

Would he come for her that morning? Winfred had said he had come yesterday and she was already gone. She ate the last piece of toast without tasting it, knowing she had made a mull of everything. She had put on her riding habit out of habit, she snickered at the pun, but although she sat in the breakfast parlor and waited and waited, he did not come. It was what she deserved. Perhaps she would have a chance to speak with him at the garden party and apologize.

Eventually she gave up, and went upstairs to read until it was time to change for the afternoon. Farnsworth arrived promptly to escort her and her aunt to the garden party.

"Good afternoon, my lady," he said, bowing over Aunt Hambridge's hand. "May I say, that shade of pink does wonders for your complexion?"

Her aunt tapped him on the arm with her fan. "Come now, Alistair. We are too old for such blatant balderdash."

Eugenia frowned. Did that mean he was of an age with her aunt? They must be closer in age than she was to him. That was a disturbing thought.

"And you, Lady Eugenia, are as bright as the sunshine."

"Thank you, Your Grace," she muttered as she curtsied, feeling more despondent as she recalled Graham had said the exact same words to her. She wore a jonquil muslin with pink roses embroidered into a pattern with a matching pink band beneath her bodice. It seemed suitably horticultural. Her bonnet was also bright. Graham had teased her about it when she purchased it, but it was one of her favorites.

"Shall we go? I had thought we could travel by boat. It is a perfect day for it," the duke remarked.

"That sounds delightful!" her aunt exclaimed. "It is quite warm for October."

After a carriage ride to the Thames, they boarded a barge that was waiting for them.

Eugenia remained quiet—a feat for her—listening to her aunt and suitor chat and reminisce about how courting had been in their day (nonexistent) and their grandchildren (he already had five). Would that make her a mother and a grandmother if she married him?

They paid her little mind, so she nodded and smiled, her thoughts in a whirl. Graham would have appreciated the oddity of the moment. If they had but realized her silence was cause for alarm, they might have paid her more attention.

Servants rowed them upstream to the string of mansions owned by the aristocracy along the waterfront. Lord Oglesby preferred to live here as opposed to in Town, and as they approached the façade from the river, Eugenia understood why. The gardens put Vauxhall and Hyde Park to shame. It was wild perfection. Eugenia assumed Capability Brown had been the one to design such a visual feast, but he had done so in such a manner that it did not look intentional nor overly manicured. The flowers were in full bloom, their colors a bright rainbow, and their mixture of fragrance strong even near the river.

"How lovely!" Aunt Hambridge exclaimed.

As they slowed and floated to dock, a wide expanse of lawn opened up before them where a cricket game was being played on one side and lawn chess on another. Further up the hill towards the house, tents had been erected for shade and tables of food. It was a pleasant contrast to Town.

The duke climbed out to hand them on to the pier, Eugenia almost being tipped over as her aunt lunged forward. She gripped the side and closed her eyes, praying that no more disasters befell her for the afternoon.

Farnsworth laughed. "You may open your eyes now, my lady." He was looking at her warmly, and she felt acutely uncomfortable. She wanted to be away. Reprieve came in the form of Lord and Lady Oglesby, who were making their way towards the duke to greet him.

Lord Oglesby (though looking much older) and Farnsworth had apparently been old school chums and had played on the championship cricket team together. His Grace was quickly recruited to play in a match they were organizing.

"Do you have any objections, Lady Eugenia?"

"Not at all. It will be delightful to watch you play."

He barely waited for her answer as he rushed off with Oglesby.

Truth be told, Eugenia was relieved. He was still handsome and kind, but she had hoped for something more when she married.

She walked up the hill behind her aunt and Lady Oglesby to join the other guests mingling near the food. Part of her was envious of the gentlemen, because she was rather a good cricket player herself. However, she was determined to behave with complete decorum, so there would be no tying up her skirts and joining a team. This was not Devonshire.

She really missed Sibyl on days like this. She was surrounded by females she was not completely comfortable chatting with. It felt as though she always said the wrong thing and she never knew what it was. They would still smile and tolerate her, but she could always sense their withdrawal.

Looking around, she spotted Graham talking to Kitty Ravenhill, this Season's beauty. Eugenia could not bear to be in her presence and had a difficult time refraining from saying so. Graham knew she thought the girl shallow and cruel, but he did not seem to think so by the way he was smiling and flirting with her. Eugenia knew the girl's heart to be as black as her hair and her name, and she found it impossible to pretend amiability when in the presence of such people.

He caught her staring and raised his glass in greeting. She inclined her head and then decided to meander through the famous rose garden. Maybe someone more pleasant was there. In fact, Lord Perth should be attending. Was he also playing cricket?

Only solace was to be found amongst the riot of roses, which was more than she could say for the tents, where it felt as if everyone was staring at her and judging her. If only one of her brothers and their wives would come back to Town, perhaps she would not feel so alone. She knew she could not escape by herself for the entire afternoon. Perhaps she could steal just a few more minutes and then she would dutifully go to cheer on Farnsworth and his cricket prowess.

GRAHAM WAS NOT enjoying looking for a wife at all. It had only been a small suggestion in the corner of his mind, which had somehow taken on too much significance after the conversations at the club the evening before. There was clearly some sixth sense amongst gently bred females to smell when a man began the search. Miss Ravenhill had cornered him from the moment of his arrival and was making his skin crawl. If that were not enough, he had noticed Farnsworth bringing Eugenia to the party in a regal fashion along the Thames, the way they had traveled in Georgian times. Could she truly be considering him? What was Knighton thinking?

He was surprised when he saw Farnsworth abandon her to play cricket, but perhaps the duke thought to impress Eugenia with his athletic prowess. Wearing the ridiculous bonnet he had helped her purchase, Eugenia walked up the hill behind her aunt. The hat had brought her such joy and he could only smile at seeing her wear it.

He frowned as he watched Eugenia walk away on her own and wondered how long it would be until he could extricate himself from Miss Ravenhill. He wanted to mend this silly rift between Eugenia and himself, and if she was going somewhere alone it was perfect timing.

Miss Ravenhill actually excused herself and he wondered how long he should wait until he could follow Eugenia. He greeted a few acquaintances, then went after her to the garden. It was odd, he thought, as he made his way between large bushes taller than his head, that he had missed Eugenia these two days they had not spoken. He had not realized how much they had confided in each other before. He wanted to share things with her that he knew she would find amusing, and he wanted to hear her thoughts on Perth and Farnsworth. It could not have escaped her notice that the duke was thirty years her senior.

When he was deep into the garden, he heard voices and stopped in his tracks.

"I must say, Lady Eugenia, that I had not thought you capable of snaring a duke and an earl," a female voice said with complete and undisguised malevolence.

Graham frowned as he moved closer to try to distinguish the voice. It was vaguely familiar, but no female of his acquaintance would speak to him in such a manner.

"I do not think 'snared' is the right word," Eugenia retorted. Good for her.

"As long as you stay away from Mr. Tinsley," the other voice snarled. "I think I will have him for myself."

"I wish you luck with that, but I have no intention of staying away from one of my oldest friends."

Graham walked faster through the maze of bushes until he could confirm his thoughts. Eugenia's antagonist was indeed Miss Ravenhill.

"I know you have wanted him for yourself," the black-haired beauty continued, "but a silly chit like you could never satisfy him."

It took all of Graham's strength to be still and not go and strangle the woman. Did she think he could not see through her spite? The whole of London knew Ravenhill was under the hatches and intended to sell his beautiful sister to the highest bidder. It would not be Graham.

"Tinsley and I?" Eugenia repeated. "That is preposterous," she said, though the look on her face was almost comical.

"Come now, I am not that bad," he muttered, without stopping to ponder any further.

Fortunately, Miss Ravenhill missed the look on Eugenia's face which he was close enough to spy through the leaves.

"When Perth and Farnsworth open their eyes and discover how..." She looked Eugenia up and down in a disparaging way. "*Unladylike* you are, they will change their minds about offering for you."

"They already have. Does that make you jealous, Kitty?"

Miss Ravenhill narrowed her dark eyes, making her look like a snake. "Be careful. You do not want to make an enemy of me."

"If this is your good side, then no thank you."

"Stay away from Tinsley," the beauty commanded, marring her features with an ugly scowl. Tossing her head, she turned and stalked away.

Graham watched her leave. "Good riddance," he said.

"Graham! You startled me," Eugenia said, one hand to her chest as he took a seat on the bench beside her.

"Is something the matter?"

She gave an unladylike shrug of the shoulders. "Just another female who does not care for me."

"Miss Ravenhill?"

She gave a nod.

"I thought the air grew warmer after she had left."

Eugenia tried to cover a laugh.

"Why do you care for her opinion anyway?"

"I should not, I know," she said, looking down and picking at one of the embroidered roses on her gown. "But what she said is true."

He turned her chin and lifted it towards his face. She really was handsome, especially with those large, dark blue eyes so reminiscent of the sea, in which one could drown.

She searched his face and for a moment he found himself tempted to kiss her. Good Lord, he was going to rot in hell for that thought.

"Is the thought of me really so preposterous?" he whispered, close enough to her face that he could feel her breath touch his skin.

"You scapegrace!" She hit him hard on the arm. "You were eaves-dropping!"

"Of course I was." He laughed.

"At least I hope you believe me now, that she is a conniving little shrew."

"I have known all along," he scoffed.

"I think that is doing it too brown, my dear, but thank God," she muttered.

He felt the same way, except Perth and Farnsworth were not bad men; he just did not think they were right for her. "Am I forgiven, pet?"

"Yes. I do not like being at odds with you."

"Nor I you. My mornings have been very lonely. I have missed talking to you."

She made a face at him. "Now who's doing it too brown?"

"I was being serious!"

She made an endearing little noise and looked straight ahead.

"Would you care for a boat ride? I saw several punts along the water—unless you had your fill while with Farnsworth. It was a rather nice, if antiquated, touch."

"Anything to escape."

They smiled in mutual understanding and walked to the water together, avoiding the crowds. When they reached the boats, Eugenia looked longingly at the one next to the one he had chosen.

"No, you don't. No racing today." He took her arm and pulled her to his boat.

She looked mischievous, then sighed. "Oh, very well. I did promise myself to be demure today."

"In your very fetching bonnet," he quipped.

"It is, is it not?" She smiled and the world seemed brighter because of it. He pushed the boat from the bank and began to row. This part of the river was shallow, and also calmer and cleaner than near Town. He began a gentle rhythm as she leaned back and let the sun fall on her face. It was so comfortable being with her—even though she was often not a comfortable person. She was simply...Eugenia.

"Tell me about your courtship thus far," he said, once they were far from the bank.

She lifted her head and looked at him with one eye closed. "Did you know Knighton gave Farnsworth permission to pay his addresses? He is the first one Rowley has accepted, to my knowledge."

"To be fair, the others were not up to snuff," Graham added.

She wrinkled her nose. "Farnsworth is nice, but he was at school with my father. He and Aunt Hambridge reminisced for the entire journey here."

Graham chuckled. "And Perth?"

She tipped her head back and closed her eyes. "He is handsome and wealthy enough that he does not need my money."

"True...but?"

"But... I wish there was not this ridiculous sense of competition about it. Do they comprehend I am more than just a prize to win?" She swallowed heavily and Graham felt a twinge of guilt inside.

He stopped rowing and took one of her hands.

"Genie, you do not have to marry where you cannot be happy."

"It is not that." She shook her head and opened her eyes. "I do need to marry. I realize that now. I am sure either one of them will be a lovely husband and treat me well."

Then why did she sound so sad about it? "Do not rush into it. Promise me, pet. Take your time to know them both before you decide. Promise me."

She bit her lip and nodded her head, then looked away.

"I will always be here for you, Genie."

She gave him a half smile and he had to be content with that.

"What of your prospects?"

She surprised him by turning the tables. "I can safely say that Kitty Ravenhill is not on my list."

"Endeavor not to be alone with her. I would put nothing past her," she warned.

"I have not managed to remain single thus far without a keen sense of self-preservation."

"Oh? Then perhaps you should look behind you."

Graham turned seconds before Sir Martin Hardy bumped his boat into theirs. Everything would have been perfectly well – they had not collided at any great rate of speed – but Sir Martin had been standing up, like a gondolier paddling through the Venice canals, in order to impress Miss Ravenhill. He lost his balance and overturned their small craft, sending himself and Miss Ravenhill into the river. An unfortunate amount of water splashed into their own boat, but at least they stayed upright. By the time the boat was turned over and both parties were pulled from the water, the entire guest list was standing on the riverbank, gawking.

"So much for a demure afternoon," Eugenia muttered.

# CHAPTER FIVE

O F COURSE, THE picture and description the next morning had not failed to include her. At least this time it was not her fault. There was a small amount of satisfaction to be had from seeing Miss Ravenhill portrayed in a less than glamorous light, with her black hair plastered to her face and screaming at Hardy like a fishwife. It was worth having her own drawing there. However, that would not satisfy her brother, she was sure.

That day, Mother Nature intervened in the form of pouring rain and Eugenia's courses, so she stayed in bed with a hot water bottle and some lurid Gothic novels.

"At least I will not be in the news-sheets for a day or two," she consoled herself while drinking some chocolate and eating an entire tray of biscuits. She was deep into the scene of Mrs. Radcliffe's *Romance of the Forest,* where Adeline was about to be tricked into a false marriage with the Marquis but Theodore was helping her escape with the Marquis in hot pursuit...when the maid knocked on the door. Eugenia scowled. She hated to be interrupted when deep into a story. Stevens entered bringing in a vase of bright pink roses. She sat them on the dressing table and brought the card to Eugenia.

*My dear Lady,*

*Forgive me for abandoning you at the garden party I hope you have no ill effects from the accident.*

*Your very obedient servant,*
*Farnsworth*

"Oh, plague on the man!" she exclaimed and tossed the card on her side-table. She turned over and watch the raindrops run down the window panes. Some of them would look as if they were going to join and then veer off and go in a completely unexpected direction. She frowned. It felt like a very apt analogy to the past week of her life. Everything was going in a different direction and she was not certain she liked being pursued. But how to redirect the rain when there were unseen forces making it go where it would?

Perhaps she should try to make more lady friends. Then she could at least have someone to talk to besides Graham. Maybe she could look at his list of potential wives and befriend some of them. That way she could help him narrow down the choices to someone she could tolerate. Unlike Miss Ravenhill, who would never allow her to speak to Graham again. She snorted with satisfaction at the remembrance of the shrew dripping with disgust when her head was bobbing in the Thames.

Just then there was another knock on her door and Eugenia tried not to groan.

"Come in," she croaked instead.

Expecting her maid, Eugenia did not turn over.

"Genie?" she heard her aunt's voice ask quietly. That lady probably thought she was disturbing Eugenia's rest. "Are you not feeling quite the thing? Stevens said you were not well."

Eugenia untangled her covers and sat up in her bed. "I am well, Aunt. It is only my monthly."

She frowned sympathetically. "I do not miss those. We have had an invitation I wanted to ask you about," she said with aplomb as she sat in one of the rose velvet armchairs near the fire.

"In this weather?" Eugenia could not help but grimace. Everything was gloomy when one had one's courses.

"No, not until the weekend. Perth is having a short house party at his estate near Brighton."

"Does he say who will be there?" House parties could be very good or very bad depending upon the company. Eugenia knew she needed to know Lord Perth better before making any decisions, and technically he had not asked her yet, after all. He had merely said he wished to court her.

"I will have to see if I can discover. I have never actually been to his estate, but I hear it is quite lovely. Perhaps he wishes to impress you."

"Why me? And why so suddenly?"

"I could not say, but they are both lovely matches for you."

*Not love matches, notice, Eugenia.*

Eugenia knew that, on paper, there were none better. Many of the young ladies had lists ranking the eligible gentlemen numerically by who was the best catch.

She was determined to get this right.

There was another knock on the door and her maid entered with an apologetic look from behind two more large vases of flowers. The maid tried to bob a curtsy when she saw Lady Hambridge.

"I did not know if you would wish to see these, miss, or if you would prefer me to take them back downstairs."

"They can go in the sitting room," Lady Hambridge directed, having taken the cards and handed them to Eugenia.

"Who now?" Eugenia asked.

"Perth and Ravenhill."

Her aunt frowned.

"Before you say a word, I have no intention of allowing Ravenhill to court me. He was one of the ones *the herd* scared away last Season."

"I thought so," her aunt remarked. "His reputation is as black as his name."

Had not Eugenia thought the same thing about his sister the day before?

"As long as you do not encourage him, then he should not be a problem," she added.

"I did not even speak with him yesterday. His sister tried to warn me away from Mr. Tinsley. I told her that was preposterous."

"And why is that?" Her aunt looked offended.

"Why does everyone keep asking me that or insinuating that something is possible between us? He is my only friend left in Town now that Sybil has married. He's like one of my brothers!" Eugenia could not believe she was having to explain.

"Well, he is one of the most handsome men in Town."

Eugenia wrinkled her face. That was true. But so were her brothers.

"And he is apparently considering taking a wife."

Also true.

"And one cannot underestimate the value of friendship. That, my dear, is the true key to happiness in marriage."

Much though Eugenia did not want to agree, the last week had shown her how much friendship mattered. Two days of being at odds with Graham had been awful. "The point is moot, Aunt, because Graham could never think of me as more than a brat little sister."

"If you say so." Her voice indicated she thought anything but.

"Besides, I thought you were on Farnsworth's side," Eugenia argued.

She had been picking at the embroidery on her coverlet while watching another raindrop slide down the window. Her aunt sighed dreamily and Eugenia swung her gaze to her aunt's face.

"He is still very handsome, but now I cannot want him for you. Not that he is in his dotage—Alistair is the very picture of health – but he does have a parcel of nephews who could very well inherit and I do not want you to feel pressured into the match when the fact is he does have heirs and he will age sooner than you."

"Then why did Rowley give his blessing?"

"Who can say? I imagine he could hardly not give it if age was the only objection."

There was yet another knock on the door and Stevens entered.

This time she held no flowers, thank goodness. She bobbed a curtsy. "Forgive me, my lady, but I did happen to discover who was invited to the house party."

Aunt Hambridge gave a nod for her to speak.

"His Grace, the Duke of Farnsworth, Mr. Petersham, Sir Martin Hardy, and Mr. Tinsley. A few guests are coming in from the country, but I could not discover who."

"There is a noticeable lack of ladies," her aunt remarked.

"There have to be some. He could hardly only invite me."

"True enough. I think if those are the gentleman, they are harmless enough. I am surprised by Farnsworth being included."

"It would not be sporting of Perth if he did not invite the competition," Eugenia said in a mocking voice.

Her aunt ignored her and stood up. "I will send our acceptance and then I am going to play cards with Lady Mottram."

Eugenia relaxed when her aunt shut the door. Mayhap she could lock it and relax for the rest of the day. She certainly did not want to think about what her aunt had said about Graham, but the thoughts kept going through her mind and would not leave, much though she wished them to perdition.

Of course, she knew Graham was the most handsome man of her acquaintance. She was not dead, after all. Next to her brothers, he looked like the angel Gabriel, with his contrasting golden locks and light green eyes. She knew all the ladies watched every move he made, but to her he was just Graham. "Is that true?" the little devil over her shoulder asked.

"Of course it is," she answered, because self-preservation lay in that direction, because she adored the relationship they had and nothing was worth jeopardizing that. 'Twas why she needed to help him find the right wife—who would not be Kitty Ravenhill.

Just when she had reassured herself, her eyes were growing sleepy, and another knock sounded on her door. She had heard her aunt leave for her card party, so Eugenia decided to ignore it. Whoever it was could go away. The door opened and she kept her eyes closed, pretending sleep.

"Genie, I know you are not asleep. You are the worst pretender I have ever met."

"Go away, Graham. You know it is not proper for you to be in my room." Her heart skipped a tiny, treacherous beat when he sank down on the side of her bed. She was still in her woolen night-rail and her plait had long since become unraveled, which she confirmed by opening one eye to see a wild, fuzzy tendril sticking up.

"Very well. I will not tell you what I have."

"You are a beast."

"But a handsome, caring beast. I heard you were not feeling well and I came to see if you were on your death-bed from the mishap yesterday."

"As if I would be so craven!" She sat up at that and winced from the pain in her abdomen.

Graham did not miss a thing. He eyed her suspiciously, with one haughty eyebrow raised. Eugenia was the only one in her family who could not do that. It was the Knight family look that apparently he had acquired and she had not.

"If I were going to be so delicate as to take a chill, I would have done so from rescuing the boy."

He inclined his head. "Shall I ring for some tea or sandwiches?"

She looked guiltily at the plate of biscuits and cup of chocolate she had already devoured that morning. But that had been at least two hours ago. "Why not?" Perhaps he wanted them for himself.

He reached over to pull the rope and she caught a whiff of his woodsy scent which was very earthy and soothing. When he sat back, he lifted something from the floor and handed it to her.

"A hat box?"

He made a motion with his hand for her to open it. She lifted the lid to see a new bonnet, identical to the one that had been ruined the day before and immediately burst into tears.

⋙⋘

"GENIE? I THOUGHT you would be pleased. I can take it away at once."

A sound like a mating fox emitted from her person. Goodness, what had he done? He put his arms around her, and she sobbed onto his shoulder. *Was this the emotion that women get during each month, that men discuss in their clubs to avoid like the plague?*

She then held a ragged breath and sat up. "Forgive me. I do not know what came over me."

"I did not mean to make you cry."

She wiped at her eyes with her sleeves. "I know. Thank you for the bonnet. I know you hate it and so that makes it more special."

Graham blinked a few times and decided not to overthink matters.

The maid entered with a tray and set it down on the bed in between them, giving him a pointed look. He had left the door open, so he smiled his most charming smile at her. He made Eugenia her tea with two spoons of sugar and a generous dollop of milk, then handed it to her.

She piled a few of his favorite egg and cucumber sandwiches on a plate, then handed it to him. They smiled during the exchange.

He took a bite, chewed and swallowed. "Were you pleased with this morning's papers?"

"Oh, yes." She nodded while trying to cover her mouth as she chewed. Then she tossed him an impudent little half grin of apology and guilt. "I hope you do not have her on your list," she said, trying to dab at her lips with her napkin daintily, as though she had just not blurted something out with her mouth full of food.

"She was never on my list, as you say. Come now, pet. Do you have a list?"

"Not on paper, *per se*, but there are certainly people I would not consider and some I perhaps would. Surely you have some idea, Graham. Otherwise you are going to find yourself trapped by the likes of Kitty Ravenhill."

He gave a mock shudder.

She hit him with one of her pillows. "I am serious! Do you think I would be allowed to talk to you if you married her?"

He chucked her under the chin. "We cannot have that. Very well, I will play. Who would you suggest for me?"

She twisted her face adorably. "I will have to think about it. Do you have any particular requirements?"

He tapped his cheek with his index finger, pretending to think. "Well-bred."

She snorted. "That goes without saying."

He scowled at her. "This is my list, is it not?"

She waved her hand for him to continue.

"Sense of humor. And a sportswoman."

"Will you clarify that?" she said, closing her eyes as if trying to conjure up the image of the ideal mate for him. It was rather entertaining, if nothing else.

"A good seat on a horse and able to shoot?"

"That will narrow your choices considerably," she pointed out. "If you say billiards or cricket then you will be completely out of luck since neither is a ladies' sport."

"You play billiards and cricket," he argued. She had not yet realized he was baiting her.

"We both know I am a poor example of ladylike attributes."

"I like you just the way you are, pet. If you simply played by the rules you would have no difficulty."

"Perhaps I should try to think of societal behavior like a cricket game," she teased, smiling mischievously.

Graham felt something stir within him when she looked at him like that. Describing his ideal mate was becoming dangerous.

"What else? Beautiful, I assume?"

"Beauty is in the eye of the beholder," he retorted. "Kitty Ravenhill is aesthetically pleasing, but is one of the ugliest people I have ever met."

Eugenia was watching him carefully. "There is no one you have in mind?"

"Not particularly. I am open-minded, but I have no desire to be trapped into a marriage of convenience or wedlock by scheming."

"I would hate that for you. I would hate it for me," she added ruefully.

"What about you, pet? You have had lots of unsuitable suitors, but now that Perth and Farnsworth are interested, will either of them suit you?"

"Say that quickly ten times." She blew out an exasperated breath, causing a stray hair to go upward. "Farnsworth is very agreeable in a paternal sort of way. Perth is handsome…"

"But?" he prompted.

"I feel like I am walking on ice when I am with him, but I admit I do not know him very well. Perhaps the house party will give me an opportunity to discover our compatibility."

Graham nodded. "I do not personally know of any faults." It was hard to know a person's true self amongst the whirl of the Season. Yet Graham knew nothing averse about Perth and he had known him since school, even though he was three years Perth's junior.

He had received a note from Knighton that morning, informing him that he would be on his way to Town, but he did not want Eugenia to know yet.

But how would Eugenia behave with her brother around? Would she feel obligated to marry to please him? Graham knew Knighton well and he loved his siblings dearly, but he might think it was for her own good to marry. Eugenia might appear disobedient, but truly she wanted nothing more than to please her brother. Graham could see how conflicted she was by these two suitors. He would have to keep a close eye on Knighton and make certain he didn't pressure her into a marriage that would only see her miserable. For all Rowley was like a brother to him, the duke could be extremely stubborn when he thought he knew best.

"I should be on my way," he said, standing and straightening his jacket. "I'll stop scandalizing your maid now and leave you to your Radcliffe."

She waved her hand dismissively. "No one is worried about you."

*They should be*, he thought instinctively.

"I will see you tomorrow, then. I have promised Lady Hambridge to escort you to Brighton."

She gave him a hesitant smile.

"Cheer up, pet. I will fight Knighton if he tries to force you into anything disagreeable."

"Promise?"

"Promise." He bent over and kissed her on the cheek, then left before he said or did something he would regret.

# CHAPTER SIX

T HE TRIP TO Brighton was uneventful. The rain had stopped the day before, so the roads were not terribly muddy. Graham rode alongside their carriage with Sir Martin Hardy and Mr. Petersham and they were charming and witty the whole way. It almost made Eugenia forget why they were going to Brighton.

When they arrived, the coastal town was different from what she had envisioned. She had grown up on the coast of Devonshire, with dramatic cliffs and strong winds, but here the scenery was much more gentle and more peaceful. The house was on a hill overlooking the Channel, but there were not a great number of trees. When she alighted from the carriage, she stretched to feel the warm sun on her face and absorb the welcome smell of the salty ocean air again.

Perth himself came out to greet them, with a matron who Eugenia suspected was the countess and a beautiful young lady who must be a sister.

"Welcome to Seaside Cottage, our humble estate. My lady, may I present to you the Countess of Perth? And my sister, Lady Emily."

Eugenia curtsied deeply. She could feel the assessing gaze, and Eugenia suspected Perth had come by his fastidiousness honestly. Lady Emily Russell seemed very sweet and almost shy. She hoped they could be friends. The rest of the introductions were made and Perth offered her his arm and led her into the house.

It was not as grand as The Grange, but this was one of the smaller estates. His primary seat was in Lincolnshire, or somewhere equally far, if she remembered correctly.

It was a charming home of white stone, and Eugenia felt comfortable there. It did not have the high ceilings or grand entrance hall like many manor houses, but it was tastefully done with pale colors reflecting the sea, and white wainscoting.

"Would you prefer to be shown to your rooms or have some refreshments?"

Eugenia deferred to her aunt. "It was not a fatiguing journey. I think tea would be just the thing."

Perth inclined his head to his butler and showed them into a drawing room. It must be the showpiece of the house, Eugenia conjectured, with its windows overlooking the spectacular chalk cliffs bordering the Channel, that she had not seen from the angle at the front of the house.

"You are the first guests to arrive," the countess remarked.

"Who else will be joining us?" Lady Hambridge asked.

"Only Farnsworth and his unmarried daughter, Lady Augusta. There are several other families, who will be joining us during the daytime as they live close by."

As long as she did not say Kitty Ravenhill, then Eugenia thought she could tolerate this for a few days.

"Do you know of Lord Ravenhill and his sister, Catherine? He is a baron and his estate lies some five miles north of here."

Her aunt shot a look at her. Eugenia thought she might be sick. *I will only be for four days*, she said to herself, and had a feeling that she would be repeating that several times a day for the duration.

"My daughter, Emily, and Kitty have been dearest friends whenever we visit Seaside."

"How lovely that must have been. Eugenia had no other girls nearby with whom to play when she was young," her aunt replied, almost sounding as though she was making an excuse. Eugenia tried to plaster a smile on her face. She would be the model of propriety if it killed her.

The countess looked at her sympathetically. "I had heard of one or two... misadventures... but nothing disastrous. I am certain that once she is wed, her husband will take her in hand," she said to Aunt Hambridge who, noticeably, did not look at Eugenia.

Having seen the gentleman settled into their accommodations, Perth joined her on a small sofa near the window. "Thank you for coming, Lady Eugenia. I hope you will find it pleasing."

"It is a beautiful property. I think I could sit here all day."

"It is not so grand as The Grange, to be sure, but it is my favorite. Nothing equals the storms rolling in off the Channel."

She smiled, thinking it would indeed be lovely to watch those.

"Is there anything in particular you would like to do whilst here?" he asked.

"I think a walk along the sea would be delightful."

"That I can manage. Is there nothing else?"

She chanced to look up into his eyes. They were the same green as Emma's, and of another handsome man she could think of, although his were a touch more blue. Perth had a few flecks of gold in his. It was odd being close enough to see the tiny nuances of someone else's eyes. "Perhaps a ride. I cannot truly do that in Town," she answered, before she became distracted and forgot the question.

"No, not without censure, at least, more's the pity. I did rather enjoy watching you." He was looking at her very warmly. At least he liked something about her.

It was strange to be flirted with in a serious manner, if there was such a thing. Could flirting be serious? It was something she could ponder later.

As servants began to bring trays of sandwiches, biscuits and tea into the drawing room, another carriage rolled up the drive.

Her eyes found Graham's and she wondered if he had heard the countess announce the other guests. He raised his brows then winked at her in understanding. It was nice to have a friend who understood her. She would miss him so when they both married. She tried not to let her sudden sadness show on her face.

Lord and Miss Ravenhill entered and polite greetings were made all around before the gentlemen took themselves off for a game of billiards.

Eugenia would give just about anything she owned to join the gentlemen instead of sitting here with the ladies. She could already feel the icy stares from Kitty Ravenhill and the assessing ones from the countess. It was hard not to squirm and fidget.

"When are you coming to London, Lady Emily?"

The earl's young sister looked at her mama.

"Perhaps next Season, when Perth has married. I do not care for the social whirl."

"That is too bad," Kitty Ravenhill remarked. "It would be much more fun to have you there."

Lady Emily smiled. "I am sure you will *take* this Season, Kitty, but selfishly I hope you will still be there."

"Even if I marry," Kitty said, casting a sideways glance at Eugenia. "I will always have time for you. I do not plan to be tucked away in the country, never to be seen again."

Of that, Eugenia had no doubt.

"And how do you feel about Town, Lady Eugenia?" Lady Emily asked softly.

*How to answer that?* If she were honest, she would call it a fickle beast. "I think it has a great deal to offer," she answered cautiously instead, "but there are many more restrictions than in the country." Eugenia hated that she had to be careful with every word.

Lady Emily pursed her lips prettily. She was the quintessential picture of a dainty and perfect lady.

Why, Eugenia wondered, would Perth be interested in her? It was certainly a conundrum. She seemed to be the opposite of what he was looking for. Did he not realize what she was really like? Perhaps this house party would enlighten him, but she was determined not to give him a disgust of her, at any rate.

"Have you any earnest suitors, Miss Ravenhill?" the countess asked.

"I have had six marriage proposals so far, but my brother is giving me until the end of the year to choose."

"How fortunate for you," the countess remarked and Eugenia was not certain whether it was a look of approval or disdain.

Eugenia sat awkwardly, waiting for the next question. The countess could hardly ask about her suitors, now could she? Eugenia did not think mentioning how many offers of marriage her brothers had turned down last year would be quite the right thing to say, either.

"Oh, look, here come Farnsworth and his daughter," Lady Hambridge remarked.

Eugenia was happy for any diversion.

"Lady Augusta is his youngest," her aunt added.

The countess went out to greet them and brought them back into the drawing room. Introductions were made, and the duke made a point of bending over her hand and kissing the air above it. She tried not to blush, but he must have sensed her discomfort, for he winked at her. Or could he tell how uncomfortable she was in a drawing room full of women? She would have to beg Graham to find a way for her to do something outdoors with the gentlemen. Otherwise, she would stick out like the complete fraud she was. She curtsied deeply and rose, only to be looking into the eyes of Lady Augusta, who cast a look of exasperation at the duke which Eugenia could only hope no one else witnessed. It certainly made her want to crawl into a hole and hide.

GRAHAM COULD NOT help but wonder how Eugenia was faring. He had not missed her look of despair when the gentlemen left for the billiards room.

She was such a conundrum. She loved dresses and bright colors, but she truly did not know how to be a lady.

"Do you have any good shooting to be had down here?" Sir Martin asked.

"Not as fine as up north, to be sure, but there is some decent grouse on occasion," Perth answered amiably. "I had thought we might go for a ride in the morning. Perhaps you might care to keep a look out?"

Several of the gentlemen murmured their approval.

"My sister wishes to have a picnic on the beach, if the weather holds," Perth added.

"And we shall not wish to disappoint the lovely Lady Emily," Ravenhill agreed.

Graham could not fathom that Perth would allow the likes of Ravenhill anywhere near his sister, but stranger things had happened before.

"You are on the hunt for a wife?" Petersham asked Perth.

"Hunt would not be the verbiage I would choose, as I have no intention of trapping or killing any prey," he remarked.

Graham caught Petersham's gaze before he looked at the ceiling in annoyance.

"What of you, Tinsley?" Ravenhill asked with a smirk on his face. Graham refused to be baited. He knew very well Ravenhill wished to cause trouble. He was just not certain how, yet, but he would have to be watched.

"I am in no rush to attain the altar. I merely remarked I was open to the right person."

"Do not say that near the ladies," Sir Martin said as they each selected their cues.

A carriage rumbled up the drive and Ravenhill looked out of the window. "Brave of you to bring Farnsworth here."

"I think it was dashed sporting of you!" Sir Martin exclaimed to Perth.

"How much do you have on whom?" Tinsley asked dryly.

Sir Martin grinned widely. "I shall not say. It will be more fun that way."

Graham shook his head.

"I am rooting for the underdog," Ravenhill said with a gleam in his eye that made him look like a weasel.

"I should go and greet the new arrivals. Carry on without me," Perth said, waving his hand at the billiards table and making his exit.

When the echo of his footsteps receded, Graham turned towards Ravenhill. "What are you about? I hope you do not mean to make trouble."

"I do not know what you mean," Ravenhill replied with an air of insouciance. Perhaps he was more of a chameleon than a weasel, Graham thought.

"It is merely that I am protective of Lady Eugenia as a sister and I am tasked to act in her brothers' stead during their absence.

"If you say so," Ravenhill retorted and took his shot at the ball on the felt.

"Are you on the hunt for a wife?" Graham turned the man's own question and turn of phrase on him. Perhaps that way he could discover his lordship's intentions further.

"Always."

"Always?" That was hardly a satisfactory answer, so Graham pushed for more. "You are rather young to be desiring leg-shackles, are you not?"

"Not when the pater left the estate in debt."

*Not to mention your own gambling habits,* Graham thought to himself.

"Marrying Kitty off will help, of course." He looked up from aiming his cue and fixed Graham with a meaningful look.

"I hope you both find who you are looking for," Graham said dryly. "Do you have someone in mind?"

"I have narrowed it down to a list of the most... appealing," he admitted.

"All of them heiresses with at least 25,000 pounds?" Petersham speculated, his voice dripping with sarcasm.

Graham actually did not know how much Eugenia's dowry was, but he knew it was probably one of the highest ones on the marriage mart at present. Perth, at least, had no need of funds, so his proposal would not be mercenary. He would treat Eugenia well too, especially compared to Ravenhill.

"I suppose Lady Emily is on your list, as well?" Sir Martin asked. "Taking little thing," he added.

Ravenhill gave a slight shrug of one shoulder, as if it mattered not to him which heiress he netted.

"Do you think Perth is coming back?" Sir Martin asked.

"Probably not. His competition has arrived," Petersham replied.

"Then I shall take his shot," Sir Martin said, stepping up to the table with his cue.

Petersham came to stand near Graham while Ravenhill and Hardy played their game. "Why did we agree to this house party? It is a matchmaking hornet's nest."

"Because Perth is our friend, as is Lady Eugenia?" Graham offered.

"I knew there was a reason." He sounded unconvinced as to whether the reason was adequate. "Do you think there will be a row?"

"Something is afoot, but I think it will come from an unexpected quarter."

"A black-haired friend? That term is used loosely, I assure you," Petersham drawled.

"He will bear watching," Graham agreed. "I will warn Eugenia to lock her doors."

"You know as well as I that will not be enough if he is determined."

Perth returned and saw that the game had proceeded without him. "Sorry, old chap. We didn't think you would be back. I hope you do not mind," Hardy said.

"Not at all." He waved his hand and took a seat against the wall with Graham and Petersham.

"Are all of the guests arrived?"

"Everyone who is staying. The vicar and family will join us for supper to even out the numbers. Do you think it would be poor form to have the ladies shoot with us?" Perth asked.

"I can only speak for myself and Lady Eugenia, but she would be delighted with such a prospect."

Perth gave a satisfied smile. "My sister is also fair with a bow or a rifle. I was trying to determine upon some entertainments these ladies might enjoy."

"Anything of a sporting nature Lady Eugenia will like. I had not realized what a sportsman you were, Perth, though I suppose you were active at university."

"I take my duties in Parliament seriously, but I like nothing better than being in the country, riding or hunting."

"It is most considerate of you to accommodate the ladies as well as the gentlemen," Graham remarked. The man was sickeningly perfect. However, anyone would be better than Ravenhill—even Farnsworth.

At dinner that evening, the vicar and his wife, and their marriageable daughter, joined the party. The vicar, Reverend Masters, was a jolly sort and his wife had a kind demeanor. They were just as Graham thought a vicar ought to be – much like Edmund was. The daughter was rather plain and looked bookish, with spectacles on her nose, but she had a good figure and a nice complexion. Why Graham even noticed was beyond him. Perhaps, next to the other ladies present, no one would look anything but average.

The atmosphere had certainly changed for the evening. Lady Augusta was deep in conversation with Lord Perth, and Lord Ravenhill was trying to monopolize Lady Eugenia.

When they went from the drawing room to the dining room, Graham was seated between Lady Emily and Miss Masters. He was grateful not to be subjected to Kitty Ravenhill's antics for an entire meal. Would that he could be so fortunate the entire weekend. Unfortunately, she was still sitting across the table from him. At least such rackety manners as talking over the tureens would not be indulged by such company.

Lord Ravenhill was on the other side of Miss Masters, and surprisingly, he could overhear them discussing something intellectual.

He turned to speak to Lady Emily. "You have a charming home here, my lady. Do you prefer the seaside to the northern estate?"

"Both have their merits," she said prettily. "The north is better for hunting and sporting pursuits."

"Your brother mentioned you were fond of sport. Do you hunt?"

"I do, sir, yet only for the riding."

"I understand we will be riding a little tomorrow."

She looked around and then leaned towards him. "My lord, forgive my impertinence, but I feel I must tell you something," she said, her voice lowered. Her gaze darted across to where Kitty Ravenhill sat.

"You have my confidence if you wish it," he said reassuringly.

She gave a little nod then picked up her glass and held it in front of her mouth. "Please be careful. I overheard the brother and sister making plans to compromise you."

Had Graham heard correctly?

"I have been in anguish over whether to tell you or not. Kitty is my friend, but my conscience would not allow me to remain silent. If nothing happens, then you will only think me an interfering fool. At least you can make your own decision."

Graham looked at her. She was young, but she was not silly. "I appreciate your candor, Lady Emily. No one wishes to be compromised and forced into anything."

He could see the weight lift from her shoulders. She was not yet officially out, but perhaps next Season he would consider her. "May I also say that I wish you, too, to be careful. The brother has mentioned his interest and also his need for a wealthy bride."

She looked taken aback that she might be considered, but then she seemed to see the sense in his warning. "It appears we might need to guard each other, my lord."

"Indeed. I will try to do my part with him, but may I also beg of you to ensure that Lady Eugenia is not left alone?"

They both looked over to where Lord Perth was making Eugenia laugh.

"That will be easy. I quite like her."

Graham rather liked her, too.

# CHAPTER SEVEN

E UGENIA WAS DELIGHTED, the next morning, at the prospect of riding and having a picnic. Dinner the night before had been uncomfortable. Lord Ravenhill had smothered her for the duration of dinner until they were back in the drawing room, and then Lady Emily had clung to her side. It was unusual for any female to spend much time near her, but the girl had been very kind and friendly. Nevertheless, she was greatly relieved to be in her element this morning. She was much more at home in the outdoors than in a London drawing room. Perth had lovely stables, she had discovered, and she was extremely pleased when he picked a lively Arabian gelding for her to ride.

Lady Emily came up beside her on an equally energetic mare. It seemed they were kindred spirits outdoors, which surprised her.

"I am so glad you have come. Finally my brother will allow me to participate, since you are also an avid rider. Normally he makes me stay behind when guests are here."

"Brothers are prone to such fustian," Eugenia said sympathetically. "I assure you, I have my hands full of overbearing ones."

"And you and Mr. Tinsley are close?"

"I consider him my fifth brother," Eugenia agreed.

"I think it is touching how he looks after your interests," she said, glancing over to where Graham was sitting atop Xerxes, looking very dapper.

The way Lady Emily was watching him was no surprise, but it was the first time Eugenia had felt a twinge of jealousy over another lady. Perhaps, she mused, that was because she was a perfect lady and would make Graham a very good wife.

Lady Augusta and Farnsworth brought their mounts forward and greeted Eugenia and Lady Emily; neither could fail to note it was a cold, barely civil one from the daughter.

Eugenia wanted to shrink into invisibility. She could not blame Lady Augusta for her dislike of her. Very likely she would feel the same way if the positions were reversed.

Perhaps she would write to Rowley and tell him she could not marry Farnsworth, although there had to be a reason he had consented to the match. If only she could speak with him about it.

Once everyone was mounted, Perth led them on a trail across the meadows towards the sea. It was lovely to be able to gallop and feel the wind in her face again. England was full of dramatic shoreline, and while more tame than the Devonshire coast, the chalk cliffs were no less beautiful. They reached the end of the track and dismounted; the wind whipped her skirts and bonnet fiercely. The waves were equally turbulent, causing a sharp spray as it hit the rocks.

Perth came to stand beside her and smiled down at her.

"It is lovely," she shouted over the wind and roar of the waves.

"Not so lovely as you, my dear."

If her cheeks were not red from riding, then they were from bashfulness.

Farnsworth and Lady Augusta joined them and effectively split their conversation. It was very neatly done.

Eugenia did not miss the fact that Lady Augusta stepped too close to Perth and entwined her arm around his.

"You have a marvelous seat, Lady Eugenia," Farnsworth said, drawing her gaze to his and thus away from his daughter.

"Thank you, Your Grace. I was brought up in the saddle. It was either that or be left alone in the nursery." She smiled sheepishly. She always felt inadequate and therefore the need to justify her gentlemanly abilities.

A gust of wind began lifting her heavy skirts, so she let go of her bonnet in order to protect her modesty. Unfortunately, that caused the bonnet to fly from her head. Without thinking, she tossed her reins to Farnsworth and chased after her hat. Unladylike oaths flew from her mouth as she came within reach and then the bonnet would pick up and fly away again as though taunting her.

No one else could really help her because they had to hold their horses, so she made a complete fool of herself. She could only be thankful that the news-sheets would not get wind of this...*literally,* she thought, as she held her skirts in one hand in order to run.

She grew tired of chasing the thing and debated letting the winds have it, but she came close enough to make a final lunge, with the result she fell to her knees in order to catch it. Hat once more in hand, she stood slowly and brushed off her skirts, not wanting to turn around and face the horrified looks. She smiled brightly and marched back towards her horse, at the same time attempting to look dignified.

"I had no idea you were to be the entertainment for today," Kitty Ravenhill sneered.

"Nor did I," Eugenia said with a charming smile.

She could not help but glance at Lady Augusta who was looking at her with disdain. At least the countess and her aunt had declined the ride.

Graham came over to help her remount. "Chin up, pet. Do not let the cats' claws leave a mark."

*Too late,* she thought, but nodded anyway.

Thankfully, by the time they had ridden down the path to the beach, she had regained her composure somewhat.

There was a nice cove, which was sheltered from the wind, where a picnic was set up for them. Grooms were waiting to take their horses, and Lady Emily approached her.

"Try not to let them distress you," she said softly, but Eugenia heard.

She let out a loud sigh. "I try not to, but sometimes it is difficult not to compare myself unfavorably with other ladies."

"I like you the way you are. You are much more fun than they."

Eugenia smiled at Lady Emily. She knew she was only trying to help, but fun was the word that always seemed to get her into trouble.

"Would you like to sit with me?" she asked. Eugenia saw that the countess and her aunt had joined them. They were sitting and laughing with the duke, who looked far more in his rightful place next to the older women. She tried not to overthink that.

Graham and Perth sat next to the ladies on their blanket and Eugenia looked at her friend with surprise, wondering how he had managed to get away from Miss Ravenhill.

He seemed to read her mind. He leaned closer and whispered, "I paid Hardy twenty quid to distract her for a few minutes."

Eugenia laughed. "Does she have you by the neckcloth?"

"It has become a nuisance," he retorted and ran his fingers around the edge as if to loosen it.

Plates were passed around and she noticed Lady Emily select a small portion of pigeon pie. Eugenia had always had an unladylike appetite, but now she made an effort to restrain herself, feeling again that no matter what she did, she was destined to do it wrongly.

"Are you enjoying yourself?" Graham asked.

"I am trying to. It certainly feels more at home here than London."

"Yes indeed," he said, as a gust of wind threatened to pick up their blanket and overturn their food. Both of them instinctively reached for the edges to hold them down.

Lady Emily saw their actions and then seemed embarrassed. "I apologize. I have picked a wretched day for a picnic."

"Please do not apologize for the weather. This is normal in Devonshire. We feel right at home, I assure you," Graham answered for both of them.

"Do you spend most of your time in London, Mr. Tinsley?" Lady Emily asked with a perfect blend of curiosity and ladylike demureness.

"I probably spend half my time in Town. Once I assume the title, which I hope is a long time away, I intend to do my duty in the Lords."

"Just like Douglas." She nodded with approval. "Devonshire is much like here?"

"Certainly more like here than London. My family estate borders Knighton's and it is, in my humble opinion, the perfect mix of ocean, rivers, meadows and hills."

"It sounds divine," she said wistfully.

Eugenia realized she should probably be asking Perth about his family seat instead of deciding how perfect Lady Emily was for Graham. "What is your estate like, my lord?" she turned and asked Perth." It is on the other side of England from Devonshire, is it not?"

"My estate is mostly fields, farms and sheep. It is charming in its own way."

"It sounds lovely," she remarked, trying not to long for Devonshire.

⤜⤛⤜

GRAHAM WAS COMPLETELY exhausted, but not from the ride. After the picnic, Kitty Ravenhill had stuck to him like the stench of a rabid badger. He was grateful this was a short house party or else he would have to find an excuse to leave early. Surely he could survive one more day. His valet had prepared a bath for him and he sank into the decadent, steaming heat that was filled with some kind of oil which helped him to relax. His mind escaped to blissful nothing until he heard his door open. "I am not yet ready to get out, Harper," he said, mildly irritated. He never required his man's services to dry himself, so why was he disturbing his rare moment of peace?

Harper did not answer, so Graham lifted his head and opened one eye.

Kitty Ravenhill was leaning against the wall, watching him with a knowing smirk.

"I do not recall inviting you into my bedchamber," he said, with more calmness than he felt. He sat up slowly and carefully, grateful for the deep tub.

"All I have to do is scream," she said. There was a calculating gleam in her eye.

Graham cursed to himself. He should have followed his own advice and locked the door.

"Let me make something perfectly clear, Miss Ravenhill. I have no intention of being forced into anything with you. Any chance at all you may have had of capturing my regard has now been reduced to nil."

"Come now, Mr. Tinsley. I think we can come to a mutually satisfying agreement," she purred, moving closer.

"I think not. You will get no satisfaction from me."

"My brother will call you out."

Graham raised a haughty eyebrow, becoming more angry by the second. "You would wish a death sentence on your brother? This is no game, Miss Ravenhill. I take my freedom very seriously."

She scowled at him.

"Nothing—and I do mean nothing—will induce me to wed you. Nor would you wish that. Your life would be a living hell. However, I have done nothing to lead you on, nor has the thought of making you my bride ever crossed my mind."

She was clenching her jaw and he could hear her teeth grinding.

"I will take my chances, with my friends supporting me. Unfortunately, scandal never favors the female and you would do well to remember that. Now, I suggest you turn around and leave the way you came. My door will be locked to you always."

"I will make you regret this," she snarled.

"Not more than I would regret being shackled to you," he snapped.

"I have my ways." She turned and marched from the room, slamming the door behind her. Graham waited to hear some sign that she had been seen or discovered leaving his room, but thankfully, he heard none. He did not breathe a sigh of relief but a shudder of disgust ran through him. He had no doubt that there would be more trouble.

Graham quickly soaped himself, rinsed and climbed out of the tub. His thoughts were extremely disturbed and it was not so much himself he was worried about. He had a sinking suspicion that Kitty meant to do something to Eugenia or Lady Emily, but he did not know what. He had just managed to fasten his breeches and was reaching for his shirt when his door opened again.

With a groan, he turned to see Eugenia shut the door and lean up against it. She looked ready to breathe fire upon him.

"May I help you, pet?" he asked casually, as if he was not standing there half-dressed.

"How could you, Graham?" she growled.

He frowned. "Would you care to enlighten me of my sin? Because I was trying to bathe and relax and, apparently, I am somehow at fault."

"Kitty Ravenhill," she nearly spat. "Of all the loose women to consort with, why did it have to be her?"

"I suppose you saw her leaving my room?" he asked, pulling his shirt over his head.

"You are lucky it was only me."

"Did she see you?"

"Oh, yes! She smiled like the cat who got the cream as she was re-pinning her hair. She has no shame at all!"

"Hmm," he said thoughtfully, crossing his arms over his chest and leaning against the post of his bed.

"Is that all you have to say for yourself? You disgust me. I wish I could be indifferent!" She threw up her hands in a tomboyish gesture so typical of her.

"You are also in my chamber, Eugenia," he pointed out.

"No one considers aught is amiss between you and me."

"Nothing more has happened between you and I than Miss Ravenhill and I."

Eugenia narrowed her eyes at him, as though trying to assess whether he was telling her the truth or not. "Truly?"

"Truly," he reaffirmed. "She was trying to compromise me."

"Can a gentleman be compromised?" Eugenia twirled and plopped down into a chair. A tear rolled down her cheek. "Oh, Graham. I am so sorry. Why did I think the worst of you? I should have known that nasty, conniving little serpent would try to do something like this."

He walked over and wiped the tear away. "I forgive you, pet. The worst part is, I expected this from her and her brother."

"You should lock your door," she said.

Graham laughed. "I had meant to tell you that and then here I am, caught by not one, but two females.

She gave him a precocious look. "Thank God I was the only one who saw."

"Yes, indeed, but I told her that no matter what she tried I would not marry her."

Eugenia jumped up into his arms and kissed his cheek before resting hers on his chest. "You are the best of brothers."

He swallowed hard. He was not feeling very brotherly at that moment, with her body pressed up against his. He would have to have a word with Lady Hambridge about this. Had no one told her about men? Those men who were not brotherly? He set her back from him before he did something extremely stupid.

"Has Perth proposed yet?"

"No. He said he is waiting to hear from Knighton."

"Do you think you will accept him?"

She shrugged and walked over to the window. She began to worry the heavy gold brocade through her fingers. She was a fidget, his Eugenia.

"I do think Farnsworth is off the table, at least."

Graham was relieved but tried not to show it. "Why do you say that?"

"Did you see him flirting with Aunt Hambridge and the countess?" She shook her head. "I think something is in the wind there."

Graham blinked a few times. He had not noticed. "I do not think they could give him an heir…"

"He has nephews. Besides, I do not think I could tolerate being Lady Augusta's stepmother. And I would be a grandmother without ever having borne my own child!"

He walked over to the windowsill and stood beside her, looking out over the park. "For what it is worth, I think you are making the right decision."

"Nothing feels right anymore. I simply need to try harder."

"Do not change for them, Genie. Perth seems pleased with you."

She snorted. "That is because he does not know me well enough. He will change his mind."

"Do not sell yourself short. You will learn what you need to know. Anyone would be lucky to have you."

"Do you mean to ask Lady Emily? I like her a great deal. She is the first female to truly want to be my friend since Sybil."

"I am glad you like her, but she is not yet out and I have not made up my mind. I think when I am ready I will know it."

"How fortunate you are to have a choice," she snapped.

"I almost did not, today," he reflected.

"You said you would not marry her under any circumstances!"

"I do not intend to, but there are situations in which honor overrules everything else."

She looked at him, completely horrified. "I cannot think of any-thing that would induce me to marry a Ravenhill."

# CHAPTER EIGHT

EUGENIA WENT DOWNSTAIRS early for breakfast the next day and Lord Perth was the only one in the room. She hesitated at the door when she saw him sitting there alone, then chastised herself.

"Good morning, my lord," she said, entering the room and attempting to be cheerful. He immediately pushed back his chair and stood up.

"Good morning, Lady Eugenia. You look lovely," he said, coming over to greet her.

She did feel rather lovely that day. She had chosen a muslin day dress the color of grass, which gave her a summery feel.

He held out a chair for her. "May I prepare a plate for you?" He waved his hand and a footman came forward. "Do you take coffee or tea?"

"Tea please, with milk and two spoonfuls of sugar," she answered, smiling up at him as he pushed in her chair. He filled a plate for her and another footman placed a heaped tray of warm scones before her.

"I trust you slept well?" he asked as he took his seat next to her.

"I did, thank you. The sound of the waves nearby soon sent me to sleep."

He gave a nod as though it was just as expected. "I always sleep best here."

Eugenia took a bite of a scone and wondered if mundane conversation was to be her lot if she married him. But that was unfair, she reprimanded herself again. Her brothers would frequently make no more than polite greetings first thing. She certainly should give him more than ten minutes to decry his conversational skills.

She dismissed her thoughts and relished the melting of the fresh scone and butter on her tongue.

"Would you care to take a turn about the garden after breakfast?"

"That would be acceptable, my lord."

"I find nature very pleasant first thing in the morning. It is a pity our society favors late night pleasure and thus misses most of it."

"I have never been able to sleep late into the morning," Eugenia admitted, and then mentally cursed herself for it. What if she decided he was not to her taste? Would she be obligated to eat breakfast alone with him every day?

"I will confess," he was saying, "that I suspected as much. I see you riding in the park when most ladies are still abed."

"Good morning," Graham said, entering the room; it immediately brightened. He patted Eugenia on the shoulder, like one of her brothers would have done, and she noticed Perth frown.

"Is your food unsavory, my lord?" she asked with concern.

"No, no. My food is excellent."

Graham filled his plate and sat down across from her.

"Did you sleep well, Tinsley?" Perth asked. Apparently this was the first question of the day for everyone.

"I did, rather," Graham answered as he accepted a cup of coffee from the footman and then selected one of the scones from the tray. He looked around and his gaze alighted on the orange marmalade.

Eugenia snatched it before he could.

"Eugenia," he warned.

"I just wish for my share. I remember a time when you took all of the jam before anyone else could."

"So you hid it from me every time I visited thereafter."

"Only until everyone else had had a chance to have some." She turned to explain to Perth. "You should know our Tinsley is a glutton for anything resembling jam. He fancies marmalade in particular."

"Would you mind taking your serving and passing the jar? I promise not to take more than my share. I was only twelve at the time," he explained to Perth.

Eugenia bubbled up with laughter. Moments later Graham joined her.

Perth stood quickly. "Would you care for that walk now, Lady Eugenia?"

"Yes, of course. Will you excuse us, Graham?"

He was chewing, but lifted his cup in salute as he began to rise.

She waved him back down. "No need for me. We will see you this afternoon?"

"Oh, yes. The shooting. I would not miss it for a pony. It seems as though we are due for a rematch."

She scoffed. "You have never beaten me before."

"Not since you were five," he agreed. "Perhaps today will be my lucky day."

Perth took her arm and practically dragged her from the breakfast parlor. "Let me fetch my bonnet, my lord."

"Of course. I will wait here," he said as he released her.

She tried to walk slowly up to her room, but slow was not her habit. She found her new straw bonnet which was adorned with dandelions tucked into a matching green ribbon.

She smiled when she saw it atop her head and thought it very dashing. When she descended the stairs, Perth was waiting there for her, smiling appreciatively.

She took his arm and he led her out into the garden. "You are very familiar with Tinsley," he remarked.

"Oh, yes, he is like a brother, "she stated as she always did. "Surely you knew that from Emma or Heath?"

He smiled pensively. "I suppose so."

He led her through the formal parterre, set below the back terrace. Some neatly patterned lines of shrubbery lay centered around a large, tiered marble fountain, where water trickled gently from the top, flowing down each layer.

They passed through the shrubbery and he led her down a gravel path. "There is something I wish to show you."

"I am happy to be shown," she replied, unable to think of anything more pithy to say.

They passed through a screen of evergreens, then the view opened up into a wide expense of cliffs and water and downs. There was a bench there for viewing pleasure, and he led her to sit down before joining her. He felt very large and the bench seemed small. Too small. She was acutely aware of him as a man. He distinctly did not feel like one of her brothers.

She felt him fuss with his hat in his hands and lifted her gaze to find him looking down at her. *Oh, my...*

"Lady Eugenia," he began and then looked out over the water. "As you are aware, I invited you here to meet my family and to ensure we would suit."

She nodded hesitantly.

"I sent a letter to your brother, and had hoped to hear a reply before speaking with you, but it appears I do not have the luxury of time."

The confusion must have shown on her face.

"Surely you do not miss the way the other gentlemen here are vying for your attentions?"

Her first instinct was to deny it, but then she thought about it.

"You do understand, I see, but the fact that you must think about it does you credit. I had known about Farnsworth, but the others..." He shook his head. "I am convinced I must speak to you now."

Others? The only other two gentlemen here were Ravenhill and

Tinsley.

He moved in front of her and kneeled on the ground, taking her hand. "Lady Eugenia, would you do me the great honor of becoming my wife?"

She felt outjockeyed. She had certainly not expected this from a morning constitutional through the garden.

"Do I speak too soon?" he asked sheepishly.

"No, no. No. I am honored, my lord."

"I should have waited to speak to your brother, like Farnsworth did. It is my deuced competitive nature," he said, rising and running his hand through his hair.

"I am very flattered by your offer, my lord." She should accept. *Say it, Eugenia.*

He held out his hands. "Do not answer me until you speak to your brother, if you wish. Only promise me that you will accept no other first."

"As Farnsworth is the only other to have offered, I can assure you I have already decided that he is better suited to my aunt than I."

He pursed his lips. "They do seem rather…"

"Smitten?" she offered.

"But he needs an heir." As if that explained everything, she reflected dryly.

"He has several nephews," she replied.

Perth sat down next to her again and took her hand. She watched the strange event feeling curiously detached. She had as good as betrothed herself to this man and she felt almost nothing except relief that she would please her family.

"I confess I feel a great sense of relief, knowing you have already decided against the duke."

She turned to smile at him and discovered he was leaning towards her. He placed a chaste kiss on her lips and gave her hand a squeeze. "May I say how happy this makes me, Lady Eugenia? You will make an excellent countess."

"Thank you, my lord."

"Shall we?" He stood and offered her his arm, but she noticed his attention was caught by something in the distance.

He immediately tried to lead her back towards the house.

"What is it?" She turned back and immediately saw what had disturbed him. "Oh. That was unexpected."

"The scoundrel!"

Farnsworth and her aunt were walking along the shore, hand in hand. He bent over to place a kiss on her lips that made Eugenia blush. It was nothing at all like the one Perth had just bestowed upon her.

"I am sorry you had to see that," he said, looking down at her with a crease between his brows.

"I am not. They deserve happiness just like we do."

"Your graciousness does you credit, my lady. However, he should not court you yet..."

She held up her hand before he finished. "It is quite permissible. I think he suspected he would not win my regard."

"It certainly eases any reservations I had with regard to trying to steal you away from him. I assure you, I would never be so careless with your affections."

"Thank you, my lord." Eugenia did not think her aunt and the duke were being careless. They were on a deserted beach, early in the morning, and had a realistic expectation of complete privacy. She was happy for her aunt. She only hoped something might come of it; then she would not feel so guilty.

"Is it to be bows or pistols, my lord?" a servant asked.

"I will defer to the ladies," Perth said, looking lovelorn at Eugenia. Graham had never thought a man could look such, but the earl appeared completely smitten.

"Why not both?" she answered. Graham knew too well how proficient she was at both.

"An excellent notion," Perth agreed. "That way, more people can participate if they choose."

There was a nice park to the east of the house where targets had been placed for their afternoon's entertainment.

"What do you say, my lady? Shall we divide into teams?"

"Ladies against gentlemen?" Eugenia suggested with a gleam in her eye that Perth would learn soon enough. He could tell that the earl did not understand he had met his match when it came to competitiveness. Felix was the only one of her brothers who could regularly beat her, which stood to reason since shooting was his profession.

"If that is what you wish," Perth answered.

The earl, Tinsley and Petersham divided on to one half of the lawn while Eugenia, Lady Emily, Lady Augusta, Kitty Ravenhill and Miss Masters lined up on the other.

"Why must we separate from the gentleman when the whole idea is to be nearer to them?" Kitty Ravenhill protested, loudly enough for the men to hear.

He saw Eugenia cast a look of disgust at the chit before masking her displeasure.

"Do you say best of three?" Perth called.

"Perhaps, rather, the winner of each flight goes against the other in a round?" she returned.

"That sounds fair."

Lady Emily was first against Ravenhill. Both shot three arrows and hit within the smallest circle of the target.

"Well done!" Perth exclaimed as he went to examine the targets. "I will call this one a draw!" he shouted down range.

Graham had to admit he was impressed despite himself. Lady Emily continued to have more depth to her than he had seen in most ladies.

The servants removed the arrows and it was Eugenia's turn to stand against Ravenhill. It would also be close. Eugenia was not quite as exact with the bow as the pistol, but he would put his money on her, any day.

As they drew their strings, Ravenhill walked over to speak to Eugenia.

Graham could not quite make out what was said, but he was quite certain it involved a boon if he won.

She glared at the baron and immediately turned and fired three arrows in succession, dead center, nearly splitting one after the other.

Ravenhill answered in kind, hitting dead center twice but one slightly off, if Graham was seeing properly. The look on the baron's face was beyond measure. It was clear he had underestimated his opponent.

The others took their turns, with respectable results, but after multiple rounds, it was clear Perth and Eugenia were the winners.

"Are you certain you wish to go compete with your future husband?" Perth asked, looking at Eugenia and smiling indulgently.

*What had he just said?* was all Graham's mind could ask. He looked around but no one else seemed to have heard or have thought anything of it if they had. Perhaps he had been mistaken?

"I am absolutely certain, my lord," she answered him coyly.

*Oh, well, 'tis best Perth be forewarned.*

"I think we should move the targets back farther," Eugenia suggested. Most people can master ten yards but thirty takes some skill. We can continue moving back by ten yards until one of us is the clear winner. Agreed?"

Perth chuckled as though highly amused. Graham hoped he would stay that way because he knew Eugenia was just getting started. She was no longer the smiling, beaming ray of sunshine, but the fierce warrior maiden intent on her task.

The targets were set to their new distance and a servant waved a flag, indicating they were ready.

"Ladies first," Perth said, as though all of this still amused him.

"Fifty quid on the lady?" Sir Martin said to Petersham.

The countess hushed him and Graham wanted to warn Petersham not to waste his money.

Eugenia stepped up to the line and took a little more time fixing her aim on the target but then she fired the three arrows in rapid succession. Graham could not see how precise she had been, but he had no doubt she was within the center circle.

Perth looked a little more serious as he took his first arrow from his quiver and lined up his mark. He did not fire them rapidly as Eugenia had, but each one carefully.

The crowd marched down to the targets to see the results and they were both astonishingly accurate.

"Farnsworth, you be the judge," Perth said.

The duke looked carefully but shook his head. "There is not a clear winner. I say either a rematch from the distance or go farther."

Eugenia had said as much when laying out the terms, but Perth still raised his brows and looked to the lady.

"Farther," she said, accepting her arrows from the servant and marching back to the starting line.

Perth watched her with a narrowed gaze but said nothing and accepted his own arrows. Graham thought perhaps he was finally seeing Eugenia for herself. The crowd moved back towards the shooting line, murmuring their thoughts.

"She is quite a marksman," Lady Emily said appreciatively.

"She is very competitive," Lady Hambridge added a bit apologetically.

"Such behavior is not very ladylike," Kitty Ravenhill put in bitterly.

The targets were reset and both competitors took their places. Eugenia repeated her process and fired her three shots methodically.

Perth took his time again and they all marched farther down the field to survey the outcome. Graham did not know if he preferred Eugenia to win or lose. However, she was a fiendishly good shot and as they neared the targets, it was obvious she had beaten Perth.

"Yes!" she exclaimed with laughter.

Perth eyed his target with disgust and then turned to Lady Eugenia. He held out his hand, clasped hers and bowed over them. "Congratulations, my lady."

Graham could tell by the look on his face what it had cost him to lose. Whether it was falling to his betrothed, a lady, or loss in general, he could not say.

Eugenia beamed with pleasure and then looked at the crowd. "Shall we try pistols now?"

Perth remained quiet, waiting for his guests to answer. Ever the gentleman, Graham thought with some displeasure.

"Tinsley? You owe me a rematch. Petersham? Hardy? I know you love to shoot," she goaded, very likely without realizing it.

"I think perhaps another time," Graham remarked, trying to warn her from doing further damage.

She looked at him with frustration, so he walked over and guided her to some trees, away from the others. "If you are trying to impress Perth with your demureness, you are instead making a spectacle of yourself."

"Whatever can you mean?" she asked with disbelief. "I thought we were having a shooting contest. Is the point not to shoot your best?"

He sighed and shook his head. Perhaps she never would understand. "The point is to have fun, and it is even acceptable to win. However, the guests have been standing out here for hours watching you and Perth."

Realization dawned on her face. Her chin quivered, but she nodded and then walked back to the assembled guests. "I apologize. I did not mean to become so impassioned."

Perth smiled. "There is no need to apologize, but perhaps every-one else might wish to return to the house for refreshments. I am happy to stay out here and shoot pistols with you."

"That is kind of you, but there is no need. We will have plenty of time for shooting later on."

She took his arm and they began walking towards the house.

Yet again Graham was left amongst the others, speculating on what the status was between Eugenia and the Earl.

"Has it been settled then?" Miss Ravenhill asked her brother, a few steps behind Graham.

"I had not heard, but not if I have anything to say about it."

"You had best to do something quickly, for my efforts have not been successful."

*Nor will they be,* Graham thought with contempt. Just what was Ravenhill about? Graham would have to remind Eugenia again to be careful—that is, if she was still speaking to him.

# CHAPTER NINE

E UGENIA COULD NOT fall asleep. After the narrow escape Graham had had with Kitty Ravenhill, Eugenia had locked her door, but nevertheless could not stop worrying. He had warned her about Lord Ravenhill and that he might possibly try something similar. The thought of either one of them being tied to a Ravenhill was beyond disturbing.

Normally, she slept dead to the world, unless something was bothering her and then she could not purchase a wink. At home she would read an entire book on such occasions, but nothing could make her stop fretting about impending marriage. Not one of her suitors had ever felt right. Oh, she liked most of them well enough, but not enough to marry. Perth was her best prospect by far.

One more day… if she could survive that then she could at least go back to London.

She tossed and turned, trying not to think about the obscure future. The moon was not even very bright, so there was little light coming through the small parting in the curtain. She flipped back over to the other side and then her sheets were entirely too tangled, so she tossed them off to reorganize them.

She climbed out of the bed and widened her curtains, in order to have enough light to straighten the bedding without having to light a taper. What she would not give for a book, a cup of chocolate and some warm biscuits, but she dare not leave the safety of her chamber. It was still hard to believe that Kitty Ravenhill had barged into Graham's room while he was bathing. Eugenia never would have thought of such a thing! What if she had been caught, as she had wished? It did not bear thinking on, but Eugenia could do little else.

A noise jerked her out of her reverie. Was her imagination getting the better of her? It sounded as though the door handle were rattling. Someone was trying to open her door!

Quickly, she scrambled to hide on the other side of the bed while she gathered her wits. She needed a weapon. No one trying to intrude during the night would do so with good deeds in mind. She crawled to her dressing table and found her dagger. Truly, she had never thought to use it on a human, but she would do so before her virtue was stolen. She also found her candlestick and crawled back behind the bed. Her eyes adjusted a small amount, but it was still not bright enough for her confidently to throw a dagger at an intruder.

There was silence for a few minutes—it must have been—but her heart did not stop racing. Indeed, when she heard the noise again her chest thumped even harder. This time, it sounded as though a key had been placed in the lock. It rattled again, but she heard a muttered curse. At least she could now say the intruder sounded male. Footsteps crept away from her door and she wondered if that meant he had given up. Did it further mean that Lord Ravenhill had come to compromise her? Who else would it be? 'Twas either he or Kitty, but her brother could do much more damage to Eugenia's reputation and future.

She waited long enough for her pulse to calm and then began to rise when she decided he had given up. Thankfully, her party was to go home in the morning—she just had to survive until then. Should she seek out her aunt for protection? No. She shook her head. If he was gone, there was no point in waking anyone when she could no doubt defend herself. Despite not approving of Ravenhill, Aunt

Hambridge might still force Eugenia to wed him to save her reputation, if she was caught in a compromising situation.

Eugenia climbed back up onto the bed, knowing there would be no more sleep for her that night. She kept a weapon in each hand and stared at the canopy over her head, wishing she had a book or anything with which to pass the next few hours.

A shadow passed in front of her window. At least, so she thought. It was hard to tell when there was little moon. Her heart began to pound again and she swore to herself that she would never again read a Gothic novel after this night.

The panes on her window rattled and she had had enough. Stealing her courage, she threw back the covers again and marched over to the window. She tossed back the curtains... and screamed when she saw a face looking back at her.

"Let me in!" Ravenhill demanded.

"Absolutely not! How dare you try to sneak into my room!"

"I will break the window," he threatened.

"Go ahead. I will be gone from this room before you can enter." She turned to run but he forced the window in, knocking her flat on her face.

She grunted with the pain and the shock and began to crawl forward. He grabbed her ankle and pulled her back, the rough carpet burning the skin on her legs as he dragged her towards him.

She screamed and tried to fight free, clawing at him in desperation. She had dropped her dagger when she fell and strove to reach it.

"Stop it, you viper of Hell!"

"I am not the one who has broken into a lady's bedchamber!"

"I should have known you would not fight like a lady."

"That was the wrong thing to say," she growled. He might be twice her size, but she found renewed strength to knee him in a place most likely to disable him. Her unconventional childhood had had its benefits. He groaned and for a moment she thought he would vomit over her, but he was not about to give up so easily. Just as she began to scramble away, he grabbed her night-rail and ripped it. Realizing she was utterly ruined if anyone happened upon them, she kicked at him, desperately searching for a way to get out of the situation with more than her life intact.

"What do you want, Ravenhill?" she asked. Shaking with fear, she crawled backward. Despite the darkness, she could still see the predatory gleam of his smile at her exposed skin and she shivered.

"You, of course," he said, taking off his coat. "I had not expected such a lively encounter."

"Please, no," she whispered as she felt around on the carpet and her hand met with metal. "Anything else. I will find a way to get you money."

"But it would be so much more *pleasurable* to have the whole package," he said, lunging for her.

Her hand curled around the hilt of her knife and as he landed on top of her, she drove the blade into his back.

She had no idea what she had hit, but Ravenhill groaned in pain and then went limp across her body at the very moment someone began pounding on the door. "Eugenia! What is happening in there?"

"Graham!" she shouted.

"Let me in!"

"I cannot!" she cried back at him.

"Are you right behind the door?"

"No," she called back.

Loud thumps and splintering followed. In a few short minutes, the door crashed into the room.

"Genie!" he shouted, running towards her and emitting a string of profound curses when he observed the situation.

"Is he dead?" she asked as Graham flipped Ravenhill away from her.

"We need light. I think he is still breathing."

*Ask and ye shall receive*, she thought bitterly, the sounds of the household waking intruded upon her notice. Then steps could be heard coming towards her room; on their arrival, most of the owners were holding tapers.

"What in the world?" Perth asked, being the first to arrive, followed by the countess, the duke and Lady Augusta. She could not see anyone else's face, but she was certain they all were witnessing her shame.

Eugenia began to shake as the horror of what had happened sank in.

"He is still alive," Graham pronounced.

Eugenia was not sure if she was pleased or disappointed by that. The man had intended to violate her. He *had* violated her, even if her virtue was still intact. The rest of the events went on as though she was an observer. Things happened around her and she just watched.

"Send for the doctor," Graham said to the gathering. "I do not believe anything vital was damaged. Perhaps he passed out from the pain."

"It appears that he climbed in at the window," Lady Augusta said. Why was she in there?

They lifted Ravenhill and put him on the bed. Her aunt came over and placed a blanket around her. "Are you hurt, my dear?"

She could not form words, but shook her head as tears formed in her eyes instead.

"Take her to my chamber, Tinsley," her aunt ordered.

Graham scooped her up in his arms and carried her out of the room. When he placed her on the bed, she wanted to cling to him, but instead she stayed curled up in a ball.

"Have her things packed. As soon as I have attended to Ravenhill, we are leaving."

"Do not do anything rash, Tinsley," her aunt said.

Eugenia could feel his gaze on her; she barely had the energy to move her eyes to meet his. He walked over and gently brushed his fingers across her face.

"Whatever happens, Genie, you did nothing wrong." He kissed her forehead and then left her. She felt utterly desolate.

⟫⟫⟩⟨⟨⟨

GRAHAM COULD BARELY contain his fury. Bruises had already begun to form on Eugenia's skin when he put her down. He should have protected her better. It should never have fallen to her to protect herself. But how would she feel if Ravenhill died? She might never recover from that. Her family would support her, of course, but no one would want to marry her and her name would be tarnished forever. Even Knighton could only pay so much to conceal the damage and anyone who could be bought did not deserve her.

He opened the door to find the Countess in the hallway, then re-entered Eugenia's room to find Perth, the duke, and Lady Augusta there with the doctor. Thankfully, Lady Emily had not been present and Petersham and Hardy were in a different wing.

Graham waited for one of them to speak as Ravenhill lay still upon the bed.

"Dr. Walters thinks he will live if infection does not set in." Perth finally spoke.

"She struck him very effectively in the shoulder, which immediately incapacitated his arm. He was awake for a few moments, but I have given him a sedative. I will call in the morning to see how he goes on, my lord," the doctor said. "I will see myself out," he pronounced and left them alone.

"Did she say what happened?" Perth asked.

"I think it is rather obvious," Graham retorted.

"Is it? Because when I arrived, you were rolling him off her."

"Good God, man, what are you suggesting? She had to fight him

93

off with a knife!"

"What lady has a knife to hand?" Lady Augusta asked derisively.

"Thank goodness she did!" he barked.

"Perhaps, when Lady Eugenia feels able, she may explain," Farnsworth said with grating calm.

"Both of you should be defending her," Graham growled. "Her aunt and I are taking her back to London immediately." He turned to leave. "Let me know if he lives, because when I am through with him he will wish he hadn't."

"Be reasonable, Tinsley. There is no sign of forced entry. Perhaps she changed her mind," Perth remarked with a frown.

"You heard the blackguard say he needed an heiress, and she is the wealthiest of them all. She made no mention to me of him courting her, other than to say that nothing would induce her to marry him."

Perth shook his head in disbelief.

"I believe you have had a narrow escape, my lord," Lady Augusta said, sidling up to the earl.

"No, I believe Eugenia has. Frankly, this disgusts me. You are not worthy of her." He stepped over the wreckage he had made of the door and directed the servants to gather Eugenia's trunks and load them into the carriage.

Dawn would soon be coming over the horizon and they could make the return journey to London before noon. He hoped Knighton would arrive soon, because this was not going to end well for Eugenia. None of this was her fault – in fact, Ravenhill had set it up that way – but now it would be she who would be ruined. He had no doubt Knighton would also see Ravenhill ruined if he lived, but nevertheless word would spread that she had been violated and Perth no longer wanted her.

Perth was certainly not the man Graham had thought he was. After he had come forward to help save the duchess, he would have expected better from him. Had Lady Augusta poisoned him against

Eugenia? Had she said something while he himself had been in the other room?

When the carriage was ready, Graham carried Eugenia downstairs and laid her across one of the bench seats. Her maid and aunt took the other. When he released her, she began to shake and he debated tying his horse to the back of the carriage in order to hold her. Instead, he took a flask from his pocket and held it against her lips. "Drink. It will help you sleep."

"What is it?"

"Brandy." She took it without a fight, wincing a little when she swallowed, but then turned over and tucked the blanket around her. Lord willing, she would sleep and not dwell on what had just happened. Hopefully, Knighton could find a solution quickly.

Graham did not know what he would do if Knighton did not arrive soon. Pray God he was already in London. He had little doubt the news—whether accurate or not—would spread like fire. The journey to London was not far enough to rid him of the pure fury he felt against Ravenhill and the injustice that was being served to Eugenia. She had not encouraged the scoundrel's attentions, yet she was to suffer as though she had. Graham vowed he would do whatever it took to right this wrong.

They reached London before most of Society would have awakened, but workers were already about, making deliveries, and vendors were setting up for their day.

Eugenia was still sleeping, so he scooped her into his arms and carried her into Hambridge House, up the wide staircase to her chamber and placed her in her bed.

When he descended the stairs, Lady Hambridge was waiting for him.

"What do you mean to do?" she asked.

"Go home and change and then see if Knighton has yet arrived."

"He is on his way?" she asked.

"Indeed. If there is a God, he will be here already."

"Please let me know. Otherwise, I will go out tonight and mitigate as much of the damage as I can. These things have a way of traveling faster than light."

"Knowing Knighton, he will wish to do whatever possible to keep this quiet. Perth made it rather clear that he considered her compromised."

Lady Hambridge gasped. "I cannot believe it of him!"

"I heard it with my own ears."

"And Farnsworth?"

It was unlikely, Graham reflected, that he succeeded in masking the incredulity in his expression. "Your niece had decided against the duke, since he seemed to favor you."

"Oh, dear." She looked as though she would faint. God save him from hysterical females at this moment!

"Indeed."

"I can speak with her and with him, of course."

"I think it is best to discuss the matter with Knighton. I will send word." He gave a curt nod and left.

Returning to his own house, he quickly shaved and changed his clothes and set out again on foot. Thankfully, Knighton's town residence was close by, because Graham did not wish to be back in the saddle again so soon after riding for half the night.

The relief he felt when he saw the brass knocker on the door was indescribable. Despite the early hour, Quincy opened the door to him with a pleasant greeting.

"I am most happy to see you, Quincy! Where might I find His Grace?" he asked.

"His Grace and their lordships are in the breakfast room, sir."

*Plural?* he thought as his feet made haste in that direction. More than one Knighton brother would be extremely welcome at this juncture.

The footman opened the door without hesitation – Graham had always run tame about both households.

"Tinsley," the duke said, standing to come and shake his hand. Edmund and Heath were also there. "I must say, you are very welcome, but I assume you did not come at this early hour just to welcome us to London?"

"Unfortunately, no," he said, taking a seat. One of the footmen brought him a cup of coffee.

Knighton perceptively dismissed the servants. When the door closed behind them, Graham spoke. "I have just returned from Brighton with your sister and your aunt."

"At this hour?" Heath asked, pausing in the middle of buttering his toast.

Edmund remained silent.

"What happened?" Knighton asked quietly.

"Ravenhill forced himself into Eugenia's room and tried to ravish her."

"Tried?" Heath growled. "Is Eugenia harmed?"

"She fought and stabbed him before he succeeded," Graham replied.

"Does he yet live?" Edmund asked.

"He was alive when we left. The doctor said the only risk to his life would be infection."

His brow creased, the duke said nothing, thinking as he did when trying to solve a problem. He'd had the weight of a dukedom on his shoulders from a young age.

"There is more, I am afraid." Graham sighed. "As you know, Farnsworth had asked to court her, as did Perth."

"I received his request," Knighton confirmed.

"I expect you also saw they were vying for her hand in a rather public manner?" he asked, brows raised.

"I did."

"We all did," Heath clarified.

"It was mostly civilized, despite the gossip columns' love for Eugenia. We left a few days ago for a weekend house party at Perth's Seaside Cottage. It quickly became apparent that your sister seemed to favor the earl's suit, but Ravenhill and his sister were neighbors and present for everything. They also made little secret of the fact that they were out to catch the largest monetary prizes to be had."

"Which would be yourself and Eugenia," Knighton said, putting the pieces together.

"Correct. Perth had already proposed and your sister had accepted, but it had not yet been announced. I overheard Ravenhill telling his sister he still had a chance, but I did not suspect he would break in through her window. I had warned her to lock her door."

Heath pounded on the table with his fist in anger.

"I also received an unwelcome visit from Kitty Ravenhill, but I was able to send her on her way, but not without threats being hurled at me. I am afraid this was partly my fault."

"No one acting like a scoundrel can excuse it or lay the blame at anyone else's feet," Edmund offered.

"Be that as it may, Eugenia is in trouble. Perth so much as denounced the betrothal and Farnsworth and his daughter were witness to all of it."

"Your brother-in-law dares to jilt our sister?" Heath asked in disbelief. "I would not have thought it of him after she rushed to save Emma from me!"

"Thankfully, nothing has been made public. I will send a note post haste to Perth, to explain and to request he keep me abreast of Ravenhill's condition. First, I would like to see my sister, then we shall determine what is to be done."

"Did Eugenia say anything to you?" Edmund asked.

Graham shook his head. "No, but I did not press her. It was very clear to me what had happened."

Edmond squeezed his arm. "Thank God you were there to support her."

"Farnsworth might still have her," Knighton said, standing.

He might, but Graham wondered if forcing that match would be even more punishment to poor Genie when she knew he preferred another.

# CHAPTER TEN

EUGENIA DID NOT wish to face the world, but she knew that at some point it would be necessary. Just not yet. When there was a knock on her door, she tried to ignore it, but it opened anyway. It was probably Stevens or her aunt, come to check how she did, but she closed her eyes, determined to ignore them.

The side of her bed sank and a hand touched her face. It was decidedly not her aunt. She opened her eyes to see her eldest brother's face looking down at her with sadness.

"Rowley!" she exclaimed in little more than a whisper. Without a word, he gathered her in his arms. "You have heard?"

"Yes, what Tinsley knows. I should like to hear the whole from you if you feel able. Edmund and Heath are also here. May I take you to them?"

"I want to go home, Rowley."

"I know you do," he said, stroking the side of her face, "but unfortunately, this must be dealt with first."

"I was afraid you would say that. May I bathe first? Graham must have put me straight into bed."

"Everything is to be prepared for you when we arrive back at Knighton House."

"Oh, I see. Very well. My aunt knows?"

"I have spoken with her. She will attend us later, once we have made some decisions."

Rowley stood up and held out a hand to her. When she moved, she winced.

Her brother scowled. "I want to know what happened, but I will not make you tell the story more than once."

"I am well enough, truly, but I do feel as if I was kicked and thrown from a horse."

Rowley said nothing, which was worse than him venting his spleen. He found her slippers and led her from the house. He helped her into the carriage even though they lived only a short distance away. Even though, perhaps, she did not look different on the outside, she felt different and exposed—as though everyone would know what had happened simply by looking at her.

As soon as she entered the doors of Knighton House, both of her brothers enveloped her in a hug. It was difficult not to feel relief. She felt safe, although she knew this was only a mild reprieve from the storm to come.

Quincy cleared his throat. "Everything is prepared for my lady, Your Grace."

"Brothers, we shall allow Eugenia time to bathe and refresh herself before the inquisition. We will be waiting for you in my study when you are ready, my dear."

She climbed the familiar staircase and entered her room, where Stevens was waiting with a tub full of steaming water. The maid gasped when she saw her mistress. Eugenia had not looked at herself, but she could not imagine it was a pleasant sight.

"You may go, Stevens. I shall do for myself."

"But my lady," she protested.

"Please go." She did not feel like arguing, nor being cosseted. "I will ring when I am ready to dress."

Stevens bobbed a curtsy and left.

Eugenia turned to look at her reflection. A deep purple bruise was forming on her chin and a cut marked her swollen lip. That was only the part which could be seen. She slipped off her gown and climbed into the tub, deliberately numbing her mind. Detaching herself seemed the best way to deal with this.

She knew her brothers wanted to discuss her future. Surely Rowley would not force her to wed Ravenhill? She would rather die than have him touch her again. She also had not missed the look on Perth's face when he discovered her, either. What would become of her?

Stevens helped her to dress and she made her way downstairs to the study. Her brothers stood up when she entered, and she walked over and sat in a chair near the fire.

Rowley closed the door and came to sit across from her. He reached over and took her hand. "There is no easy way to speak of this, but if we delay, it may cost us dearly. I have asked Tinsley to be here to fill in those parts of the story of which you might be unaware."

Eugenia had not noticed him there, but turned her head and saw him lurking in the corner. His gaze pierced straight through her and she had to look away.

"He has told us that Ravenhill broke into your room and you were fighting him off when he himself discovered you."

She nodded. "Ravenhill tried my door first, but I had locked it as Graham advised me to do." She swallowed hard. "I heard him walk away and thought he had given up, but then I found him at my window. Somehow he managed to force the sash. I thought I could get away but he caught hold of my ankle."

"Did anything else happen?"

She lowered her gaze to her lap. "We struggled and he ripped my gown. I reached for my dagger about the same time Graham burst through the door." She looked gratefully up at her best friend. "After that, I remember very little."

"That is much as we suspected."

"What happens now?" she asked, her voice shaking.

"I have sent word to Perth, but Tinsley thinks he is being unreasonable. He did propose to you?"

"Yes," she whispered, "but nothing has been announced."

"I am afraid, dear sister, that he is not inclined to view this situation in your favor."

"Gentlemen never do," she said bitterly.

"If this is the case, I am most disappointed in him. Emma will be devastated by what she will view as his betrayal."

"He is only human and cares a great deal for what others think of him."

"You are far too generous. This is not something I will easily forgive," Heath snarled.

"Your aunt is inclined to believe that Farnsworth will still have you."

"No!" she shouted. "I cannot marry the duke."

Rowley looked taken aback. "Why ever not? In your situation, you would do very well in deed to become a duchess."

"At what price, brother?"

"I realize it may not be a love match, but your reputation—your good name – would be saved."

"Did my aunt also tell you she is very much in love with him and he with her?"

"What does that have to say to anything?"

She looked around at the other faces in the room. "The three of you have made love matches, yet you would settle for a cold, loveless union for me?" Angrily, she jerked to her feet "I have done nothing wrong, yet you would punish me? No, I would prefer your efforts go towards proving Ravenhill the blackguard that he is."

"Do not fret yourself on that account," Heath assured her. "However unfair it is, Sister, it will not be enough to replace the doubt that he damaged you."

Eugenia shook her head. "I cannot believe you would force me into this."

"I am not forcing anything yet. I will speak to Perth and Farnsworth and consider the situation again," Knighton said.

"Let me assure you, Brother, nothing—and I mean nothing—will persuade me to wed Ravenhill."

"That was never in question," he replied.

She gave a conceding nod, too grateful to speak. She knew in her heart that he wanted what was best for her, but Society still dictated what was considered acceptable and what was not.

"I will consider your wishes as much as possible. However, life as a pariah would be worse than marriage to such as Farnsworth."

Eugenia was not certain. Life would be lonely, but that would be preferable, in her opinion. There had to be some remote village in England or Scotland where she could settle without notoriety.

Emma strode into the room. "I have just heard! Oh, my dearest!" she exclaimed when she saw Eugenia's face. "This cannot be tolerated!" She turned to her husband.

"I am doing what I can, my dear. We are making a plan."

"If I were a man I would call him out!" The duchess's anger on her behalf was touching.

"You can hardly call out a man who is already injured. Eugenia took care of him herself."

"I am glad to hear it, but she will be the one to suffer for the scoundrel's actions."

Eugenia saw her brothers wince.

"Do not tell me it is not so."

"Their plan is to marry me off as quickly as possible. Your cousin no longer wishes to be betrothed to me."

Emma spun around to face her. "My cousin?"

Eugenia could no longer speak. "Please explain things to her. When you have more information, please let me know." She retired to take a walk in the garden, too angry and upset to speak any longer. She had known this was what would happen, yet it did not make it any more palatable.

Graham touched her arm as she tried to leave the room, but she shook it away. She did not need to see the pity in his gaze. She needed to be alone and the garden was the closest to somewhere peaceful she could find within the environs of the house.

GRAHAM REMAINED IN the corner, more disturbed than he would like to admit about Eugenia's situation.

He listened to Knighton explain to his duchess everything that had happened, including Perth's involvement and rejection.

"You cannot mean to force her to marry somebody just to hush up a scandal!"

"I hope it will not come to that," Knighton replied. "I—we—all want to see her happy."

"What does *she* want?" the duchess demanded.

"To return home. But you know what will happen if she does not face the situation." The duke threw up his hands as if he knew there was no good solution.

"She is welcome to live with us at The Grange, if that is her wish. The people there will not shun her."

"She did nothing wrong and if she runs away, Ravenhill wins," he countered.

"There has to be a better way," Edmund said thoughtfully.

Graham agreed, but remained quiet.

"Perth would have been the best way, but I refuse to twist any-one's arm for the privilege of wedding my sister," Knighton pronounced.

"What do you plan to do next?" the duchess asked.

"I sent an express to Brighton as soon as I heard from Tinsley. I expect a messenger back soon."

"I will go and discover if he has come," Heath said as he stood. "I do not think Quincy would have interrupted our family meeting."

Graham wanted to find Eugenia, even though she doubtless wanted to be alone. The brothers overwhelmed him at times, and she may well have felt outnumbered.

He left the study, where the duke and duchess were still debating what was best to do with their sister. Truly, he did not wish to be part of that conversation at present, except it was amusing to watch her stand up to the duke without hesitation.

Quincy seemed to know Graham was looking for Eugenia. "She is in the garden, sir."

Graham gave an appreciative nod and then walked slowly across the marble floor, past the ballroom towards the terrace doors. He opened them slowly and looked around. She would probably be at the back of the garden.

The bright, sunny day was a blunt contrast to the dark, dire situation they were facing.

He walked quietly—thoughtfully—through the lush green grass and flowering bushes, where bees were buzzing about their business.

When he reached the end, he paused to watch her on the wooden swing Knighton had had placed there for her, beneath the large birch tree.

She was twirling aimlessly in the swing, looking completely distant and lost. And young and innocent.

He shuddered to think what would have happened had he been a minute later last night, but she has done a rather good job of defending herself. He had not been quick enough though, he thought regretfully, since Perth had still misunderstood the situation. How anyone could think Eugenia capable of such duplicity was beyond him. She was the most pure soul he knew. Not purely perfect, but certainly not deceitful. It was untenable to see her spirit crushed.

"I know you are there, Graham," she said after a few minutes, still not looking at him.

He stepped forward, then behind her, and began to gently push the swing. She leaned her head back and closed her eyes.

"How can I help you, Genie?"

"I wish I knew," she answered, barely above a whisper.

"Are you contemplating something rash?"

She chuckled, but with a bitter humor. "You know me too well, Graham. Of course I am considering something rash."

"Such as?"

"I shall tell you only if you give me your word not to squeak beef on me."

"I would not be out here offering to help you, if I intended to plot against you." He stopped. "Your brothers are only trying to help, but I cannot agree to you being handed over to Farnsworth as a means to save your reputation."

He heard her swallow hard and saw a tear run down her face.

"Thank you." She pushed off with her feet and the wooden swing twisted around. "I am trying to weigh my options. As you say, if I remain, I will be married off quickly to whomever will have me. I cannot think that even the Duke of Farnsworth would be so desperate."

"But he saw, as I did, and would have to know you were being attacked against your will."

"Perth did not."

"Perth is a coward," he growled. "He is too worried about appearances. I believe Lady Augusta may have poisoned him against you."

"Then she is welcome to him."

Graham pushed her a few more times before she spoke again.

"I think I might like to go away for a while," she said after a time.

"And where would you go?"

"That, dear friend, is the stumbling block I have. Moreover, the herd would be after me before I reached Hounslow Heath."

Graham could not but agree with that conclusion.

"I do think it would be best if you made appearances, head held high, with the support of your loving, powerful family."

"Sporting my lovely bruises," she retorted.

"It will support the fact that you were attacked," he reasoned.

"And when all of the gentlemen reject me?"

"You will always have me."

She smiled sadly and squeezed his hand. "I do not know what I would have done without you. My brothers cannot see the forest for the trees at the moment. We must protect the Knighton name at all costs," she mimicked in a stern voice.

"Where would you go if you could go anywhere you chose?"

She pursed her lips, looking thoughtful. "The West Indies sounds delightful," she replied, continuing to tilt her head back as though the dream was a reality in her mind. "Think of the exotic food and animals—and warm sunshine all the time."

"Think of the bugs, the malaria, being too hot and sticky to sleep at night."

"Very well, spoilsport," she said sharply, opening her eyes to look up at him. "Where would you suggest?"

"I think I would choose somewhere along the Mediterranean. You still have the warmth and sunshine but less of the annoyances. And mountains are nearby if you desire a change of scenery."

"That does sound pleasant. I have always wanted to travel."

"Realistically, where would you go? Just for a short repairing lease, mind you."

"Now you make it sound as though I have lost an estate at the tables or killed a man in a duel."

Graham waited for her to realize what she had just said. Eugenia often spoke before she thought.

"Oh, gracious! I might have done just that."

"You were defending yourself. It is hardly the same thing."

"To rational people, maybe. It is the *ton* we are speaking of, Graham."

"To return to my original question, where else would you go?"

"Perhaps to Heath's farm in Kent, or one of the smaller estates if Rowley would allow it? Because we both know that he would know the moment I arrived there."

Graham absolutely, without hesitation knew he should not say what he was about to. However, last night he had seen what Eugenia had suffered, and he knew he would do practically anything to protect her choice in the matter.

"I have a cottage in Bexley," he said quietly, "not far from here. I go there myself when I need to escape."

She dragged her feet to stop the swing and turned to look him sharply in the eye. "You would do this for me?"

"Only as your last resort," he replied, holding her gaze. "And only if Knighton knows you are safe."

She nearly launched herself at him, but he caught her. She clung to him as though her life depended on it, and he held her tight as her body began to shake with sobs. Graham had been contemplating marriage to some unknown lady, vaguely, in his mind, and he did not know why he had not thought of the solution before.

"You could marry me."

# CHAPTER ELEVEN

E UGENIA CEASED SOBBING immediately, but a few shuddering breaths escaped in spite of her best efforts to control them. "What did you say?"

"I said that you could marry me," he repeated.

"There is no need for you to be a sacrificial lamb. You have already done more than necessary."

"I need to marry someone."

Eugenia released Graham and stepped away. The thought of him sacrificing himself for her was simply too much. "I thank you for even forming the words without choking on your tongue, but I could not do that to you. Everyone would pity you."

"Eugenia," he said in the same tone Rowley used when he was taking her to task.

She held up her hand. "I will accept your generous offer of visiting your estate, but that is where your obligation will end."

She wiped at her eyes and tried to straighten her dress. "We should go back inside. I am certain the herd has everything decided for me in any case." She began walking, needing to be away from him. If she stayed, she would give in and take him up on his offer. It would be such an easy, comfortable solution and it was so very tempting. However, this was her tangle, not his and it would be both selfish and unfair to chain him to her for the rest of their lives.

"Eugenia!" Rowley called to her when she reached the house. She tried not to be annoyed, but she hated the way everyone had gathered to determine what happened to her.

She returned to the study, determined to be calm but firm. However, she was not expecting her aunt and the duke to be there. She paused at the study door, unable to move.

Graham came up behind her and put his hands on her shoulders. "Remember what I said. We have not finished discussing this."

She could not look up into his green eyes nor would she lose her resolve. She moved forward into the room and curtsied, feeling as though she were about to stand trial, her brothers and their wives the jury.

"Your Grace."

Farnsworth stood and came over and took her hands. He searched her face, examining her wounds. "I should have killed him."

"Nonsense. He is not worth the blood on your hands, but I appreciate your concern. He is in a far worse case than I, I assure you."

"I am glad to hear it." He led her to the seat next to her aunt, and gathering her skirts, she sat down, assuming a demure pose.

Were they to have tea and a tribunal, she wondered as Quincy brought in a tea tray. Apparently, they were to discuss her future like any other matter. How very civilized.

Once the duchess had served everyone, Rowley cleared his throat. "Farnsworth was kind enough to bring news that Ravenhill appears to be recovering."

"He declared it was a mere scratch," the duke agreed.

"However, Genie, Perth has written to confirm that he does not believe you will suit after all," Rowley added.

"That is no surprise, Brother," she said with far more calm than she felt. Her blood was boiling.

Farnsworth set down his teacup with a clink. "Ravenhill means to try to have you, still. When he awoke, he made many outrageous claims, including your acceptance of his betrothal."

Eugenia dropped her scalding hot tea in her lap and immediately jumped up. "Never! I will never marry that... that cur!" She wished she had a wider vocabulary at that moment.

"Eugenia, do but consider," her aunt said, taking her hand even though she was distractedly trying to mop up the tea from her dress. "You will be ruined if you do not wed quickly."

"I know you might find this distasteful, my lady," Farnsworth said softly, "but I am still willing to have you."

Eugenia bit her lip and closed her eyes. They all seemed to consider she should be grateful for being purchased like a lame broodmare! She turned sharply to look at him and her aunt. "While I am exceedingly grateful you believe the truth, that I did not encourage Ravenhill's attentions, or lose my virtue, I cannot, in good conscience, marry you."

"Eugenia!" Rowley scolded.

"No, dear brother, you do not know what I know and you have not seen what I have seen."

She looked kindly upon the duke and her aunt and spoke quietly so only they could hear. "I saw you together, walking along the shore. There is no need to sacrifice your happiness for mine."

The duke looked down at his hands. Her aunt's eyes filled with tears. "I am sorry, Genie," she said, her throat choking on her words and rising, she hurried from the room.

The duke looked up. "I had not intended for that to happen, my lady. Seeing your aunt again brought back something lost long ago."

"Then you should take that rare second chance given to you," she replied.

He gave her a thoughtful nod. "Would you at least let me openly court you for a time until the scandal blows over?"

Eugenia was quite taken aback by that proposition. It was very unexpected.

"That is rather a good idea, Genie, if you will not marry him in truth." Edmund finally gave his opinion.

"This is not just a ploy to change my mind, sir?" Her eyes strayed to Graham's; he was lurking in the corner again. He made a little half shrug with his shoulder, but it seemed as though there was hurt in his eyes. She frowned.

"Why do we not all close ranks at Almack's tomorrow night?" Farnsworth suggested. "No one will dare snub Lady Eugenia in the presence of two dukes."

Eugenia could barely stop the groan from escaping her mouth. She loathed the insipid Assembly Rooms as much as any gentleman did. "That will certainly put all of the cards out on the table."

"There is nowhere better to dispel rumors and garner support," Rowley agreed reluctantly. Eugenia had no doubt he would rejoice more than any other once she finally wed—if she ever did wed. He hated London and he had never known how to handle her. She felt for him, she truly did. How could he be expected to understand her when she could not explain her actions to anyone—let alone herself—most of the time.

"Eugenia, will you agree to this?" Emma asked kindly.

"What choice do I have? However, if the plan does not work quickly, I beg that I be allowed to have some time away, to be by myself." She looked at her brother with grim purpose.

He looked back long enough that she had to struggle not to squirm, but gave a reluctant nod. "We will discuss the terms of that request later."

Farnsworth went to shake Rowley's hand and then left, presumably to seek out her aunt.

Emma, Cecilia, and Isabella, her brothers' wives, came towards her. "We must make sure you look absolutely perfect tomorrow night," Emma said, beginning to lead her from the room. Eugenia turned and saw Graham still watching her from the corner. He raised his brows at her in question, but she looked away quickly before she did something they would both regret. Curse him for putting that thought into her head, she reflected miserably, because now it was all she could think about.

She hated being the family's project, but it seemed inevitable.

"Now I have fulfilled Rowley's prophecy for me," she said as they all entered her room and she dropped onto the chaise longue.

Eugenia knew that the sisters were just trying to distract her from the doldrums. She had never worn that emotion well, regardless of the gravity of the situation. She played her part as best she knew how, but she was very likely the worst actress of her entire family. It would have served her well many times had it been otherwise.

Alas, she knew that charade would never work.

"This purple," Emma remarked, holding up Eugenia's favorite dress.

"I wore it a week ago," she remarked sadly.

"'Tis too fresh in Society's minds, then," Emma said and went back into the dressing room.

"Perhaps something more demure?" Cecilia asked tactfully as she followed Emma.

Isabella sat next to Eugenia and took her hand. "Try not to worry. We will not let you marry anyone horrid. Was there anyone you had eyes for before?"

Eugenia blew out a breath and shrugged. "Lord Perth."

"The one who proposed and then withdrew?" Her voice was laden with disgust.

Eugenia could only nod. What would people say when they discovered she had been jilted?

"That will never do," Isabella said, wrinkling her brow.

Cecilia and Emma strode back into the room, holding a pretty blue silk gown that Eugenia had not seen before.

"This one is perfect," Emma said holding it up.

"Where did you find it?" Eugenia asked.

"I commissioned it before I found out I was increasing," Cecilia answered. "It will never fit me now and it would suit the occasion perfectly."

Eugenia had to agree. It was a perfect blend of alluring and demure. "I thank you, Sister."

Cecilia waved her hand. "You may thank me by finding your perfect match despite this ridiculous scandal."

"I wish I could be more like all of you," Eugenia said, disheartened.

"You need only to be yourself," Isabella added earnestly.

Somehow, Eugenia knew that her preferred extravagant headdress would not be suitable for Almack's. A certain image of Graham, presenting her with the bonnet he referred to as garish, came to her mind. A small smile came to her lips.

Emma misunderstood Eugenia's smile, of course, but she would not enlighten them.

"That is more like it. Do not let them defeat you, Genie," Emma said. "Revenge will be sweet."

"I feel I should say something like, 'vengeance is mine saith the Lord,' but I confess I agree with Emma," Isabella added with a wry smile.

The sisters planned her appearance from head to toe and Eugenia tried to pretend that she was interested. The only thing she cared about was surviving the evening without being a complete outcast... or taking Graham up on his offer.

➤➤➤◄◄◄

NO SINGLE GENTLEMAN in his right mind enjoyed going to Almack's. They were all only there for one reason—either they were desperate to marry, or they were there supporting someone in their family who was desperate to marry. Otherwise, they were demented. Graham arrived earlier than he normally would have done, in his ridiculous knee breeches and dancing slippers. He could glide about the floor as well as any gentleman, but he did not like his entire ensemble being dictated to him by shrewish Society matrons.

Few people wanted the Knighton family as their enemy, but even a ducal family could not stop the tittle-tattle. This was the juiciest morsel of gossip to be had this Season, and it would take a great deal of behind-the-scenes effort in order to keep Eugenia from being shunned.

There was a hush when their party arrived. Every member of the Knight family arriving together was a scene to behold. Those people who were not dancing turned to watch.

Graham also turned to look and saw Eugenia on the arm of the Duke of Farnsworth; they were standing beside Knighton and his duchess. Behind them were Edmund and Isabella, with Heath and Cecilia and Lady Hambridge.

Eugenia looked magnificent, wearing a blue silk that was simply elegant. She must have taken advice from her sisters-in-law, he thought with a rueful smile as his feet began to lead him towards his second family.

He bowed before them. "Your Graces, Lady Eugenia."

"Good evening Tinsley," Knighton said, as though he hadn't known perfectly well that he would be in attendance.

"I have come to beg Lady Eugenia for a dance, if she has any dances remaining?"

His gaze slid to hers, not missing the slightly annoyed yet amused glint in her eye. She hated this pretense as much as he, but it must be done. They had decided to cover her bruising with cosmetics, he noticed.

"Let me think; I might have a dance or two available."

"But the first shall be mine," the Duke interrupted. "And one of the waltzes."

"Then I shall be next," Graham remarked as he watched the duke lead Eugenia to the floor. The rest of the party began to disseminate amongst the crowd. They knew their duty was to prevent further scandal, such as anyone having the audacity to snub Eugenia, and to dispel any nasty rumors. For indeed, the latter were already circulating. He had heard them with his own ears.

"Mr. Tinsley," a familiar voice said in his ear.

Graham turned to bow to Lady Jersey, also known as the biggest gossip in Town. "Good evening, my lady." So, Sally Jersey thought to pry titbits from him, did she?

"Is it true?" she asked, finally looking at the duke and Eugenia, who were now dancing.

"To what do you refer, my lady?" he asked smoothly. He could play the game better than she, he was sure.

"You make a nice attempt, Tinsley, but you are thick as glue with the Knight family, do not deny it."

"I will not," he agreed.

"Was Lady Eugenia compromised and is she to marry Ravenhill?"

"No and no. Will that suffice?" He looked at her with his brows raised, daring her to argue.

"Not quite, sir. There is always some element of truth in every rumor, and I will discover what it is," she answered, and glided away towards the duchess. Clearly she was not satisfied with his answer, but she would get even less purchase from Emma. He almost followed her just to enjoy the set down, but instead he made his way towards Petersham and Hardy, whom he had never seen grace any assembly, let alone the august rooms of Almack's.

"And to what do we owe the honor of your presence here?" Graham asked dryly. "Frankly, I cannot believe they allowed you two through the doors."

"You are no more surprised than we," Petersham agreed. "Apparently they are desperate."

"We are here because Heath threatened our lives if we did not come and support Eugenia," Hardy said good-naturedly.

Graham gave a nod. This was certainly the time to call in favors. Hopefully, others would follow their lead by dancing with Eugenia. It was as good a plan as any. This would assure she had at least four dances from gentlemen who were not her brothers.

Petersham cleared his throat and moved a little closer. "I heard Ravenhill is returned and means to cause trouble."

Graham turned and looked sharply at his old friend.

"Where did you hear this? Has he been seen in Town?"

"I have not seen him with my own eyes, but we stopped by White's on the way and it was all anyone could talk about."

"We must tell Knighton." He scanned the crowd, hoping there was time before the set ended. This was the worst possible place for a confrontation and there had not been enough time for them to assure their allies that it was but a rumor. Dancing with Farnsworth was certainly in Eugenia's favor, but would it be enough?

"He is on the floor with his duchess," Petersham pointed out.

Graham cursed under his breath. "You will have to tell him, then. I have the next dance with Eugenia."

"Do you think Ravenhill will be allowed in?" Sir Martin asked.

"The two of you were," Graham retorted.

"Good point," Hardy answered, not taking offense.

"The question is, would Kitty Ravenhill have been granted vouchers?"

"That is beyond my expertise," Petersham drawled.

"Edmund and Heath are not dancing," Graham said, spying the two brothers with their wives. They made their way across the ballroom, not stopping to greet acquaintances. This was far too urgent.

When he reached the brothers and their wives, they immediately stopped their conversation.

"What is it, Tinsley?" Heath asked, eyeing Petersham and Hardy behind him.

"We must talk. I would rather your wives hear this as well, because we will need their help."

They were all staring at him, waiting.

"We have heard rumors that Ravenhill is in Town and means to cause trouble tonight," Petersham spoke.

"Then we must protect her at all costs," Edmund said.

"I am to dance with her next," Graham said. "Then I shall lead her to Petersham."

"And then I to Hardy. That should take us to eleven o'clock," Petersham remarked.

"If he has not appeared by then, we will be in the clear for tonight at least," Heath said, knowing the doors would be barred to anyone not present by that sacred hour.

"And if he puts in an appearance?" Cecilia asked.

"We must keep him from her at all costs, but we cannot control his mouth or his sister's, unfortunately."

"I will tell Knighton as soon as the dance ends," Heath said. "If he can waylay the man before he engages with anyone else, perhaps Rowley can produce a miracle."

Graham thought it was their best chance, but there was more than money involved now. Ravenhill would have the pot of gold, and sufficient power and influence were here to enable him to ally himself with a ducal family. And with an audience, Graham fully expected a performance worthy of Drury Lane.

As the dance ended, dozens of people were watching and murmuring, but no one had turned their back on Eugenia. At least she had not been tried and condemned at the hands of Society—yet. However, they were as fickle as the wind and would turn as quickly.

As Farnsworth led Eugenia from the floor and to Graham himself, he could see the strain on her face, but she was making a good effort to hide it. Only those who knew her well might see that her smile was not genuine and did not reach her eyes.

They did not speak until they were on the floor. Thankfully, it was the first waltz and they would be able to converse.

Once the orchestra began the three-quarter measure, he took her in his arms.

"What has happened?" she asked.

He hesitated. He fully meant to inform her, but he had not realized she would have been so observant. Perhaps her senses were more than usually acute at the moment.

"Do not tell me *nothing*," she continued.

"I will not," he responded, meeting her eyes. "There are rumors that Ravenhill is back in Town and means to cause trouble tonight."

He watched her face assimilate this proclamation. The smile fell from her face.

"No matter what happens tonight, will you promise to trust me, Genie?"

She looked up at him with those large midnight eyes, and knew that Ravenhill was taking his life in his hands if he darkened those doors tonight. The wave of protectiveness for Eugenia that swept over him was like nothing he had ever felt for anyone else. He might not love her romantically, but she was one of his dearest friends and he would do anything for her.

"Of course I trust you, Graham, but I will hear nothing more about a proposal."

He was saved from answering by a commotion at the entrance to the ballroom. The blackguard had arrived and it took every ounce of his will not to sweep Eugenia away through another door.

# CHAPTER TWELVE

I F EVER THERE were a justifiable moment to swoon or have a fit of the vapors, this was it.

"Steady," Graham said. "Look at me."

She somehow obeyed and her eyes met his.

"That is the way. You are a Knight. Lift your chin and show them you care not a whit. This is when you prove to everyone who you really are."

"My knees are shaking, Graham."

"They cannot see that. I will not let you fall."

She believed him, yet she was sure she must be squeezing his fingers so hard they would lose feeling, but he smiled down at her as though nothing and no one else in the world existed. He was a much better actor than she, she reflected somehow as he twirled her about so quickly it was difficult to think about what else was going on. Yet, if she allowed herself to be lost in the comfort of Graham's arms, she might just lose her wits completely. There could be no happiness down that path, because she would want his heart if they were to marry. Friendship with him would never be enough. Without question, it would be better than Ravenhill or Farnsworth her conscience argued. Although she knew Farnsworth wanted one thing from her—and it was not friendship—she did not think he would be cruel... but she could not do that to her aunt.

"What is happening?" she asked, hoping Graham could see. He was much taller and could view everything in the room.

"Ravenhill is wearing a sling and a plaster on his forehead," he told her, adding sardonically, "he looks quite the martyr."

"Who is he talking to?"

"He is surrounded, but your brother is trying to pull him aside. I fear we may not have much luck. We must keep him from reaching you at all costs."

"But how? Shall you form a barrier around me?"

"We will, if necessary. You are to dance with Petersham and then Hardy after me."

At least those were not waltzes, she mused gratefully. Graham was the only one, besides her brothers, with whom she thought she could even exchange a single word at this moment.

"Smile, pet. You must show everyone Ravenhill is not affecting you."

"What if he is putting it about that we are betrothed?"

"Then we will simply dispel that notion. You promised to trust me, remember?"

She fought back tears. He made it sound so simple. She just wanted this whole ordeal to be over. "I might have to escape to Bexley," she whispered. "I do not know how long I can go on."

"I sent word to my caretakers, Mr. and Mrs. Prudy, that they were to welcome you. I would feel much better, however, if you would not go alone."

"I promised Rowley I would not go anywhere straight away."

"I think that is still the wisest course of action." Graham frowned.

"What is it now?" She could not keep the panic from her voice.

"Kitty Ravenhill is also here," he snarled. "Now you must force yourself to smile at me or people will think I have angered you."

His face transformed and he looked down at her with a look she had never seen from him before. Her insides warmed. Good heavens.

She needed a fan. It was all an act, she had to remind herself.

The music drew to a close and Graham bent over her hand and kissed it.

"What are you doing?" she asked through a smile.

"Letting the *ton* know that you are desirable," he said, raising one brow.

"Like a Cyprian?"

"Like a prospective wife." He nearly choked through his false smile.

"I need a drink," she said, feeling breathless.

"You are not the only one," he muttered.

Thankfully, the orgeat and watered-down lemonade were across the room from Ravenhill.

"Hopefully, Petersham is paying attention and will come over here for you."

Eugenia could not think about her next dance partner. She swallowed the tasteless liquid and took the opportunity to look about her. Eyes were upon her; she could feel the not so subtle stares to her core. "I would do anything to be able to leave this very minute," she said, gritting her teeth through her smile.

"That would be disastrous and you know it."

"I feel as if there is about to be a confrontation, and everyone is waiting to watch the farce."

"So long as it remains a farce and not a tragedy," he remarked with wry humor. "Petersham is walking this way; good man."

Moments later, Petersham bowed before her. "My lady, I believe I have the pleasure of this next set with you?"

"Indeed." She took another swallow of her cold drink, wishing it were something stronger for false courage.

"Knighton has not been able to have a word alone with Ravenhill. He is positively swarmed with people asking about his injuries," Petersham said quietly.

"Just as he wished," Graham drawled.

Eugenia wished the music would hurry and begin so she could at least be doing something.

"Were you able to catch anything Ravenhill was saying?" Graham asked.

Petersham looked sideways at Eugenia.

"Please speak freely. I have no delicate sensibilities."

"Very well. He pronounced that upon accepting his proposal, you were swept away by emotion and accidentally injured him."

"I beg your pardon? I am certain I misheard you."

"You did not mishear, my lady." His voice was laden with distaste.

"I am going to finish what I started." She moved forward and Graham took her arm.

"Not here," he commanded.

"Did you hear what he said?" She was completely stunned.

"I heard. We must beat him at his own game, however."

The music began, thankfully. "Go out there and be your usual joyful self. It is vital that you do not look at him or pretend that you know what he saying. Can you do that?"

"If I must."

Petersham led her to the floor and, thankfully, it was a lively country dance which required her to concentrate.

As she curtsied to her partner and he bowed to her, he smiled reassuringly. "You must only continue for a little longer and then your brothers will deal with him."

"Pray it will be that simple."

For an entire twenty minutes she was able to dance without anyone speaking to her or causing any major catastrophes. It was a welcome relief.

Her partner led her back to the safe haven of the Knight clan where Sir Martin Hardy was waiting to dance with her next.

Her brothers and sisters smiled at her as though nothing were wrong, and she could not help but wonder if something was happening without her knowledge. Graham would tell her, if no one else would, but she did not know when she would have a chance to speak with him again.

"Remember, Hardy, return her to me," Rowley commanded.

"Yes, Your Grace," Sir Martin parroted. He was a pleasant dear, if a bit simple. At least, she had never had a serious conversation with him.

The next dance was a quadrille and as they took their places, a hush fell over the room.

"I beg your pardon, Hardy, but I really must insist upon this dance with my betrothed," a voice drawled from behind her.

Oh, no. This was one of those rules Eugenia was supposed to remember. It was something about not refusing to dance, but it was unpardonably rude of Ravenhill to cause a scene like this. She turned with undisguised fury.

"I say, Ravenhill, I awaited my turn and you can wait for yours," Sir Martin said nervously.

"I am not your betrothed," Eugenia growled in a quiet voice, but the orchestra had stopped and she had no doubt everyone in the room heard.

Ravenhill laughed. "There is no need to be shy, my dear. Everyone already knows about our inability to control our passions."

Suddenly, Graham was at her side and she saw Knighton and her other brothers walking towards them.

"Why do we not move this off the dance floor so others may enjoy themselves?" Graham asked calmly, yet he was already leading her away.

Eugenia was mortified. Trouble always found her even when she behaved well. All she wanted was to be normal. Was that too much to ask? Now there was to be no privacy for this discussion. All of her shame was to be laid open, bare for all the gossips to feast on like vultures.

"You, Ravenhill, are a coward," Graham said with quiet savagery as soon as they were off the floor. "You knew she would never agree to dance with you or ever be alone with you again, so you accosted her when she already had a partner."

"I would prefer we remove to Knighton House for this discussion," Rowley declared as soon as he reached them.

Petersham, Hardy, Farnsworth and her brothers all surrounded Ravenhill, Nevertheless, he would not yield.

"Of course I am ready to discuss settlements, Your Grace," he announced loudly—and, of course, Lady Jersey and Lady Cowper were close enough to hear and witness every word.

"I am not betrothed to you, Lord Ravenhill," Eugenia stated, grinding out the words as she tried to maintain some semblance of decorum.

"I have witnesses to say otherwise."

"Nonsense!" Graham exclaimed, stepping forward.

"Do you deny you found us in an embrace?"

"Most vehemently!" Graham answered.

"How dare you thus insult my sister!" Knighton said with icy disdain, stepping forward.

Eugenia could not allow Rowley to challenge this scoundrel. She had to do something. No one else should have to suffer. Before allowing herself to think about it, she grabbed a glass of orgeat from the nearby table and took several steps towards the black-hearted villain. "We are not betrothed. I am not compromised, and I will never marry you." She threw the punch in his face.

"I will have satisfaction!" he demanded as the liquid dripped down his face.

"You will have nothing," Graham announced, stepping between Eugenia and Ravenhill. "You cannot possibly be betrothed to the lady when she is already betrothed to me."

⫸⫷

GRAHAM FELT EUGENIA tense beneath his hand, but he squeezed her arm and looked down at her with the most love-struck expression he could manage.

Ravenhill began to sputter with indignation, but Petersham and Hardy took him by the elbows and started to escort him from the hallowed assembly room halls before he could issue any challenges.

The image of ducal reserve, Knighton turned to usher his herd from the ballroom as well. They could hardly resume dancing as though nothing had happened.

Eugenia still had not said a word. He imagined she was storing up quite a tirade to spew at him once they were private.

They left with no further ado, and Graham joined Knighton and his duchess alongside Eugenia in their carriage. It was not far to Knighton House, and no one said a word between the two places. They helped their ladies to alight and up the steps, where Quincy held the door open for them.

"In my study, please. I would like a word before everyone else joins us," the duke commanded.

Graham squeezed Eugenia's hand, offering reassurance, but she looked up at his touch, disillusioned.

"One moment, Knighton."

He pulled her aside and whispered in her ear. "You may jilt me later if the thought of marriage to me is so abhorrent, but I am in earnest."

He turned and joined Knighton in his study, closing the door quietly behind him and leaning against it. Knighton was propped against the edge of his desk, with his arms folded across his chest. They stared at each other for a moment before Rowley moved and went to the cupboard and poured them each a glass of brandy. Graham knew better than to speak first.

"Is this something you came up with on the spur of the moment or was Eugenia aware of your betrothal?"

"She was... aware of my proposal, shall we say," Graham answered.

"I see," Knighton said, staring into the amber liquid in his glass.

"I could hardly allow Ravenhill to continue as he was. I saw no other solution."

"And you have taken it upon yourself to be completely responsible for Eugenia? Did it not occur to you that Farnsworth would have come to her rescue?"

"It was far worse than we had anticipated, Row. A false courtship would not have redeemed her good name."

"Farnsworth was prepared to marry her. Who knows what he will say now?"

"You would force her to marry him? Knowing he loves your aunt and how Eugenia feels about him?"

Knighton waved his hand. "The duke has the maturity and stability she needs to become settled in life."

Graham began to pace across the Aubusson carpet. "I cannot believe this of you. How could you sentence her to a lifetime of unhappiness? If she is that much of a burden to you, then yes, I will take responsibility for her."

"Did Eugenia agree to this?"

"Now you care for her opinion?" Graham was outraged at the hypocrisy of his oldest friend. "Do you truly object to this match or is it me you find unworthy?"

"I object to this entire situation. I should not have let this happen to her. I knew her unsuitability for Society." He shook his head.

"There is nothing unsuitable about Eugenia!" Graham slammed his glass on the table with more force then he intended, but why did they always think it was her fault? She was a duke's daughter, she had an enormous dowry, she was beautiful, but she had been brought up without a mother. If anyone was to blame for this, it was Knighton, but he had done what he thought was best, and truly it did no good to apportion blame.

Knighton sighed heavily. "I do not wish to argue with you, Graham."

"Nor I you. But I cannot stand by and allow Eugenia to be married off to someone she loathes, merely to avoid scandal."

"Why must you be the one? I was trying to save you from what you profess to disdain for her."

"It will be no hardship to wed Eugenia. I care for her more than almost anyone I can think of. And I like her. I adore her whimsicality."

He had already been chasing after her and keeping her out of trouble, so what would be the difference? He had not minded so much. There would also be perquisites to being married, he began to think, but he digressed.

Knighton was eyeing him thoughtfully. "We will speak with Eugenia before anything is decided. She could hardly jilt you immediately anyhow."

Graham opened his mouth to protest, but the argument was saved from escalating by the appearance of Heath and Edmund.

Heath slapped him on the back. "Now you will be a brother in truth, eh? I must say, I am relieved."

"I think it is a splendid match," Edmund added.

"But is it real?" Rowley asked with menacing calm.

"Of course it is," Heath said, pouring himself and Edmund a glass. After he handed his brother a drink he raised his in the air. "He would hardly sacrifice himself for no reason. To Tinsley and Eugenia."

Graham would never admit otherwise, for he could not completely answer that question himself.

Heath turned to Graham with a knowing smile. "You sly devil! I never would have thought you would offer for her, but there was no one I'd like better as my brother." He walked over and shook Graham's hand with fervor.

Graham smiled, knowing Knighton was watching his every move. He would not look him in the eyes. He needed to speak with Eugenia before Rowley did.

Edmund also stepped forward and patted him on the back. "I am very pleased by this as well. Whether you did it out of principle or love, I honor you for it."

Graham inclined his head. This was taking on a life of its own.

"A toast to Eugenia and Graham: may you have the happiness the rest of us have been so fortunate to find," he said, lifting his glass.

Graham took a drink and realized he was feeling the effects. Perhaps he was becoming soft in all manner of things. He frowned.

"Why the solemn face?" Knighton asked.

"No reason. It has been a busy few days and I find I am rather tired." Graham excused himself from the brothers' presence, then inquired of Quincy if Eugenia was available to talk. It was late, but he would prefer to resolve this before she could overthink everything and come up with reasons why they should not marry.

"I am sorry, sir. Lady Eugenia has retired for the evening and begged not to be disturbed," Quincy said apologetically.

"Thank you, Quincy." He accepted his hat and gloves and set out to walk home. It was just as well, he thought. It was rather late, and he had had more brandy with the brothers than he had intended. He wanted to have a clear head before he attempted to convince Eugenia of why this was right. He stopped at the corner and looked up at the sky. Nothing was falling down on him, he mused. In fact, he felt quite surprisingly content.

Somehow it mattered that Eugenia accept him—not to prove Knighton wrong, but because it felt right. He stumbled a little and grabbed onto a lamp post to steady himself. He looked up at the house and it swayed a little. He shook his head. He could not remember the last time he had had enough spirits to make him bosky. But he could hardly refuse to toast with the brothers over his good fortune, could he?

He chuckled and began to hum a tune. This was certainly not how he thought his bachelorhood would end, and would have laughed at anyone who had said Eugenia would become his future viscountess.

He looked up to where her window was. At least, he thought it was her window. He began to count one, two, three... no, hers was the fourth room—or was it?

He picked up some pebbles from the street. Would it not be romantic to serenade her by darkness? The devil! He was becoming a milksop! Was it the brandy or had Eugenia done this to him? Now all he could think about was her smile and seeing her happy again.

He had to talk to her before Rowley, anyway, so he began to concentrate hard on remembering which room was hers. He was saved from guessing by the opening of a window. At least he still had enough wits about him to step back into the shadows in case it wasn't his fair Juliet come to profess her undying love for him. A hiccup had just escaped his lips when a large valise came flying down and dropped not five feet in front of him. That was soon followed by a rope and a delicious bottom in breeches being flung over the windowsill.

If he'd had time to think, he might have realized his fair damsel was trying to escape him. But brandy has a way of muddling proper thought and when she slid down the rope he was waiting to catch her at the bottom.

He decided the best way to silence her screams and convince her he would make a good husband was with a kiss.

# CHAPTER THIRTEEN

E UGENIA'S SENSES WERE stunned. First, there was the shock of someone grabbing her when she jumped to the ground, then the realization that it was Graham, and then the feel of his warm arms surrounding her. The last thing she ever would have expected was for him to kiss her. He tasted of fire and brandy and she could not help but respond.

She liked it very much, but was he trying to convince her that they would be compatible?

Reluctantly, she pulled away. "What are you doing?"

"I will ask the same of you. I am not the one coming down into the road from my window in an attempt to escape."

Well, she could not argue with that. "I meant the kiss. What do you mean by that?"

He looked as though he was trying to catch his breath, as indeed was she. She wriggled to get down from his arms.

"Stop that!" he squawked.

"Then put me down," she insisted.

"I do not want to," he answered, almost sounding petulant.

"Very well." She settled against him as though she could stay there all day.

He turned and leaned back against the wall. "I will hold you until you explain why you were running away."

"I should think it to be rather obvious," she murmured, rather liking the feel of being in his arms.

"You are running away from me," he said. There was a hint of anger in his voice.

She answered carefully." I am leaving for a time, in order to reflect—and to allow all this chaos to go away. Scandals always die down if one only waits." She hoped.

"True enough, but only to a certain extent. In this situation, it will only go away if you marry."

"That may be the way of the world, but it is so very wrong."

"I agree, but your choices of Ravenhill or Farnsworth will hardly make you happy, unless you have changed your mind?" He left the query dangling, but he knew very well she had no interest in either man—she would not term Ravenhill a gentleman—as a spouse.

"How could you even ask that?"

"Because you seem very opposed to me, and I want to know why."

"It is not you, Graham. I cannot have you make such a sacrifice for me."

"I would do anything for you, Genie. Do you not understand that?"

Her heart thudded, and she was surprised how much she wished that she could ask him about his heart, his love. But even she could not be so bold. "Then allow me to leave. I left a note for Rowley so that he would not come looking for me. If you reassure him, then there will not be a fuss."

Graham slowly set her down on her two feet and looked her in the eye.

"There is absolutely no way I will let you run away in the dark of night, alone. If you think that, and that your brother will not come looking for you, then you have lost your wits, pet."

"I will find a way to leave, Graham, and I will not tell you where."

She crossed her arms over her chest.

He cursed, a long string of words, and ran his hand through his hair as he began to pace about while having a conversation with himself. She thought perhaps he might be a little bit intoxicated, but he seemed to have sobered now.

She debated picking up her valise and slipping away, but that would only make matters worse. Fervently, she hoped he would come to the right conclusion. If she were male, there would be no question that she could go away to think.

He finally stopped and turned. "There is only one solution."

"Only one?" She frowned.

"I will go with you. You leave me no choice in the matter."

She would be well and truly compromised if he went with her, unless they could keep it absolutely quiet.

"Will you escort me there and then return to convince Rowley to permit me this indulgence?"

"And what did you write to him?"

She sighed. They had already been standing outside the house too long. It was a wonder no one had discovered them. "I wrote that I needed a little time and that I was going somewhere safe. They could pretend I had a head cold until I returned. I told him you could explain." She looked at him sheepishly, hoping he would agree.

"Why, thank you," he answered, not disguising the sarcasm.

"Graham, are you going to let me go?" He now had a hand on either side of her, against the wall.

"Yes, yes. Let us go to my house so I may pack some necessaries. I will escort you to Bexley, but I am must leave the Duke my own note."

"Thank you, Graham!" She reached up to kiss him on the cheek.

At the same moment, he turned quickly and their lips met again.

"You can stop doing that," she said as he picked up her bag and they began walking.

"What if I want to?" he countered, not looking at her.

"If *you* are wanting to kiss *me*, then I am convinced the Thames has frozen over. I know you think of me as the obstreperous little sister. Or is it true that gentlemen really do not require feelings to... to..." She twirled her hand in the air, too embarrassed to say the word.

He chuckled. "Well, gentlemen are certainly less discriminating, I will grant you, but there are still some standards."

"Why, thank you, I think," she said, trying to decide if that was a compliment or not.

"Eugenia, I do not think of you as just the obstreperous little sister."

She absorbed that statement for a few steps. "Then does that mean you want to... to..." She twirled her hand in the air again.

"It would certainly be one of the benefits to marriage."

He had to be jesting with her. Surely, he could not think of her in that way? Nonetheless, a little voice in her own mind told her she was attracted to him. She had never thought anything might come of it because every woman in London was attracted to Graham. It was simply who he was. He liked women as well; that was also no secret.

"Does the thought of me scare you because of that, pet?"

She pursed her lips. "I do not think so. I did rather enjoy your kiss."

He laughed. "Thank God for that!"

"But that is not reason enough to marry you. Every woman in London probably thinks that way of you."

He was still laughing at her. "What is so funny, Graham?"

"You are completely without artifice. I will know you are never lying to me, at least." He bent down and placed a kiss on her nose. "I think we will have one advantage that most marriages do not."

"I have not agreed to this," she reminded him shortly, despite feeling her head spin.

He ignored her remark. "We are the best of friends and I cannot think of any other lady whose company I enjoy more."

What could she say to argue with that? He seemed sincere. "I will agree you are my best friend. But do you not comprehend that that is why I cannot bear to see you give up your chance of love—for me?

"But I do love you, Genie."

Her heart jumped so hard it felt as if her chest would explode.

"Not in the romantic, infatuated way you mean, perhaps... but the way I love you will last forever."

"Oh," she whispered. She knew he was right, but it still did not feel good to hear him say that. But in truth, was that not how she felt for him?

"You are being unusually, unnervingly quiet," he said as they stopped on his front steps.

"It is so much to take in. A few days alone will help me sort through my muddled thoughts."

He shook his head and put a key in the lock. The house was quiet and he showed her into a small study off the entrance hall. For how well she knew him, she had never been in this house. The study was dark and masculine, with mahogany paneling and a large desk of the same wood. A fireplace was flanked by two armchairs and a portrait of the viscount with his hounds looked down at her.

"You can wait here while I gather what I need. If we leave soon we will reach the cottage by dawn. We really must not make a habit of escaping Town in the dark," he mused. "Is there anything you require while you wait?"

She shook her head. "No, thank you."

He left her alone, which was what she had wanted, but now she had time to think before she acted. She curled up in one of the armchairs. Was it a poor choice to run away? What she truly wanted was to go to bed, wake up and find this was a nightmare. If she left with Graham, however, then they risked more than a fake betrothal to her—for that is what she thought of it. When he'd had time to sleep on it, surely he would change his mind? For all Eugenia knew people thought her reckless, the gravity of the situation was very real to her.

She closed her eyes and was tempted to sleep. As long as she could convince Graham to leave her at Bexley, even if just for a few days, then that was what she would do.

⤞⤝

GRAHAM SAT AT the escritoire in the drawing room, trying to think of what he could possibly say to convince Rowley to leave Eugenia to her rustication. In the end, he decided on complete honesty. He had caught her running away and had decided to use the few days to convince her they were well-suited. Even though he knew his duty, he wanted her to be convinced.

He sealed the letter with a note to his butler to have it delivered to Knighton first thing in the morning and then hurried back to Eugenia because he feared she would go on her own anyway.

She looked like she was sleeping. She was his. He let that thought germinate while he watched her in repose, but her eyes opened when he entered the room. It was one of the few moments where Eugenia was calm.

"Are you ready? The horses are waiting."

She smiled and nodded as he helped her to her feet. "I am glad we are to ride. I was afraid you would bring the carriage."

"I know you better than that, my dear."

"Yes, you do." She was clearly surprised, however, when they went outside to find her own mare."

"How did you manage this?" She turned to look at him in surprise.

"I sent my groom."

"Quite. Thank you," she said as he assisted her into her saddle.

They navigated the streets of London to the Dover road with ease at that time of night—or early morning, as it were. As they reached the open road and gave the horses their heads, Eugenia began to laugh.

"Dare I ask what is so humorous at this moment when I would much rather be sleeping in my warm bed?" As he said it, he realized it was not true. He was very much enjoying himself and often he did not reach his bed until dawn, anyway.

"Stop being such a kill-joy! You may sleep when we arrive."

"Am I allowed to stay, then? At my own house?" he teased.

"Long enough to sleep. I would not want you to have an accident on my account," she countered.

"How gracious of you! I must warn you, however, this is a cottage in truth. I do not use the term loosely as Perth does. There are but four bedrooms."

"However shall I manage?" She cast him a look of exasperation and then pulled ahead of him.

Watching her ride was a thing of beauty, even in the dark, but it was not yet a full moon and many things could happen in the dark. Many things could happen in the daylight, for that matter. He urged Xerxes to catch up and was relieved when he saw the flash of her comely form ahead.

"Eugenia!" he called, but at that moment he saw her horse slip and they both went tumbling down. "Eugenia!"

He had never known panic such as he felt in that moment. He felt as though his chest were being crushed and he could scarcely remember dismounting and rushing to her. "Eugenia!" He stripped off his gloves and knelt beside her. He cradled her face in his hands for a moment and slid his fingers down to find a pulse at her neck. "Thank God," he whispered as he began searching her for other injuries.

She let out a ragged gasp and opened her eyes. "Graham?"

"You fell from your horse," he explained.

"Not I, surely?" She lifted her head and looked around with a puzzled frown. "I do appear to be on the ground."

"But you are not hurt?"

"I do not think so. Mainly the breath was knocked out of me."

She sat up and moved as though a little sore, but she did not seem to be hurt. Graham could not imagine how he would have explained that to Knighton.

"Where is Cleo?"

"Hopefully nearby. If she has run back to London riderless, your brother will turn the kingdom upside down and strangle me when he find us."

That brought her to her feet quickly and she began calling for Cleo. They found her a few minutes later, lazily grazing on a patch of grass.

"She does not appear to be lame. She threw a shoe!" Eugenia said with relief, lifting one of the mare's forelegs.

Graham also felt the noose around his neck loosen a bit. He was still going to meet with the Duke's displeasure, but this was no laughing matter.

"How much further to Bexley?" she asked, already beyond being thrown.

"Not above a mile or two."

"I did not realize this was so close to London."

Graham wondered if he should mention how often he and the brothers had used to come here for a few days, to relax and fish...and it would probably be the first place the Duke would look.

"I suppose we will have to lead Cleo. Hopefully it will not pain her to walk that far," Eugenia remarked after a thorough examination of her mare.

They gathered the reins and began to lead the horses. As if throwing a shoe were not enough, England decided they had had dry weather for a few hours. Big, fat drops began to fall on their heads, and while his hat was slightly more substantial than Eugenia's, neither one of them would emerge at Bexley with a square inch dry upon them.

There was no point in trying to talk over the rain, which was now pouring down, and Graham was not about to leave Eugenia to walk on her own, even though it would have served her right.

When they finally trudged through the gates to his cottage, the sun had risen enough that they could see.

Graham looked up at his cottage and frowned. It did not appear that anyone was home nor had been in some time. "What the devil?" The gardens had not been cut and the hedges were wild.

"When was the last time you were here?" she asked skeptically.

"Before the Season began. I have not had the time to come down here since," he replied as they led the horses down the overgrown path—and that was because he had been squiring her around, he thought wryly, but refrained from saying so out loud.

"I hope nothing bad has happened your caretakers."

Graham could not help but think the worst. "It certainly looks abandoned," he said as they led their horses around the back to the stable. There was water and some hay, at the very least. They removed the saddles and saw their horses rubbed down, and then turned towards the house.

He strode to the back door and began to knock. There should have been some sign of life by this time of morning. As he had feared, though, there was no answer.

"Is no one here?" Eugenia asked having crept up beside him.

"It does not appear that way." He tried the handle and it was locked. "If the Purdys are on holiday, I failed to receive word. Come to think of it, they had not replied to my note about your possible visit." He cursed under his breath.

"We should try the windows and see if there are any loose latch-es... unless you have brought a key?" She looked at him sideways and he began to laugh.

She put her hands on her hips and it only made him laugh harder. "Graham," she growled. "Tell me this minute why you are laughing!"

"You should see yourself!"

"I am sure I look a fright, but this is hardly the first time you have seen me soaked to the bone and covered in mud."

"No," he agreed, "but this whole situation is such... If I do not laugh, then I might do something drastic."

"More drastic than telling the whole of London you are betrothed to me?"

"Indeed." He pulled off his hat, then untied the strings to hers and tossed them on the bench near the porch. "It looks like I will be buying you another bonnet," he said softly before cradling her face in his hands and lowering his lips to hers.

She gasped with surprise but then quickly gave in and returned his kiss. *Good girl*, he thought, as he became more and more comfortable with the idea of her as his wife. When he pulled back and let her go, she stared at him as though seeing him for the first time. "Why are you doing this?"

"Are you going to pretend you did not enjoy that?" he asked, with just a little self-satisfaction.

"That is beside the point," she sputtered.

"No, that is exactly the point. We are compatible, not just friends. Shall I continue to teach you? There is a great deal more to learn."

She hit him. Hard. Then she began to walk away.

Chasing after her, he took her arm. "I am unwilling to leave it at that." He spun her around. "Can you truly tell me you would rather marry one of the others than me?"

She was fighting off tears. That was why she had turned away. The look on her face undid him and he pulled her into his arms. He let her cry, despite the rain soaking them. They had to come to an understanding now.

"I do not understand," she muttered against his chest.

When she had calmed, he tilted her face up to look at him.

"Will you not give me a chance? At least consider it until Rowley arrives?"

She sighed heavily—just the sound every suitor wished to hear from his perspective bride.

"At least no one else is here to know we are alone together."

"True," he said cautiously. "And you know I would not force you to do anything if you truly did not wish it."

"I still do not know how you think to change my mind. We have been as brother and sister our entire lives."

"Not entirely," he corrected. "You became a woman while I was away."

She gave a tiny shrug of her shoulder. "Do you think we might find our way inside now, Graham?"

He burst out laughing and tweaked her on the nose. "Put me in my place, pet."

# CHAPTER FOURTEEN

E VERYTHING HAD CHANGED. Eugenia was now aware of every movement Graham made and she was not sure she liked it. She watched as he started a fire and then went back out to the stables to haul in their valises. He then began stripping away his outer garments and tossing them over the table.

"Why are you looking at me like that?" Graham asked.

Eugenia had not realized she had been staring, but she shook herself. "Everything has changed," she answered.

"Well, yes," he said, furrowing his brow as he sat down and pulled off his boots. "You decided to run away on your own terms, Genie. Not the ones you had agreed upon with Rowley."

"You kissed me," she said, still unable to shake it from her thoughts, although there was the whole adventure of running away that she was only now beginning to feel the repercussions of. It was not supposed to be like this.

"What did you think it would be like?" he asked, standing and walking towards her. She had seen her brothers in their shirt sleeves and stocking feet hundreds of time, but this did not feel the same. She could no longer think of him as a brother.

She swallowed hard as he came near. "I thought it would be a short holiday to a cottage where I would be alone with your caretakers and I would sit in the garden and watch the river and solve my problems."

He raised his brows and made a face as though that were not a bad plan. "Well, you have me instead of the caretakers. And as your self-appointed caretaker, I must insist you remove your soaking garments. You are making quite a puddle on the floor."

She looked down and realized what a state she was in. Besides being drenched, she was covered in mud. "Goodness. 'Tis a pity it is too cold to jump in the water. That would be the simplest solution."

He chuckled and reached up to unbutton her cape. Her breath hitched as his fingers brushed her neck. She felt as though she had little control over her traitorous body. She did not want to react to him. It was wrong. Yet she stood there like a statue, unable to move.

His hands brushed her shoulders and as he slid her cloak off and tossed it over onto the table with his. Next was her coat and then he knelt down to remove her boots.

"I suppose this was an appropriate time as any for breeches," he remarked dryly. "Skirts would have been the devil at this moment."

"Yes." She barely mustered a whisper when she normally would have enjoyed arguing the point. He seemed wholly unaware of how alarmed she was as she stood before him in shirt sleeves and stockings.

Graham walked away and put a pot of water over the fire. "I doubt I will be able to warm enough for you to bathe very soon, but at least we may have a pot of tea and clean ourselves." He looked back at her. She had not moved; she was still standing where he had left her, watching him being so capable.

"Genie, come closer to the fire. You must warm yourself!"

She was shivering and forced herself to move towards the warmth. How could he be so unaffected? For her world had turned upside down and yet he was acting as though nothing had happened.

He rubbed his hands together and then moved about the kitchen. He opened the larder. "There is not much to be had, I am afraid. I will need to go into the village for some provisions. Thankfully, there is tea," he said merrily, pouring the water over the leaves. "There are probably some eggs in the hen-house, unless the foxes have helped themselves to the hens."

After the tea had steeped, Graham poured her a cup and added some sugar for her. They sat before the fire, on the bench next to the table, and drank. It was all so very domestic.

"Would you care to go to the village?" he asked.

"All I want to do is sleep."

"That is not a bad idea, either. Come, let me show you to your room."

Eugenia was too tired to think anymore or notice her surroundings. She quickly changed into a clean, woolen nightrail and crawled under the coverlet and fell asleep.

When she awoke, it took her a few minutes to realize where she was. The bed was strange, the room was strange, and she felt strange. She squinted at the window and could not remember what had transpired until she saw her clothing on the floor. Then, all that had occurred in the past four-and-twenty hours flooded back.

Reluctantly, she climbed from the bed and searched through her valise for her hair brush. It was an abomination, how tangled her hair was. She dealt with the knots, tied her hair back with a simple ribbon, and then made her way back downstairs.

She did not know if Graham had also slept or would have gone to the village. She was not particularly comfortable staying here either with him or without him. She had not expected the cottage to be abandoned.

It was a charming cottage, she thought as she finally took the time to look around. It reminded her of the squire's home back in Devonshire, with its coziness. Low hanging ceilings, small rooms with worn draperies and furnishings, and patterns from decades ago gave it charm.

She did not see Graham, and walked through the house looking for him. There was a note left on the table in the kitchen.

*I have gone to the village to find food and the smithy.*

*~G*

She sat down at the table and put her face in her hands. She had made a muddle of everything yet again. All she had wanted was some time alone to think – to make her own decisions. And now she had made a mull of someone else's life. Perhaps she should just return to London and agree to be Farnsworth's broodmare. Apparently he was able to overlook everything else for a chance of his own heir.

She would either have to marry Farnsworth or be ruined. What a stupid, stupid society they lived in, where her word of honor and purity meant nothing! Part of her wanted to defy their dictates because it was so very wrong.

"But you would break your aunt's heart," she said, feeling more miserable by the moment. "Yet can I make this right?" she argued with herself. "There is no good answer."

Regardless of these concerns, she could not leave until Cleo had a new shoe, so she hoped Graham was able to find the farrier in the village. If they returned to London that day, perhaps no one would be the wiser.

In that moment she really wished she were a male. Everything was so unfair for women. Standing, she went to look out of the window. The rain was still coming down and she felt bad that Graham was out in it. She could not even tell the time because the sky was dark and heavy with clouds.

Her stomach growled, reminding her that she had not eaten since the day before. Thankfully, Graham should be back soon with some food. She wondered what he would say if she told him she was ready to return to London. He might strangle her and put her out of her misery.

"There you are, pet," Graham said, coming through the door and startling her.

"Here I am," she remarked.

"I have good news. I have food and the farrier is replacing Cleo's shoe as we speak."

Graham pulled out a block of cheese and a fresh loaf of bread from his saddlebag and began cutting her a slice. "Why so maudlin?" he asked as he sawed back and forth with a knife he had taken from a drawer before handing her a jagged piece of the cheese.

"I cannot speak before I eat," she said and placed a chunk of cheese in her mouth.

He laughed. "Grumpy in the mornings duly noted." He leaned forward to impart more personal knowledge, causing an errant blond lock to fall over his brow. "I am grumpy before I partake of coffee."

She smiled a little, unconscionably wanting to cry at the thought of being married to someone else and missing these moments with him.

She finished her cheese and bread and watched as he took a second helping. Now she was noticing all the little things about him as though she had never seen him before.

"You are far too serious, my dear. Should we see what the scandal sheets say?" He wagged his brows.

She looked up at that. "You found a paper?"

"Bexley is not so far from London. I was able to purchase one at the tavern where I found the cheese and bread."

She stole it from his hands and flipped open the pages greedily. He knew she read them every morning, mainly because she was always in them.

He sat back and folded his arms, watching her.

She groaned. It was much worse than she had thought. A beaten Ravenhill was shown begging at Eugenia's feet with one of her brothers dragging him away at gunpoint, while Graham was shown as a knight in shining armor charging in to save her.

"Well?" he asked impatiently.

She tossed the paper at him. "As usual you are made out to be chivalry itself."

"And what, pray tell, is wrong with that?"

"Because I am always the one you are having to rescue!" She stood hastily and ran out of the door. Eugenia hated losing her temper. She liked being merry... but nothing was going well these days and it was hard to think clearly with Graham in close proximity. She took a deep breath, preparing to go in and apologize, when she heard the thunder of horses approaching. She closed her eyes and braced herself. The herd had arrived.

GRAHAM HEARD THE stampede coming. "Well that took less time than I expected," he said, as he slowly stood up from the table. He stepped through the door at about the same time Rowley pulled up in front of Eugenia.

"What is the meaning of this?" Knighton demanded as he dismounted, Heath and Edmund close behind.

Instead of raging at her brothers, Eugenia turned to berate him. "How could you, Graham?"

He met Knighton's gaze.

"Tinsley did not tell me your locale. When I read that you had left with him, this was the first place I thought to look."

Knighton was staring at him as if he were keen for a fight. He sighed. He should have known it would come to this.

"Eugenia, go inside."

"What?" She looked back and forth between him and her brothers. "No. You will not engage in fisticuffs over this—over me."

Eugenia stepped in between them with an arm stretched out to both Graham and Rowley, as though she could hold them off. It was not the first time they had engaged in fisticuffs—after all, they were male—yet never before had she been the object of dissension.

"I will not have you fight because of me!" she shouted. "Graham did try to convince me not to leave, but insisted on accompanying me rather than have me travel alone at night."

"He should have brought you to me," Rowley said quietly, still looking at Graham.

"Really? So that you could make my life more miserable?"

"Eugenia, you know he wants only what is best for you."

"As long as it runs in harmony with what Society thinks," she snapped.

"I do not deny it," Rowley defended himself. "I have lived longer amongst these people than you. I have seen people be ruined and shunned. Is that what you want for yourself, for your children?"

"If I am ruined, there will be no children," she argued. She threw up her hands and paced back and forth for a moment. "Do you not understand that I only wanted a day or two away to reflect and consider?"

"I had agreed to give you some time after you were seen in public, Eugenia. Why sneak away like a thief in the night?"

"Because he insisted on saving me." She flung herself around and pointed a finger at Graham.

He watched the exchange, trying to leave the siblings to sort through their discordance, but that was too much. "You would rather have Ravenhill?"

"You do not wish to be saved by Graham, I take it?" Rowley asked.

"He saved me last night, and for that, I am truly grateful but I cannot see him shackled to me for life."

Graham threw up his hands in surrender. She always made it about him...not herself.

"You must maintain this charade for some time," Knighton said. "It will forfeit your chance with Farnsworth, however."

She glared at her eldest brother, looking very much as though she were about to plant him a facer for mentioning the duke.

"Very well. It is coming upon the festive season. I do not think the town would speculate wildly if we all returned to Devonshire. Would you be agreeable to that, Tinsley?"

He inclined his head, but he was quite angry nevertheless. "We will need a few days in Town in order to make it plain we are not running away."

"I agree that is best," Rowley responded, adding, "There is one last bill I would like to vote upon before we leave anyway."

"Gather your things, Sister. I would like to be back in Town before nightfall."

"Yes, brother."

Eugenia gave Graham a look which he could not quite read before she marched back into the house to collect her belongings. Whether it was apologetic or defiant, he could not quite determine.

"I would still like to pummel you," Knighton said when she had gone inside.

"The feeling is mutual, but we both have her best interest at heart."

"I appreciate your regard for her, my friend. Yet I cannot have you sacrifice your own freedom and happiness for her."

"What if she is my happiness?" Graham asked angrily. "I am no martyr, I assure you. Genie and I deal quite well together. If it were anyone else, you would march us to the altar before the week's end!" He ran his hands through his hair and looked to Heath and Edmund with a plea of frustration.

Edmund stepped forward. "If this is what you truly want, then use this betrothal as time to convince her," he suggested.

Graham glanced at Heath who gave a slight shrug. "You are certainly preferable to Ravenhill or Farnsworth."

"Thank you," he answered dryly. "Will you allow it?" He turned to Knighton.

"You have my blessing if you can convince her."

"Why is your surview so different with me?" he asked. "Why do you question my sincerity? The two of you were pleased enough a few hours ago," he said to Heath and Edmund.

"That was before you helped her to run away."

"You know her as well as I. She would have gone alone. I cannot believe you think I would harm her in any way. It was the safest thing I could do!"

"Would you give up other women?" Rowley asked, taking him off guard.

"Is this your true objection? That I would flaunt mistresses and conquests in front of Genie?"

"You do have rather a reputation with women," Heath murmured.

"You of all would know," Graham retorted.

"That is in the past," Heath defended himself.

"Yet I am not to be granted that opportunity as well?"

"Of course, you are," Edmund said, stepping forward, giving Knighton a look of warning.

"Row?" Graham wanted to hear it from his friend's own lips. He wanted a chance with Eugenia without interference.

Knighton gave a nod of acceptance.

"I shall still want some time at Jackson's with you," Graham said. "I think we both have some frustrations to give vent to."

"I will see you there tomorrow morning at eleven, then," Rowley agreed.

Eugenia appeared in the doorway and looked at each of their faces, not disguising her disgust. "What is the verdict, brothers?"

"We will return to London for a few days. You will remain betrothed to Tinsley and we will show ourselves at the engagements we have already sent acceptances to."

"And then?" she asked defiantly.

"We will spend the festive season at The Grange. That should give you time enough."

Graham watched her face closely. She seemed more hurt than anything.

She turned to him. "And you agree to give me time to consider?"

"I will be at Lovell Abbey for Christmas as well. Am I to avoid you?"

Her eyes searched his and then she seemed to release her anger in a sag of her shoulders. "No."

"Come, Eugenia," Rowley started, taking her arm. "We will see you in London," he said to Graham.

The brothers turned to gather their horses, which had wandered off to graze.

"A moment, Genie?" Graham asked. Rowley eyed him askance. "Only a moment."

Graham was grateful for any concession and time alone. He did not wish for them to part like this.

"I deeply regret what has happened, Graham," she said, before he had the chance to speak. "I do not wish to ruin your relationship with my brothers."

"You have done nothing. I knew exactly what I was doing," he said.

"I do not wish to ruin our friendship, either." Her big blue eyes looked pleadingly up at him.

"Genie," he said, stepping forward to grasp her arms. "Promise me you will not dismiss me out of hand. Will you give me a chance?"

"I wish I might understand why you are doing this, Graham," she said, gazing up into his face.

Graham was angry that this beautiful creature had been so woefully misunderstood and that no one saw her for who she truly was. He vowed to change that.

He kissed her softly on the lips, then pulled slowly away. "I will visit you back in London." She gave a nod and turned away quickly, but not before he saw tears pooling in her eyes.

Soon after, he watched four horses charge down the drive. Turning, he punched the wall.

He had no idea how he would convince her, but he knew it would be worth his time and energy. His father had often said anything worth having was worth working hard for, and that certainly appeared to be the case. However, he knew one thing for certain—Eugenia Knight was worth having. And he meant to have her.

# CHAPTER FIFTEEN

E UGENIA DID NOT speak to her brothers on the ride back to Town. Besides being angry with them, she was too confused and did not trust what words might tumble forth. Graham seemed sincere, but she did not want his offer to be out of some misguided sense of chivalry. How would she know one way or the other?

It seemed she would have to accept this betrothal for now and make it believable. Would it be so hard to enjoy Graham's company, now that she was aware of him in a completely different way? He had opened her eyes to new sensations and feelings within her which she had not even known existed. It was both fascinating and horrifying. Yet could she ever be satisfied now, for she could sense that her own feelings were changing?

When they arrived back at Knighton House after an uneventful journey, she was quickly ushered upstairs to bathe and dress for the evening. The last thing she wanted was to attend an evening party, but she did not argue.

Stevens came to dress her as though nothing had happened. Eugenia did not demur when the maid brought out a bright, rose-colored gown which was entirely more cheerful than she felt. Eugenia did not even object when Stevens dressed her hair in an elaborate style and placed flowers in the curls around her head.

"Stop this, Eugenia!" she chided herself. She was not one to dwell on misery; she had always been a happy person and she did not want that to change. Lifting her chin at her reflection in the looking-glass, she determined to enjoy herself that evening, and give the gossips little to speak of.

When she arrived downstairs in the drawing room, Edmund was the only one ready and, unconsciously, she breathed a sigh of relief.

"You look lovely, Sister," he said with a kind smile as he came forward to kiss her cheek.

"Where are we going this evening?" she asked.

"The theater, I believe. I am here to play the supportive brother."

"You are not playing, Edmund. You are always supportive."

"I do try," he agreed with a wink.

"By the by, what happened to Ravenhill when you and Heath escorted him out?"

For a moment, Edmund flashed her a look of pure deviltry.

"What did you do, Edmund?" she asked more forcefully. "Did you mean to keep everything delicious from me? At the very least, I deserve to know he will be punished!"

"Oh, I think it is safe to say he will leave you unmolested in the future."

"Do not make me beg, Edmund," she warned.

He held up his hands in surrender. "His debts have been purchased, in agreement for his never again darkening your door and also his absence from the metropolis until you are safely married. There is also the added disclaimer that he is not to try such tricks again with other ladies, nor besmirch your name."

"I was hoping for more bloodlust, but I suppose that will have to do."

"Is it so very wrong that I delight in his misery?" Edmund pretended to ponder. "It is quite a beautiful solution when you have time to reflect upon it with less anger," he added.

"If you say so," she said doubtfully. As she spoke, other members of the family began to join them.

She was collecting her wrap from the back of a side table when Quincy opened the entrance door to let Graham in. Eugenia should not have been surprised. For how else would they carry on as a betrothed couple before the eyes of the *ton*, if not in each other's company? She had seen him hundreds of times in evening dress, but now she saw him as a *man*—rather than a gentleman or brother—and it made everything more difficult.

Very firmly she reminded herself that nothing was to be different between them. She smiled brightly. "Good evening, Graham." She curtsied.

He stepped forward and bowed over her hand. "My lady."

"Shall we?" Knighton asked. "Shakespeare waits for no one."

*"All the world's a stage, and all the men and women merely players,"* Graham quoted.

"As you like it?" Eugenia asked as Graham handed her into the carriage and took his place beside her.

She was most definitely not in the mood for a romantic comedy about a duke's daughter who had been banished, or the protagonist who had to pretend to be someone she was not. It was all rather too close to the truth, although the hero was hardly in love with her as Orlando was with Rosalind.

On countless occasions she had watched plays with Graham and enjoyed the witty, sarcastic banter they exchanged. Would the ladies continue to seek him out, as they always did, now that the two of them were engaged?

"You do look lovely, pet," Graham leaned over and whispered in her ear. His warm breath tickled her neck and a shiver ran down her spine. How was she to stop her body from reacting to him? He had merely whispered in her ear.

Rowley and Emma were having a lively discussion about George and something new he had done. Eugenia turned to speak, but

Graham's face was still close to hers.

"Stop that," she scolded in a soft voice.

"Stop what?"

"You know very well that you are flirting. You may save it for an audience. We have our own play to perform, remember."

"I do not intend to put on a performance, Genie."

She relaxed a little. "That is good to hear. I have also resolved to go on as before. Did you hear about Ravenhill?"

"I did. I stopped at the club on my way home this afternoon, to apprise myself of the latest news."

"And what was the gossip?" Graham had always kept her abreast of the happenings inside the Gentlemen's clubs. Very likely, she reflected wickedly, things her actual brothers would never tell her. "And what is the verdict?"

He paused, then raised his brows and leaned forward as though to impart something beyond secretive. "They are saying we are a love-match."

"I beg your pardon?" she asked loudly enough to cause Rowley and Emma to look up from their conversation.

"*Love is a madness.*" Graham laughed.

"'Tis nothing," she said hastily, so Rowley and Emma would resume their conversation. She turned back to him. "And, *most friendship is feigning, most love mere folly!*" she tossed back at him. "Was there anything else about Ravenhill?"

"Mere speculation, fortunately. Most think he was digging for gold and created an elaborate ruse to entrap you."

"I would agree with that."

"Of course, there is also talk that Knighton paid him off, which is partly the case."

Eugenia was absolutely furious that Ravenhill would be allowed to succeed with his heinous behavior. Even if Rowley held his debts, it was still an insufficient punishment, for the effect the attack was having on her future. Her choices had been stripped away. "What of Kitty Ravenhill? Has she fled with her brother?"

"I would be very surprised if that were the case. She needs to marry quickly before the full extent of their scheming becomes known. There is gossip in that quarter already."

Eugenia knew some satisfaction that perhaps Kitty might be made to suffer as she was. "Who do the books favor?" She could not help but ask.

"She was setting her lures for Perth or myself, but neither of us will be caught."

"*I pray you, do not fall in love with her, for she is falser than vows made in wine.*"

He barked a laugh. "Indeed."

"Besides, Lady Augusta appeared to have her hooks into him," Eugenia muttered.

"Other than us, the only ones with enough blunt would be old Lord Summerton or Sir Horace Kemp."

"That would serve her right, although she would soon be a widow, which would then give her the freedom to strike fear into the hearts of all marriages everywhere."

"I've never known you to have such a malicious streak, pet."

"*Do you not know I am a woman? When I think, I must speak.*"

He laughed again. "Thank God we are both free of them." The carriage pulled to a stop in front of the Drury Lane Theatre.

"Shall we?" he asked, handing her down from the vehicle.

"Do not overdo it," she warned.

"Not even to make Kitty Ravenhill jealous?" he asked. She watched his eyes glance beyond her and then back at her with a look which suggested he was ready to devour her.

She turned to see Kitty Ravenhill a few feet behind her. Even though she knew it was for the waiting crowd's benefit, she could not help but relish the look on Kitty's face. It was a small, petty victory, but a victory nonetheless.

They made their way through the crowd and passed into the theatre, only to be stopped in the foyer by a large assemblage of persons offering their congratulations. It seemed as though every member of the *ton* was present.

When they had finally reached the stairs on the far side, in order to enter their box, there was a stir behind them. Why, Eugenia wondered miserably, could they not be left in peace?

"Oh, Lady Eugenia," Kitty Ravenhill called, smiling falsely as she caught up to them.

Eugenia could hardly give her the cut direct, though she very much wished to. She turned and inclined her head, not feeling the need to do anything further.

"When is the wedding to be?"

Eugenia swung her gaze from Kitty and looked up at Graham with a smile that she hoped conveyed all of the things a female in love should for her betrothed.

"We have not yet set the date," Graham answered. "We shall make plans while in the country for Christmas."

"I think that is a wise choice, sir. You certainly would not want to be *hasty*."

There were enough gasps heard around them at the implied insult that Eugenia knew the remark had been made for everyone else's benefit, not just to harm her. Eugenia realized she was being provoked, but she refused to give in and plant the scheming wanton a facer as she deserved.

"Have you heard of Miss Bell's school for young ladies?" she asked calmly. "I hear they have most excellent lessons in deportment," she drawled and pointedly turned her back on Kitty Ravenhill.

"WELL DONE, PET."

"It was that or throw her *cross buttock* in the middle of the theatre, which would have been much more satisfying."

"*The fool doth think he is wise, but the wise man knows himself to be a fool,*" he said in her ear.

Eugenia laughed. "Perhaps this play is better than I remembered."

"I think we have already covered the highlights. She certainly gives kittens a bad name."

"I cannot think of a greater misnomer."

They took their seats at the front of the box and Emma and the duke seated themselves next to her, then Heath and Cecelia, Isabella and Edmund sat behind them.

Eugenia appeared far more conscious of everyone staring at her than usual. Normally, she paid scant attention to such scrutiny. Graham noticed her pretend to read the play-bill for a moment, but this was one of her least favorite works by Shakespeare, and she quickly tossed it aside. At that moment Graham knew she could not have cared less about who the actors were.

Again the crowd stirred, which was something he could tell even over the roar of the bucks in the pit, and he looked up to see what the fuss was about. Directly across from them, Farnsworth was ushering in her aunt, along with Lady Augusta and Lord Perth. Graham saw Eugenia's cheeks burn, though very few knew the true story. Nevertheless, they knew her two suitors had been replaced by him...

Graham put an arm around her chair in a possessive fashion and leaned towards her. "This would be an excellent moment to smile at me."

She looked up at him and complied. "*Oh, how bitter a thing it is to look into happiness through another man's eyes!*"

His eyes crinkled appreciatively at the humor. "Does it truly bother you, pet? Were you more attached to Perth than I suspected?"

"No," she answered truthfully. "My heart is not affected. My pride, on the other hand, is dreadfully bruised."

He laughed heartily. "That's my girl. Anyone who defects so easily is not worth another thought."

He watched her gaze move over to where Lady Augusta was practically hanging on Lord Perth's arm. "May they enjoy their cold, proper marriage together."

Then her gaze drifted to her aunt and the duke. "Now my aunt may have her happy resolution. I hope the duke will do right by her, and give up the silly notion of marrying someone he does not love."

Graham gave her hand a reassuring squeeze as some singers took to the stage for the opening act before the play. Three plump men began singing in Italian and bumping in to one another, then trying to push the others out of the way to vie for the audience's attention. Eugenia laughed appreciatively.

"It is good to hear you laugh again. You have not been happy these past weeks."

She sighed regretfully. "I am determined to make the best of things."

"I am pleased to hear it. It is lowering to think that one of your dearest friends might rather have married an older duke for convenience."

She cast him a look of exasperation. "Do not speak such fustian."

"Need I remind you, you did run away after I announced our betrothal?"

"That was nothing to do with you specifically, and I did not object when you insisted on accompanying me... or, at least, not much," she added.

"Still, it was not quite the scene I had imagined when I pledged my troth to my beloved." He held his hand over his chest dramatically.

She looked heavenward and he could tell she was still unconvinced of his sincerity. "Speaking of scenes...the first act is set to begin."

"You do not like this play," he reminded her. "You should be delighted that I am here to distract you."

"I said it was not my favorite. That does not mean I will not watch it," she countered.

"I can take a hint," he said, turning his attention to the stage, but it did not stay there for long. He wanted her attention and she seemed bent on ignoring him. "I wish to do something entertaining tomorrow."

Her eyes, not her face, moved sideways. "Such as?"

"The Tower? Burlington House?"

"You know how I feel about the Tower," she murmured.

"But how else would you have been able to see those fantastic creatures?" he argued, though it was really sad to see the beautiful beasts locked up in small cages. "Besides, there are other things at the Tower apart from the menagerie."

"Very well. We can go to the Tower.... if you promise to stop at Gunter's on the way home."

"If you insist." He smiled inwardly. He would win Eugenia over one day at a time. He would convince her that they were meant to be together. Frankly, he did not know why he had not recognized it before. People were going to continue saying unpleasant things such as Kitty Ravenhill had, because it made little difference. He would do his best to distract and woo her at the same time, while Society watched.

The first act began, and he felt Eugenia begin to squirm. Some of the parallels were uncanny, but no one besides her would have made them.

In the first act, Duke Senior was deposed as the head of the court. Then Orlando and Charles fought and Rosalind fell in love with Orlando. Graham wished he had been the one to fight for her.

Rosalind was shunned and banned from the castle at the same time that Orlando left to hide from his brother.

"No witticisms to offer?" he asked.

"I do believe we exhausted all the good lines before the play began," she replied.

"Perhaps. What are you thinking of, then?"

"Truthfully? About being ruined and going into hiding—of disguising myself as someone I am not."

"Ah." It was more uncanny than he had realized. "Are you considering a disguise, then?"

"I am considering any number of things, but if this is not a disguise, then it is a ruse at the very least."

Graham turned and eyed her. "Perhaps for you, but not for me."

"Please stop saying that. I do not want you to find yourself married to me in some great act of heroism and then wake up one day full of regrets."

Graham was angry. He had to take a deep breath before he could speak without shouting. "You profess to know my own mind better than I?"

She looked at him somewhat warily. Good. "Of course not, but I do believe you deserve every happiness."

"And you do not think you make me happy?"

She frowned. He could see her mind racing as she chose her words carefully. "There is more to marriage than friendship."

"Friendship is the most many marriages ever aspire to. We are comfortable together. I think it offers many more advantages than if I were to, say, choose one of the young misses from the Season's crop and marry her in the next month. Or, if you were to have chosen Farnsworth or even Perth."

She snorted.

"If you are telling me that I would make you unhappy, then that is another matter altogether." He learned even closer and dropped his voice to a whisper. "But I do not think that is the case. You responded warmly to my kisses."

He smiled when he saw her cheeks burn crimson and she swallowed hard.

*Time for the final blow:* "Eugenia, there is much, much more that I will show you when you become my wife."

# CHAPTER SIXTEEN

E UGENIA HAD HAD a restless night, thanks to some of the things Graham had said to her. Could he truly wish to marry her? He seemed earnest and yet it made no sense to her.

Then she had gone down to breakfast and opened the morning news-sheets, relieved to find she was not the center of attention. That honor went to Lord Perth and Lady Augusta, along with the announcement of their betrothal. Eugenia and Graham had still warranted a mention in the column, but that was to be expected. Would Society lose interest with them now that they were betrothed? The world was such a fickle beast. Speaking of beasts, Edmund and Isabella had asked to join them on their outing to the Tower that day. Eugenia was grateful not to be alone with Graham, because she had needed time to reflect. At least Rowley was off to Parliament to vote on the bill he had been waiting for. That meant they could leave London soon.

Edmund and Isabella came into the room, looking absurdly cheerful. It was hard not to be jealous of what they had, while at the same time she could not be happier for them.

"I am so excited," Isabella beamed.

"About going to the Tower?" Eugenia asked.

"My wife has never been. Such time she has spent in London has been very brief," her brother explained.

"So are you saying you appreciate that my propensity for trouble has brought you to London?" she asked Isabella with a wry grin.

Isabella laughed. "I suppose I am."

"No need it to announce me, Quincy," Eugenia heard Graham say from the entrance hall.

"Edmund and Isabella will be joining us," Eugenia told him when he walked into the room. "She has never visited the Tower."

"Excellent. I am always pleased with more company. By the by, Genie, that is a fetching bonnet. Is it new?"

"I bought it at the beginning of the Season, but have not had anywhere in particular to wear it." She attempted to hold her head high and not blush. She knew it was a bit outlandish, even for her, but the small pieces of fruit looked so real that she had been unable to resist.

"It looks very...edible," Graham said, looking amused.

They made their way down the front steps and out to the carriage. Once settled inside and on their way, Eugenia spoke to Isabella. "Did Edmund warn you that they keep animals in cages there?"

"Well," Isabella answered carefully, "I had heard there were exotic beasts from all over the world there. Are they dreadfully mistreated?"

Graham groaned from the seat beside her.

"I suppose you will see for yourself."

"We could bypass the menagerie and look at the armaments or the crown jewels," Edmund suggested, ever the peacemaker.

"But I was so looking forward to seeing lions and tigers."

"Then you shall." Edmund patted Isabella's hand. "Why did you wish to come if it bothers you, Genie?" her brother asked.

"Because Graham thought it would be fun and we must be seen together."

"I promised her ices at Gunter's afterwards," he added, as though it were his idea.

When the driver pulled up to the gates of the Tower, one of the lions moaned loudly and Isabella jumped. "Is that one of the beasts?"

she asked, wide eyed.

"Yes, they are moaning to be released from their misery," Eugenia retorted.

"Oh, cut line, Genie. He is just talking. Probably singing the woes of his beloved ignoring him," Graham countered pointedly.

"Do let us go and see!" Isabella said excitedly like a child, just as Eugenia had been the first time.

They paid their shilling apiece and went inside. Graham gave Genie his arm and she took it willingly. What would it be like to be married to Graham? To touch him whenever she liked? She could not help but muse upon the idea.

They soon found the moaning lion, which was pacing back and forth in the stone enclosure.

"What do you think is the matter?" Isabella asked Edmund.

"He wants to be roaming the grasslands in Africa," Eugenia muttered under her breath.

"You must admit he is spectacular," Graham said as he admired the large cat.

"I think he is pining for Duchess," Edmund said indicating a female lioness in the next cage.

"Can they not be together?" Isabella asked. "How lonely it must be for them, not to mention cold and damp."

"I told you it was pitiful," Eugenia agreed.

They continued walking and saw an array of cats – more lions, tigers, and leopards. Eugenia did think they were amazing, she just felt incredibly sorry for them.

"I read that there used to be an elephant and a polar bear here," Isabella remarked.

"That was several hundred years ago," Edmund told her. "I would love to see them both, but I am not certain I would enjoy the Arctic."

"Shall we see the monkeys? They are my favorite species," Graham said. "I find their intelligence fascinating."

"I remember Lady Babcock had a pet monkey at her ball last Season, and it was all the rage," Eugenia said. "It used to sit on her shoulder and chatter at everyone as if it were human."

"I would have loved to have seen that," Isabella said, watching the little creatures swing about on some ropes.

"It was quite the spectacle until the monkey decided to swing on the chandeliers. He caused the candles to fall and one of them caught Lady Babcock's wig on fire!"

Eugenia turned around to describe the scene when a loud screech sounded behind her and the bars began to rattle.

She screamed and jumped as something grabbed onto her bonnet and whipped her head back.

"The monkey wants your hat!" Isabella called.

Graham began to swat at the monkey. Eugenia did not give a fig for the hat; she just could not untie the knot on the ribbons beneath her chin.

"I need a knife!" she cried urgently.

"You cannot kill the monkey," Edmund said.

"I want to cut the ribbon beneath my chin," she growled.

The commotion attracted more monkeys to vie for the fake fruit on her bonnet, as well as a crowd to see what was happening. The monkey had a death grip on a banana, and nothing would compel the knot beneath her chin to loosen.

"There is a knife in my boot," Graham said to Edmund.

Her brother found the knife and opened it but as the blade came near, the monkey continued to try to pry the fruit from her head.

"Be still!" Edmund commanded. Eugenia was not sure if he was speaking to her or the monkey.

Graham continued to swat and tried to pry the little hands—or were they paws—from her hat. Eugenia felt the blade against her skin and closed her eyes while her brother tried to free her.

She heard the cutting of the ribbon and felt the bonnet release from her head. She sagged with relief and Graham pulled her away as the monkeys chattered wildly at their new possession. To her astonishment, they managed to pull it into their cage, and taking it to the far corner, attacked the thing.

"Are you quite well?" Isabella asked, leaning close to study her face.

"Yes, yes," she reassured everyone. She could not wait until Graham began to tease her about wearing food on her head.

"Do you wish to go home?" he asked.

"I certainly feel no compulsion to remain amongst the menagerie, but you did promise me an ice."

Graham was never one to leave an opportunity for wit untouched. "As long as you promise not to wear it on your head," he said quietly, just to her.

She scowled at him. "I knew you would be unable to resist teasing me."

"Would you have held your tongue if the tables had been turned?" he asked skeptically.

"No, of course not," he agreed for her, eyes twinkling with amusement.

"If you do not mind very much, I would like to show Isabella the rest of the Tower," Edmund said.

"We shall send the carriage back for you, then," Graham said.

"Excellent," her brother agreed. He looked at Eugenia before she asked the question. "You are betrothed now and, I assume, will not leave the carriage," he said with a pointed look at her head which must be a fright.

Once back inside the conveyance, she unpinned her hair and pulled it into a simple knot. Graham watched her in silence.

"What is it?"

"Your hair is beautiful. I think it a shame ladies must keep their hair up at all times."

She gave a lift of her shoulder, unused to hearing compliments from him. She understood the performance in public, but they were alone. She put the last pin in and looked back at him. "Will I do?"

"I cannot produce a bonnet out of thin air, but you no longer look as though a monkey attacked your head," he said, but could not keep from laughing.

"Then I suppose after Gunter's you shall have to take me shopping."

※※※

EUGENIA HAD A sweet tooth and Gunter's was, without question, one of her favorite places to satisfy her cravings.

"Now, this is what I call fun," she said as they drew up at the confectioners.

"What flavor shall it be today?" he asked before the waiter approached.

"I think I shall have the elderberry. No, wait, something with cream."

Graham smiled. She did this every time. There was not a flavor she did not like. "Shall I choose for you?"

"Yes, please."

He ordered her the Lavender and the Gruyere for himself. While they waited, he debated where they should go from here.

"Genie, I think we should talk."

"We are talking; we have been talking," she said, accentuating her words expressively with her hands.

"We did not finish discussing our betrothal."

"There is nothing to discuss. We will leave soon for Devonshire, and I will jilt you when we return."

"No," he said firmly.

"I beg your pardon?"

"You heard me quite well. I want you to consider me as a serious suitor."

She opened her mouth to object, but he held up his hand. "Hear me out. Is your only objection because of my feelings?"

The waiter interrupted then, bringing them their servings of ice, artistically arranged in silver dishes with delicate spoons.

He gave her a moment to take the first spoonful and relish it as she always did. That was yet another point in favor of their union. They knew each other better than anyone else and enjoyed each other's company. He simply had to make her see it.

"I trust your selection is satisfactory?"

"Of course it is," she said. "This is one of my favorites."

"All of them are your favorites. Now answer my question, please."

"I do not want to. I do not know if I can. It seems wrong, somehow." She frowned and two lines formed between her brows.

"You and me, together?"

"Yes," she said sadly, staring at her ice.

"We are always together. Consider, if you will, the scandal sheets."

"Must we?"

He ignored the question. "We are together in them more often than not."

"But not in a scandalous fashion," she argued, as if she had no idea where his remarks were leading.

"We are together because we are friends. We enjoy each other's company. What better prospect could there be for a marriage?"

"Love, attraction," she began as her face flushed. "It is different," she managed, the last word ending on a squeak.

"Surely, it is better to be different than not to have each other at all?"

"You will only ever see me as the hoydenish little sister, Graham. Friends, yes, but I know there is more to marriage."

*I see you differently now*, he wanted to shout. He would make her understand.

She ate her ice in silence and then she set it aside, the spoon clinking in the dish.

She drew a deep breath and then spoke. "I think we need some time apart, Graham."

Before answering, he watched her fidget and avoid his gaze. He had not expected her to request time apart again after the last debacle. "I also planned to visit my family for Christmas, if you recall."

"Devonshire is big enough for the both of us. We shall not be sitting in each other's pockets. You won't feel the need to watch out for me every moment, like you have done here with my brothers being gone."

At this very moment he felt like strangling her. She was not seeing reason. She had been willing to martyr herself with Farnsworth or Perth, but she could not accept him. He was becoming more infuriated by the moment.

"Very well, I can leave you alone for a while in Devonshire.

"Hallo," a voice called. "Eugenia, my dear, are you in there?"

"It is my aunt," Eugenia said as she slipped across the seat and looked out of the window.

Graham saw the Duke of Farnsworth standing nearby. Eugenia took another deep breath and put a smile on her face.

"Good afternoon, Aunt," she said. "Your Grace."

"Will you come down and take a turn about the square with us?" Lady Hambridge asked.

"Of course," Eugenia answered.

Graham climbed down and then helped Eugenia to alight.

"Fetch your bonnet," her aunt scolded, as though she were a small child.

"My bonnet had a mishap. If it is bothersome, then we may talk later. I am certain the whole of London will have heard of my bonnet's fate by tomorrow morning, at any rate."

Her aunt sighed heavily. "Come along, then." She took Eugenia's arm and began to promenade. "Farnsworth and I wished to inform you of our betrothal before you heard it elsewhere."

"That was not necessary, but may I be the first to offer you my most sincere congratulations. I think it is the right decision."

Farnsworth beamed down at her aunt. "I gave her up once, I could not bear to do so again. Thank you for helping me to realize it, my lady."

Eugenia dipped a small curtsy.

"We intend to be married during the Christmas season, at my country estate. You are, of course welcome to attend."

"Thank you. I am not certain what our plans are, but I assure you I wish you every happiness."

They circled back to the carriage and her aunt and the duke took their leave, looking like two youngsters in the throes of their first calf-love. Graham chuckled. "Shall we go and find you another bonnet?"

She shook her head with a half-hearted smile." I do not need any more bonnets," she answered.

"The situation is dire indeed if the lady refuses a new bonnet," he teased.

He caught her watching someone across the square. Kitty Raven-hill was promenading on the arm of old Lord Summerton.

"Well," she said, "it seems as though everyone is finding their matches."

He handed her up into the carriage. "Do not despair, pet."

"How can I not?"

"You may console yourself that you do not find yourself wed to old Lord Summerton."

Graham suspected he could profess his dying love, spout a great deal of nonsense to her, but it would be a lie and she would certainly not thank him in the long run. He had been infatuated and mistaken it for love before, and it was the most uncomfortable he had ever been in his life. But how could he make her understand that that was not a desirable way to begin a marriage? How could he persuade her that only heartache and disappointment lay in that direction?

"You have me," he answered instead.

"I do not know how to make you understand." She threw up her hands in a typically Eugenia display of frustration.

"Nor I, you. Perhaps we have been together too much. I can only hope, after some time apart, you will see I am right."

"Absence makes the heart grow fonder?" she asked doubtfully.

"Why not? I certainly missed you when we were at odds for two days. I cannot see why it would be different for longer."

"Because, at length, you grow accustomed to it. The beginning is the hardest," she explained.

"And how long shall this self-imposed break from each other be?"

"I do not know," she whispered.

"So I am to devote myself to the estate and await your leisure— await my fate? My father will be beside himself with joy."

She reached over and took his hand. "I am sorry, but so much has happened that I am confused. I do not trust my judgment, and I must ensure that this will be best for both of us."

"Should this not be a mutual decision?" He could not mask the irritation in his voice. He wanted to shake her.

"I am pleased you feel you know your own mind, but I do not know mine."

"As you wish. We will no longer be under the scrutiny of Society, so you may have your distance."

"Thank you." She leaned forward and kissed him on the cheek. It took a great deal of effort not to pull her into his arms and show her what she was missing. He could only trust that the truth would out in the end when her every movement was not being judged and her character tried in the broadsheets.

# CHAPTER SEVENTEEN

THERE WAS A reason Cornwall and Devonshire were considered the ends of the earth. It took a ridiculous amount of time to travel there. It also afforded Eugenia a great deal of time in which to reflect. It was what she had wanted, but it was a frightening thing to be alone with one's thoughts—especially when one's heart and one's mind were not in agreement.

Watching Rowley and Emma with their son, George, along with Heath and Cecilia, full of joy for the impending birth of their child, and Edmund and Isabella, who were newly wedded and smelling of April and May, Eugenia could not help but be a little envious. All of them were so very much in love—why was it wrong to want that for herself?

She could not tell the precise moment when her feelings for Graham had begun to change, but she knew that it would be difficult to be married to someone who did not reciprocate her love. On the other hand, he was right—most marriages did not even have mutual affection, let alone friendship as a foundation. Was she being ridiculous? Very likely so; it was something she was often accused of, one way or another.

It was a relief to be gone from London. These last few months had become a trial. It would be a relief to be herself again. Let the gossip columns pick on someone else for a while. Kitty Ravenhill would no doubt pick up the torch with alacrity.

The first thing Eugenia intended to do was gallop across the open meadows of the estate as fast as she liked—and in breeches!—she proclaimed loudly to herself.

Then she would visit Granny and repeat all the sordid gossip for her and hear what she had missed whilst away.

It was hard not to think about what Graham might be doing. He was her best friend and they had done almost everything together since Sybil had married. The thought reminded her that Rowley had given her a letter before they left Town and having pocketed it to read on the journey, she had forgotten about it.

She pulled it out with anticipation and unfolded several sheets of double crossed, neat script and settled down to enjoy her friend's missive.

*Dearest Genie,*

*I promised you I would write and tell you everything, and I do not know where to begin! Marriage is not at all what I expected, but do not let that frighten you.*

"You know me better than that, Sibyl," Eugenia muttered.

*I can hardly write what occurs on the page, but it is not as bad as you fear.*

"I am overflowing with comfort by your words," she said to the page.

*I will admit, I did not know Lord Darling very well before our wedding, but he has been all that is kind and very patient with my ignorance. Oh, how I wish I could tell you things in person, but I would not trade this wedding trip for anything.*

*My fervent hope is you may find someone special to fulfill your dreams and make you happy.*

If only Sybil knew how much had happened in the short time since she left England.

Sybil went on to describe the villa in Italy where they were staying, and yet again, Eugenia felt that burning of jealousy in her heart. It was a cursed emotion and it shamed her to feel it, not only for her brothers but also her best friend. Yet what could she do about it? Was it possible to make Graham feel that way about her? She was the least likely female of her acquaintance to inspire passion in any gentleman's heart. Nonetheless, that was what she wanted. She folded Sybil's letter away, unable to bear any more of it at the moment. Besides, she had left out all of the salacious bits which Eugenia needed to know.

Maybe her grandmother would tell her? It was certainly worth asking. She looked at the time—half-nine—and decided to visit her grandmother before riding, when she could normally be relied upon to be awake. Sending a message to the stables for Cleo to be saddled, Eugenia then mounted and cantered the mare all the way to the Dower House.

She let herself in when the door was not answered quickly, as she could not wait.

"Grandmother!"

"Eh? Come closer so I can hear you."

Eugenia moved forward and knelt before her grandmother. "It is Eugenia."

"Rusticating because of a scandal, eh?"

"Not precisely," Eugenia said halfheartedly.

"Order tea, I want to hear everything." Her grandmother sat up, a spry look in her eyes.

Eugenia went over to pull the bell-rope and order refreshment. Her grandmother's companion answered the call. The meek, slight woman had been with the dowager since before Eugenia was born.

"Oh, my lady..." She curtsied. "I thought her ladyship was resting."

"I came in unannounced," Eugenia said. "Would you be so kind as to ask the kitchens for tea?"

"Of course, my lady," she answered, bobbing her head as she left the room.

"Now sit down and tell me what has happened in the last week. You know it takes an age before the papers reach us."

"What was the last you heard?"

"Knighton had a letter from Perth, requesting permission to court you. And Farnsworth had been here not long before, asking the same."

"Oh," Eugenia said, surprised. "A great deal has happened since then."

"Are you engaged to Perth, then? I shall never forgive you if you chose Farnsworth."

"No, indeed. It is rather a long story, though. Shall we wait for the tea?"

"That could take forever. You might as well begin now."

Eugenia went through every detail, from Perth's house party to Ravenhill attacking her, to Perth withdrawing his offer and Aunt Hambridge becoming betrothed to the Duke.

Her grandmother sat and listened, not even noticing when her companion brought in the tea tray and served her. Almost without heeding what she did, Granny ate her biscuits and sipped her tea, rapt with attention.

When Eugenia paused to drink her tea, her grandmother finally spoke.

"Ye gads, gel. Single handed, you have kept the *ton* in scandal this Season."

"I know it," she murmured.

"Well, I assume that is not the end of the story? Knighton would not have let you leave in shame, nor would he have allowed Ravenhill to succeed with such villainy."

"Indeed not." Eugenia took a deep breath.

Her grandmother rubbed her hands together. "This must be better than I thought!"

Eugenia chuckled. "How I wish you could have been there with me, Granny."

"As do I, my dear," Her grandmother gave a long-suffering sigh. There were decades of reminiscence in that sigh. Her granny had been the belle of Society.

"Mr. Tinsley took my aunt and me away from the house party in the middle of the night."

"So I should hope!" her grandmother exclaimed.

"Thankfully, Rowley had arrived back in London by the time we did. The herd collectively decided that I must be seen in public. Farnsworth also agreed to continue to court me publicly, to help dispel the rumors."

"You have run ahead of yourself, gel."

"I have, a little," Eugenia agreed, "but I knew at that point that the duke and my aunt were in love. However, we agreed to this charade and all went to Almack's together. My brothers had arranged for several gentlemen to dance with me, but we had not anticipated that Ravenhill would put in an appearance that evening."

Her grandmother gasped. "No!"

"Oh, yes. He wore a sling about his arm and a plaster on his face and milked the situation for every bit of sympathy he could."

"The cur," she growled.

"That is only the beginning. He tried to cut in on my partner during one of the dances and proclaimed loudly that he and I were betrothed."

"Did Knighton call him out? How was I not informed that there was a duel?"

"I am sorry to disappoint you, Granny, but it was Mr. Tinsley who saved the day."

"How did that rogue save the day?" she asked, with a gleam in her eye. She might call Graham a rogue, but she adored him and flirted with him as though she were twenty again.

"He announced to the ballroom that I could not be betrothed to Ravenhill because I was already betrothed to him."

"Bravo, Tinsley!" She raised her cup in the air to salute, and tea sloshed over the back of the chair.

Eugenia took the moment to eat a biscuit, wondering why she did not laugh as she normally would have done.

"Why do you look so dismayed about it?" Her grandmother eyed her keenly.

"Because the truth is he does not really wish to marry me. He says he does, and that being friends will be more pleasant than most unions, but I fear I will give him naught but disappointment."

"What would make you change your mind? I think it is an excellent match."

Eugenia paused to think. What would change her mind? "I wish I could say. I see my brothers so content and I want what they have."

"Humph! You have moonbeams in your head, gel."

"I know it. That is why he deserves someone else."

"Balderdash!" Granny slammed her teacup down in her saucer.

"Lady Emily Perth would be perfect for him. She is beautiful and demure, and I saw the interest in his eyes when he looked at her."

"Gentlemen will look at anyone in a skirt that way. Some hide it better than others, but I assure you Tinsley has noticed you." She leaned forward and whispered loudly. "Has he kissed you?"

Eugenia could feel her face burn with humiliation.

"He has, has he?" She nodded her head with a gleam in her eye. "I imagine it was glorious. He has that look about him."

Eugenia could not answer.

"And that was not enough to allay your fears of your compatibility? Are you daft?"

"Perhaps I am." Eugenia had thought her grandmother would

understand, but apparently she was the only one who wanted more than a handsome face and a talent for kissing.

⇾⇾⇾⤛⤛⤛

GRAHAM WAS SHOCKED by the decline he saw in his father when he arrived home. The change was enough so that he wondered if his father would survive until the new year. His mother and sister had not yet returned from France, but were expected any day.

He spent some time with his father, but the viscount slept for much of the day. Graham therefore studied the accounts with the steward, but they were in good order. How was he to be so close to Eugenia and unable to speak with her, to see her?

It would be difficult to convince her how much he wanted their marriage if he could not be near her. He debated ways to circumvent her edict, but he always talked himself out of it. It would be easy to visit The Grange on the pretense of seeing one of the brothers, but he did not want to push her.

He wondered whether to send letters or flowers. Is that not what he would do to woo any other lady?

But this was Eugenia. What would it take to convince her?

He had to treat her differently, not as if she were one of his friends. If they continued as they were, she might never be convinced.

The one thing he was certain of was that he could no longer stay holed up in the house; it was nearly devoid of life. The servants dared not make a sound and the sick room was unsettling at best.

He decided he had to do something, because the path to insanity lay between these walls. He called for Xerxes and mounted, giving the horse its head until they reached the village. His first call was at the baker's shop, to see if he could arrange for some of Eugenia's favorite biscuits to be delivered. He knew The Grange's chef was very likely supplying the family with Edmund's pastries of choice, but what of

Eugenia?

It was a small village, but he was able to find a few items he thought she would like and had one particular thing in mind to give her at Christmas.

Flowers, sweets and bonnets... what else could he woo her with?

He stood on the High Street, pondering. He tried to think of other ladies and what they might desire. *Jewels. Most definitely jewels.* However, there was hardly a Rundell and Bridge in the small village of Clovelly. However, he had been remiss in not making a proper proposal or bestowing upon Eugenia a betrothal ring, and for that he would shop in the family vaults.

"Talking to yourself, Tinsley?"

Graham looked up to see Edmund walking towards him.

"As you see," he said, holding his hand out to shake the vicar's hand.

"And are you shepherding the flock here, now?"

"Guilty as charged," Edmund agreed. "I have been in London for weeks and wished to ensure the welfare of some people in particular. Speaking of such matters, how is your father? I had intended to travel to the Abbey this afternoon."

"He is ailing. I fear he will not survive long."

"I am grieved to hear it. I know he will be comforted by your presence."

Graham swallowed hard. Somehow it was more real to hear his friend say it aloud.

"Are you shopping?"

"I could not endure to be in the house any longer. It is quite dreary," he admitted.

"You are welcome at The Grange, you know, at any time you wish."

Graham laughed. "I think not."

Edmund looked at him strangely.

"Had you not heard that your dear sister asked me not to pursue my suit until she better understands her feelings?"

"What a ridiculous notion!" Edmund exclaimed.

"I am inclined to agree with you, but I am acceding to her wishes for now, although I confess I was shopping for her. There is more than one way to woo a lady."

Edmund smiled. "That explains why I have not seen you of late. I had assumed it was to do with your father's decline. She must realize that you are to marry."

"I cannot say what she realizes. Be that as it may, I am allowing her to come to that conclusion on her own."

"Wise man. How may I assist you in this endeavor?"

"I wish I had a good answer. I have been unable to convince her by treating her as a friend, so I thought to court her like any other lady. Sweets, flowers, jewelry; even love poems if I must!"

"No." Edmund shook his head. "She would believe that to be flummery."

"Perhaps, but treating her as though nothing were extraordinary about our relationship will not change her mind."

"Perhaps you are right," Edmund answered thoughtfully. "I will think on it and perhaps ask Isabella for advice."

"I am much obliged."

"I have not seen a great deal of Eugenia myself, come to think of it. I see her flying past on Cleo every morning and I know she has been spending a good deal of time at the Dower House."

Graham smiled. The Dower House bordered his own property and he had been tempted time and again to visit the dowager.

"I see you have been tempted to call also." Edmund read his mind. "The restriction only applies to Eugenia, and you must know we all consider you to be one of the family."

Graham inclined his head in appreciation.

"In fact, why do you not come to dine with us this evening? It will be the perfect opportunity to see if Isabella has any ideas."

"As long as my mother and sister have not arrived. I will send word when I return, if that is the case."

"Actually, I will join you on your way back now, unless you have other business to attend to in the village?"

"No, I do believe I have accomplished all I can here. I might need to make a trip into Bideford for more fripperies. It is too bad there is not a Gunter's nearby." Although he had spoken in jest, that gave him an idea.

Edmund laughed. "Sweets will only help your cause," he agreed. "She and I are much alike in that regard."

"Except that Cook bakes your preferences."

"Does she? I had not thought it to preclude anyone else's. I shall have to remedy that."

"No, not before I have won my suit."

Edmund looked at him sideways.

"It gives me the opportunity to shower her with her favorites."

"Ah. Yes, of course."

Just as Edmund and Graham were about to leave to go back to Lovell Abbey, Mrs. Miller, the squire's wife, hailed the vicar.

"Reverend Knight, Reverend Knight!" she called, holding her skirts in one hand and hurrying towards him.

Edmund looked at him apologetically. "Forgive me, I will have to visit later, it seems."

"No apology necessary. I will send word about dinner."

Edmund doffed his hat and went to discover what it was that Mrs. Miller needed.

Graham turned his horse towards home, but decided to skirt the property and go by the Dower House. Edmund had been correct. He wasn't banished from the entire family – just from Eugenia.

When he reached the Dower House, however, Eugenia's horse was grazing lazily in the small paddock bordering the carriageway.

Graham pondered what to do, but he was not yet ready to irritate Eugenia. It had been only a week. Did she miss him as much as he missed her? Instead, he tied his horse to a nearby tree and stood and waited. What did it say about him that he was so desperate just to catch a glimpse of her?

# CHAPTER EIGHTEEN

S INCE EUGENIA HAD returned home, she had done nothing but ride almost every day. She had even lost interest in eating, which was highly abnormal.

In the name of attempting to be more ladylike, she decided to try her hand at flower arrangement. She went to the hothouse to gather a few blooms and greenery, then went into the ladies' parlor with a basketful to arrange them.

Carefully, she placed the greenery in first, then put the flowers in one by one, spreading each kind out so not as to have all of them on one side or the other just as she had been taught. She picked some jasmine and pansies because those were abundant, and she picked three Christmas roses because they were her favorite. However, those made her think of Graham and the day at the garden party when her bonnet had been ruined and he bought her another... Then that made her think of the day at the Tower when the monkeys had thought her bonnet to be made of real fruit and attacked it.

She stood back to view the arrangement and it looked dreadful. Rather than giving the effect she had desired, of a harmonious arrangement of colors and shapes, her efforts more resembled a jar stuffed with daisies by a child. "Only you could take nature's beauty and spoil it, Genie," she said to herself.

Was there anything ladylike that she could do? She could wear a dress, but that was about the sum of it. Even that could not be called graceful. She growled in frustration and hurled the vase across the room. It made a satisfying crash as it shattered into tiny pieces. Covering her face with her hands, she fell to her knees. Of course, the gut-wrenching sobs which burst forth were not ladylike either.

"Eugenia!" Rowley exclaimed as he rushed into the room. "What happened? Are you hurt?" He dropped down beside her.

She shook her head but did not look up. She wanted to be ashamed in private, but there was no such thing amongst her family.

"I can see now that this was no accident. Would you care to tell me what has upset you so?"

"No." She pouted.

"Shall I fetch Emma for you? Is this something that would be easier to tell another lady?"

"A lady? Ha! I am no such thing."

"I see," he answered in a flat voice. "Hence this display of theatrics?"

"You may leave if you only wish to preach to me," she snapped. "You have no idea how unnatural this is for me. I have no feminine accomplishments; not one. I am an utter failure at being a lady."

"That is my fault. I do know it."

"At least you admit I am a failure," she muttered.

"Not at all. You mistake my meaning. I meant your lack of confidence in female virtues."

"I know you tried, Rowley, but I wanted to be with you and the others."

"By the time Emma arrived, you were already grown."

"I have tried, brother. Even when I vow to be very careful and demure, something happens which is beyond my control."

"Tinsley seems to be earnest, Genie. Why are you so troubled with these matters when you have made a match? People are much more forgiving of eccentricities once you are wed."

"Oh, Rowley, it is still a sham. Can you not see that? He had no other choice but to make that announcement."

Rowley got to his feet and went over to the window. "I suppose I should have known, but I thought better of Tinsley."

"Do not blame him! He does not insist upon my breaking the betrothal."

"He is honor-bound not to. But I fear you do not fully comprehend, Eugenia," he said, turning back to face her. "No one will have you after all these scandals."

"Even though Ravenhill was not my fault?"

"Especially after what happened with Ravenhill, my dear."

"Perhaps it is my destiny to be unwed. I would only shame my husband. Graham, for instance, has a promising political career. How could I host a formal party without bungling it when I cannot even arrange a simple vase of flowers?"

Rowley took her hands and looked her in the eye. "He will hire a brilliant secretary who will undertake those matters for you. By this time, people will have come to expect uniqueness from you. Perhaps you should simply be yourself. As I said, as a married lady, you will have far more freedom than you do now."

"Perhaps," she said absently because she did not wish to argue with her brother, but he was only trying to make her feel better and convince her to marry Graham. Yet how could she make her best friend miserable by shackling him with her as a wife?

"Are you to dress for the assembly soon?" he asked, taking out his pocket watch and looking at it.

"What assembly?"

"The one in the village. The one we attend every year."

"Oh." He meant the one where he had first danced with Emma a couple of years ago and fallen in love. Actually, that had been the first time she had seen Graham again after he had returned from Vienna. What a silly chit she had been then. It felt like a lifetime ago. Had she known then what she knew now, perhaps she could have done better. Everyone had tried to tell her, but she had been so fresh and excited, convinced that the world was hers to conquer, that she had not understood the ton's expectations of a duke's daughter.

She fully understood them now, she thought bitterly, yet she still did not wish to be that person.

Rowley was watching her carefully. "Come, it will help you forget your woes. The villagers look up to you, yet they know you well."

"You mean they know I am a hoyden," she retorted.

Rowley smiled one of his rare, precious smiles. "Perhaps rather a partially polished gem. You are certainly not the wild hoyden you were two years ago."

"Thank you, I think," she replied warily.

"It is a compliment, Genie. But do not become too polished. I like you the way you are, even if it does not always seem so."

She felt her throat go thick with unshed tears. It was true that she had never felt she was meeting his expectations.

"I will support you, whatever you decide, but I have only wanted what I thought best for you. I think it is more difficult to be a spinster within the confines of Society, but if anyone can do it, you can."

She bit her lip and went into his open arms.

What she should do, she did not know, because being a spinster had little appeal next to being Mrs. Tinsley... but when you loved someone, you did what was best for them. "How will I know the right course to take?"

"Try to listen to your heart. That sounds trite, especially from me, but there is truth in it."

"In all honesty, I am weary of my heart and my thoughts. I have been riding a great deal, hoping to experience an epiphany—that some great revelation will happen and I will have the answer."

He barked a laugh. "If only it were that simple. My last piece of advice is to throw pride out of the window when it comes to your feelings for Graham. I would not normally advise such a lack of caution with respect to the Knight name, but I believe matters lie differently between the two of you."

"I think that is what makes this so difficult."

"I understand. And Genie, for what it is worth, I am sorry."

He kissed her on the forehead and quietly left the room, leaving her more confused than she had been before.

"How am I to know what to do?" she whispered as she bent down to pick up the pieces of shattered glass. The fate of the cut-glass vase seemed an excellent analogy to the way her insides felt at the moment. Now she had to dress for the local assembly and paste a smile on her face as though she had not a care in the world. How she had pestered Rowley to let her go to that same assembly two years ago, and then she had almost ruined herself at her first proper party! Was there ever such a cruel teacher as naivete?

She finished cleaning up the disorder she had created and took the flowers to one of the maids to arrange instead before going to her chambers to dress for the evening. At least here she could wear one of her favorite gowns again without censure!

⇛⇚

GRAHAM WOULD HAVE been pleased to attend the assembly that night knowing he would have a chance to see Eugenia. However, he felt as though he were going to a boxing match without knowing who his opponent would be.

He decided to go anyway, wondering if he might have an opportunity to dance with her even if she did not wish to speak with him. Any contact with her was better than none.

By the time he arrived, the village assembly rooms were crowded. He had been in London so long he had forgotten that country folk did not play such games as timing their arrival for a grand entrance or being fashionably late.

Despite the number of bodies in the room, he found her instantly. She was wearing a bright jonquil gown which reminded him of one of her riding habits—the one that made her look like sunshine. The color suited her perfectly. She was smiling up at her dance partner, a soldier who, Graham surmised, must be home on leave. He had heard that the Allied Army had crossed into France at last. Very likely there would be more soldiers arriving home for Christmas as well. Graham found he was happy for England, but he was also perfectly happy to strangle the captain who was looking at Eugenia as though she were a tasty dessert.

"I was wondering when you would arrive," Knighton said, sneaking up beside him—if one could do such a thing at a crowded dance.

Graham knew a moment of *déjà vu* from when he had first returned from his diplomatic post and had seen Eugenia again, no longer a girl.

"I lost track of time while visiting with Father," he remarked, not removing his eyes from Eugenia.

"What are your intentions towards her?" Knighton asked, not mincing words.

Graham did turn to gaze at his oldest friend then.

He raised a hand in defense, which was about as much in the way of dramatics as one would get from the duke. "She seems to have some doubts."

That was an understatement. "My intentions are true," Graham said carefully.

"Do you wish for the match, however? Answer me as your friend, not as her guardian."

Graham turned his gaze back to Eugenia and watched her twirl and exchange partners. "I wish for it."

"Then erase her doubts," Rowley said simply.

*Commanded, more like.*

If only he could achieve such a thing. "I intend to."

Rowley inclined his head and then returned to his duchess. Graham decided to continue watching Eugenia for a while before deciding whether or not to approach her. He looked around the room and greeted the familiar faces. The squire's young daughter was a little plump and still had spots on her face, so he asked her for the next dance.

He did his best not to stare at Eugenia, but it was the old moth to a flame adage. He seemed to be drawn to her light as though it were necessary for his survival.

Gentlemen flocked to Eugenia when the first dance was over, and he knew he might find himself without the opportunity to secure one for himself. Yet neither of them had met the other's gaze and he dared not be the first to renege on his agreement with her. He was not certain she had even noticed he was there.

The next dance was a quadrille, and he went over to claim Miss Miller. He led her out onto the floor and they took their places. He bowed to his partner and when he straightened, his eyes met Eugenia's deep blue stare. Their gazes held, as if she also were unable to look away, and then he saw her sadness even when she turned and smiled at her partner.

Even if he was unable to claim her as a partner that night, he would, at the very least, be able to touch her as they exchanged partners in the movements of this one.

How many times had he taken for granted the smallest touches? *No more.*

He came forward and took Miss Miller's hand, finding nothing remarkable at all in it. When they exchanged partners and his hand met Eugenia's, and he looked down into her face, it was one of the most enthralling conversations he had ever had without words. The touch, the warmth, the glove to glove and the looks of longing suddenly made him understand the madness of poets. He was greedy for more, yet he would not speak words. Every sense was heightened, and he memorized them as though they might be his last smell or feel, drinking them in like a fine wine.

When he returned to Miss Miller, it was an effort to recall his gentlemanly manners, though he would have sworn before that they were second nature.

When he had another chance to touch Eugenia, she broke the spell. "You should not look at me like that," she said quietly while they watched each other through their turn.

"How do I look at you?" he asked, finally free to speak since she had spoken first. "Like you are the most beautiful woman in the room?"

"Certainly not," she said sharply and turned away.

He had a great deal of work to do to convince her, but tonight was not the night. She was not yet ready—he could see that.

He returned Miss Miller to her mother and went to the refreshment table. He was not prepared to risk any more encounters with Eugenia. By now, her dance card would be full, which was for the best.

From the corner of his eye he saw a swath of green velvet sidle up beside him.

"Good evening, Mr. Tinsley," said the Duchess of Knighton.

He turned and made a bow. "Your Grace. Lemonade?" He held up a glass. "It is superior to that to be found at Almack's."

"Thank you." She accepted the offering. "Is something amiss with Eugenia?" she asked, guiding him off to the side, away from listening ears.

"I do not believe so." He answered vaguely, not wishing to betray Eugenia's confidences. However, the duchess was very keen and she considered him carefully. "I noticed you did not ask her to dance this evening."

"The night is still young, Your Grace."

"Let me know if I can help," she said softly before she walked away.

"If only I knew what to ask for," he murmured into his glass of lemonade.

He saw Edmund and his new bride, Isabella, coming near, so he quickly set down his glass and sought a new partner. He was not ready for the full Knight assault. It was looking increasingly as though it was going to be a very long evening.

Hurriedly, he asked the nearest unattached damsel to dance, even though Miss Gardner was past her prayers, and one of the village gossips. He swung her into a lively reel, thankful it required little speech.

Frankly, anything was better than having to explain his relationship with Eugenia to her family. He could not explain it to himself.

Miss Gardner cast a glance of disbelief at her sister, Hattie, then blushed furiously as Graham led her out to take her place on the floor.

When she behaved as though she were shy, he found it hard to believe she was actually capable of such gossip. In the end, however, the gossiping side of her won the day.

"Is it true, sir, that you are betrothed to Lady Eugenia?"

Graham should have guessed the news would have reached here by now. Of course, none of the rest of the Knight family knew it was to be kept a secret.

"You have had news?" he asked, trying to determine the source. While it was true some of the London newspapers reached Devonshire, for the tale only now to be spreading was surprising. Perhaps that was the nature of an assembly in the country, he mused.

"I had it from Hattie, who heard it from Mrs. Morgan, who heard it from Mrs. Miller, who heard it from the duchess herself!" Miss Gardner exclaimed breathlessly.

"Who am I to gainsay the duchess?" he answered as the music began, thus preventing further speech. *Thank God.*

The moment the reel was over and he deposited Miss Gardner

back beside her sister and the other matrons, she was well-nigh bursting with the news. She gave a knowing nod to her sister.

"It is true then?" Hattie exclaimed. "Congratulations, sir! What a perfect match the two of you will be! Did I not always say so, Dorcas?"

"You did, Sister. You said, one day when my lady was riding about the countryside in breeches, that she would be well matched with someone who knew her well, like Mr. Tinsley."

What could he say to that? He made a bow to the sisters, feeling a swift exit was the wisest course. Once Eugenia found out the news of their betrothal was all over the district, he would be distinctly uncomfortable. He turned to leave and almost ran headlong into her.

She had a look of fury on her face—ire that he could tell she was about to unleash on him.

He proffered her his most charming smile. "Not here, pet. This is not the place. You may rail at me all you wish later."

She glanced around and saw that all eyes were upon them and gave him a tentative smile.

"I think the newly betrothed couple should waltz," Miss Hattie said in a penetrating voice, and Eugenia gasped. This, if you please, from the harridan who thought the new dance come straight from the devil to earth to lure innocent maidens into sin? Graham barely swallowed a pithy and contemptuous set down.

"I think it is acceptable since you are to be married," she explained primly.

"Then how can we refuse if Miss Hattie wishes it?" he said in a crisp tone instead. He held out his hand to take Eugenia's and she accepted it. For a moment he was not certain if she would regale the entire village with their personal issues.

He took her into his arms, taking special care to keep her at a proper distance, but it was still too close with an unhappy partner.

"Why did you tell them, Graham?" she asked, looking up into his face as though he had betrayed her.

"I am afraid I cannot take credit for that."

"I should have known." Her chin fell.

"Look at me," he commanded. "Be the duke's daughter for a few more minutes. We are still friends, after all. I am only allowing you some freedom to make the right choice, but I will not wait forever."

He twirled into some tight revolutions, leaving both of them unable to speak. For now it was for the best, because if he forced her decision tonight, he knew he would not like her answer. When the music ended, she curtsied to him. Bowing politely in return, he took her arm to lead her from the floor. He did not think she would speak again and then he wished she had not.

"I was not ready," she said, disappointed. "I need more time."

# CHAPTER NINETEEN

THE NEXT MORNING, Eugenia left the Dower House and had the strangest sensation as she led Cleo to the mounting block. She had been missing Graham horribly just as he had predicted, and she had been debating sending over a note to see if he wanted to go riding. Somehow, she felt his presence. She had always known when he was around. She looked up now and could see nothing but trees. Perhaps it was the closeness of his property. She mounted Cleo and skirted the property, stopping at the bridge that linked The Grange with Lovell Abbey.

She wished she knew the right thing to do, but her heart was heavy with an ache that time apart from him had not healed. Her grandmother had been no help, stating baldly that Graham was her perfect match in every way and refusing to hear otherwise. Knighton and Heath would not understand, either, but perhaps Edmund would. He would at least listen first without judging her.

Taking one last look at the gables on top of the Abbey, she turned Cleo and headed towards Primrose Cottage, hoping for some wise guidance.

When she reached the house, she left Cleo to graze again. Eugenia was shown into a small parlor at the back of the house, where Isabella was embroidering.

"Genie!" Isabella said, rising to greet her. "How lovely to see you."

"I was visiting Grandmother, and I thought to call on my way home."

"Shall I ring for tea?" Isabella asked, waving Eugenia to a seat.

"I have done nothing but drink tea with Grandmother. I am positively swimming in it!" Eugenia laughed. She fidgeted with her skirts, then caught herself. "Is my brother at home? I actually came to seek his advice."

"I expect him soon. He was visiting some of the villagers."

Eugenia was unsurprised.

"Is there anything I can help with? Is this about Mr. Tinsley?"

Eugenia nodded. She had not told anyone of her request for time away from him and it seemed silly to speak of it. "I feel as though I am trapping him," she blurted out instead.

Isabella frowned. "Was it not he who announced your betrothal, when the Duke of Farnsworth had already proposed a solution?"

"Yes, but he knew Farnsworth intended to court me only for a short time and Ravenhill forced the issue at Almack's."

"And what does Mr. Tinsley have to say about this? I must say, he did not behave as though he was a man being trapped and forced into marriage with you, Genie."

Eugenia pursed her lips. "I suppose not. He professes to want this marriage."

"You are very good friends. I think you will be very happy with him."

"I wish I could be sure of that."

Isabella's face softened. "There is very little we are sure of or guaranteed in this life, Eugenia. If you care for him, and he for you, it is a beautiful gift and not to be wasted."

"But he does not look at me the way my brothers look at their wives; the way Edmund looks at you."

"Be that as it may, everyone shows their feelings differently, and to be fair, your relationship began differently. It does not mean it is not just as special."

Hoof beats came trotting down the drive. "That must be Edmund," Isabella said. "Perhaps he will have better advice for you."

When Edmund presently strode into the room, he had eyes only for Isabella. He did not notice Eugenia and promptly kissed his wife in a way to make Eugenia blush—the way Graham had kissed her.

When Isabella was allowed to speak, she quickly informed Edmund of Eugenia's visit. Instead of apologizing, he considered her, a devilish gleam in his eye. "How are you, Sister?" He kissed her on the cheek. "I saw Mr. Tinsley in the village today."

Her traitorous heart skipped a beat just at hearing his name. "And how was he?"

"He looks well, if a bit strained. The viscount is very near the end. I had intended to visit there today, but Mrs. Miller delayed me on my way."

"His father is ill?" Why had he not said anything?

*Because I was too wrapped up in my own selfishness!* she answered herself with disgust. Immediately, she felt like the lowest sort of friend—not to mention a fool. At a time like this, nothing could be further from his mind than a silly chit, she was certain.

"His father has been ill for some little while. You may not remember, but that was why Mr. Tinsley returned from his diplomatic post."

Eugenia did not recall, though she had rarely seen the viscount. He preferred to keep his own company – so much so that she knew Graham's mother and sister spent a great deal of time in France. She walked over to look out of the window at the dusky sky.

"He asked after you, you know." Edmund voiced the words she did not dare to ask. "I am surprised at you, Genie," Edmund went on, and she turned back with surprise. "How could you treat him so after he saved you from ruin?"

"What did he tell you?"

"Only that you asked for some time apart." Edmund shook his

head. "I made it clear that he was welcome to visit the rest of the family. I hope you come to your senses before he does pay a call."

Eugenia gasped. Edmund had never spoken to her thus before. "You do not understand." Her voice cracked. "I was trying to do what is best for him!"

"I think you are the one who is confused here, Sister. He was in the village, trying to think of things to buy for you—of ways to woo you, whilst respecting your wishes."

Edmund rarely reprimanded her and she felt as low as the dirt beneath her boots. Tears streamed down her face at those words. "What have I done?"

Edmund took pity on her and put a gentle hand on her back and began to soothe her with up and down motions. "Can he truly forgive me so easily?" If what Edmund had said was true, Graham *was* thinking of her at a time like this.

"I have no reason to doubt otherwise," he said kindly.

"I do not deserve him." She turned to put her face against her brother's shoulder, feeling as though she had been kicked in the stomach, although that would feel better than the agony coursing through her at the moment. "Why is it that my best intentions always cause trouble? I either say or do the wrong thing or, now, hurt the one I love?"

"It is not too late to make things right, Genie," Edmund said, in his way of suggestion mixed with command.

She backed away and nodded, then turned and left the room, wanting to bear her shame in private. Had she truly hurt Graham—the person she loved the most in this world?

She took Cleo's reins and began walking back to the manor house. How had she been so cruel? Eugenia had not known his father was dying. Now Christmas was also fast approaching. She could only hope she had not damaged their relationship beyond repair.

When she arrived back at the house, Barnes handed her a small box which had a bunch of posies, tied with a ribbon, on top. She immediately burst into tears.

"My lady?" Barnes enquired.

She shook her head, unable to speak, and hurried up the marble staircase to her chambers.

Eugenia could not ever remember feeling so much pain, except when her parents had died. Graham was not dead, however, and the weight of the shame she felt was unbearable.

She slipped the bow loose on the ribbon and released the posies. She lifted the lid from the box and looked inside at her favorite Maidenstone biscuits from the village baker, in the shape of hearts. How had he remembered such a thing? She fingered one delicately, though was too upset to eat. She did not deserve them, but her eyes were certainly opened.

She placed the lid back on the box, and a small note slipped to the floor.

*Genie,*

*Even with time apart, you are always in my heart.*

*Ever yours,*
*Graham*

Eugenia threw herself across her bed and sobbed miserably.

GRAHAM ENTERED HIS house, relieved finally to be able to visit The Grange, even if it was not with Eugenia specifically. She would come to the right conclusion eventually, he was sure of it. He hoped she enjoyed her favorite almond and rosewater biscuits and the posies he had had delivered for her. It made him smile to think of her opening it. He hoped she had as much joy from receiving the gift as he had had from sending it to her.

Davies opened the door for him. "Good evening, Master Graham."

"Have my mother and sister arrived yet?"

"They have not."

"Then I shall be dining at The Grange this evening. Has the doctor been to see my father this afternoon?"

"He is with his lordship now," the old butler replied.

Graham gave a nod and went up the stairs. Perhaps his father would be awake.

The door was open and Graham stepped inside. Graham waited for the doctor to leave so he could speak with him in private.

"Mr. Tinsley. How do you do?"

"I am well, thank you, but how is my father today?"

"His lordship has had a good day, from what his man has told me. He was asking after you when I first arrived."

"Thank you," Graham said, holding out his hand to shake the doctor's.

Graham walked over to the bed and sat down beside it. He took his father's hand in his, wishing he were still whole. Graham was not ready to lose him, nor take on the burden of the viscountcy.

"There you are, son," his father's voice said quietly.

"You are awake," Graham said. "I did not mean to disturb you."

"I do nothing but lie in a bed all day. I am happy for the company. Have your mother and Caroline arrived?" His father's voice betrayed his anticipation.

"Not yet. I expect them at any moment."

His father gave a disappointed nod. "Have you any news for me? I feel very out of touch with your life in London."

Graham smiled. "That is what I wished to speak with you about. I have become betrothed to Lady Eugenia."

"The youngest Knight girl?"

"The only Knight girl." He chuckled. "But she is no longer so young."

"I have not seen her in an age," his father remarked.

"She is quite beautiful and lively. You would enjoy her."

"Perhaps she will come to dinner when your mother and sister arrive."

"I am sure she would like that."

His father's expression turned sad. "I am happy to know you are thinking of becoming settled at last. It was my hope to see your children one day. I do not know if that will happen."

"Father…" Graham began, having a hard time speaking over the tightness in his throat.

"I have good days and bad, but I cannot conjecture how much longer I can go on like this. I am happy to know I will see Caroline again. I must confess I am tempted to return south with them. The warmth is most appealing now. I feel as though I can never be warm enough."

"Does the doctor say what is wrong? I did not ask."

"He believes it is something with my heart. It beats very strangely—irregularly he says. He is giving me foxglove, of all things, for it."

"Is that not poison?" Graham asked.

"Indeed it is, but at very small doses seems to settle the heartbeat. I must confess, I do feel better."

"Then I am glad for it, so long as you are careful with your dosing."

"Martins takes it very seriously. He will not let anyone else near the vial." He chuckled. "I would like to be strong enough to greet your mother when she arrives."

"I will help you however I can. Have you had dinner?"

"My man went to put up a tray for me. Eating is about as much as I have stamina for these days."

"I was to dine at The Grange, but I would be happy to sup with you instead."

"Not at all. Go and charm your young lady. I cannot wait to see the two of you together," he said with a kind smile.

Graham stood and gave his father's hand a squeeze as Martins brought in the dinner tray.

"You had better eat it all, Father, if you want to have strength."

"I will do my best," he said, giving Graham a small salute.

As he walked to his chamber, Graham could not help but wonder about his parents' relationship. Was that why he thought love was the philia kind of love? Friendly, amicable and sweet? His parents were fond of each other, and his mother and sister spent most of their time in France for Caroline's weak lungs.

Graham dressed for dinner, hoping Eugenia did not become upset. He had given her a week and he had been invited by Edmund, but he could not wait to see her.

He wore Eugenia's favorite green waistcoat that had golden monkeys embroidered into it. He laughed as he buttoned it. Would she still find it her favorite? If that did not make her smile when she saw him, then perhaps it was a lost cause altogether.

He was early, like a nervous schoolboy would be. When he was shown into the drawing room at The Grange, Edmund and Isabella were first to greet him.

Isabella burst out laughing when she saw the monkeys on his waistcoat. "That is marvelous! I cannot wait for Eugenia to see it."

"She has asked to take a tray in her room," Knighton announced as he entered the dining room.

Graham felt as though frozen in place. "Shall I leave? I do not wish to cause any strife within your family."

"Nonsense. You are part of the family. I do not believe she was aware you were joining us for dinner. Emma has just gone to tell her."

Graham nodded absently. "I hope she is not ill. I would not wish her to feel obligated to join us on my account."

"I believe she might be heart-sick and rather chagrined. We had rather an argument this afternoon after I saw you," Edmund confessed.

Graham closed his eyes. It was not what he wanted.

"Please do not feel as if I betrayed you. It was bound to come out one way or the other. You would have been invited to dine by one of us this week, regardless."

"What has happened?" Knighton asked. "I seem to be missing some vital piece of information."

"It is nothing. Eugenia merely asked for some time to think," Graham explained.

"What is there to think about?" Knighton asked in his caustic tone.

Edmund stepped forward. "I have already spoken with her, Rowley."

The duchess entered the room and gave Graham a brief smile. "Eugenia will be down shortly."

A footman handed each of them a drink, and Heath and Cecilia joined them.

"'Tis good to see you, Tinsley," Heath said. "I was wondering where you have been this week."

"Tending to the estate. I fear my father is rather ill. Thankfully, we have an excellent steward."

"My sympathies. Anything we can do?" Knighton asked.

"Actually, the doctor is trying a new treatment on him and he feels much better. He is endeavoring to regain some strength."

Eugenia entered the room then, wearing an aubergine-colored gown with a simple scooped neck trimmed with gold and a matching ribbon around her waist. Her hair was pulled back in a simple knot similar to the one she had created that day at Gunter's. She looked perfect, but there was sadness in her eyes. His own heart felt it.

He stood back, waiting for her to give him some kind of signal as to her wishes. He would stay where he was unless she indicated she wished to speak with him again, though it was the worst kind of agony to believe that this betrothal might have caused an irreparable rift between them.

She walked tentatively over to him, as though she were afraid. She dipped into a formal curtsy. "Good evening, Graham."

"My lady." He bowed.

"Might I have a few minutes to speak with you?"

He looked to Knighton for confirmation and the duke inclined his head. "Dinner will not be served for a few minutes. You may use my study if you wish."

She bit her lip and gave a nod and then turned to walk to the study. He followed her inside and she shut the door with a loud click. Her blue eyes looked up at him, large and pleading. Without warning, she launched herself into his arms—and he wrapped them around her and held her tight. He could hold her there forever. She felt right, and it was difficult to imagine any other fulfilling the role of his wife. Did that mean this was love? Perhaps it was.

# CHAPTER TWENTY

E UGENIA COULD NOT speak. She was trying dreadfully hard not to cry, even though she could not say anything at all.

"I am glad to see you too, pet," Graham said, in that way he had that was sarcastic but at the same time amused.

She inhaled deeply. Her face was still buried in his chest and she caught notes of starched linen, bergamot and... Graham. "Forgive me," she pleaded, her words unavoidably muffled.

"What was that?"

She pulled back a little, yet was unwilling to remove herself from his arms. "I said, forgive me. I have been a fool. This has been the most miserable week of my existence. Then Edmund told me about your father and now I am ashamed."

He lifted her chin and gazed into her eyes. "I missed you, too. But I am not sorry if it helped you realize how well we will deal together." He leaned down to kiss her briefly on the lips.

"How is your father?"

"He is somewhat improved. I visited him just before I came here. He would like to see you again and was delighted with our news."

Eugenia tried not to react to that.

"I would be delighted to visit him if he is up to company."

"Mother and Caroline are expected at any time. Perhaps you could call?"

She pulled away and wrapped her arms around her waist, steeling herself to speak. "Graham, are you absolutely certain about this betrothal?"

He stopped talking to her, as if he needed to touch her. It was fascinating that he could want her. "I have no doubts whatsoever, Genie."

She exhaled a sigh of relief. "We might have to reconsider your choice of waistcoat in the future."

"I think not. I have very fond memories of monkeys."

She gave him an arch look and shook her head. "Too soon."

"Ah, very well. I had hoped you might laugh. Would you walk with me after dinner?"

"Oh, yes, dinner. I suppose we should not keep them waiting." She took the arm he offered. "Yes, I will walk with you."

Eugenia scarcely paid attention during dinner, she was very anxious about the walk after dinner. What could he want to say? In the study, he had professed to have no doubts. Perhaps there were conditions to be placed upon the betrothal? In all honesty, she had no idea. It was silly to speculate, but she could not help herself.

"Are you sure you are not coming down with some malady?" Isabella asked. "You have hardly eaten a bite."

"I am sure. I am only unsettled. Today has been rather taxing on my nerves," she answered.

Isabella patted her hand. "I understand."

"I had a letter from Felix today," Rowley said to the entire table. "Unfortunately, it was dated from July, just after Vitoria. Thankfully, my contacts in the War Office keep me apprised of Felix's doings, but he says Wellington hopes they will be in France by Christmas."

"Does that mean he might be able to visit?" Eugenia asked.

"I think we would be more like to see him before we read of it," Knighton replied.

"Then that shall be my Christmas wish," Emma said.

"All of us together is always a welcome occurrence," Knighton agreed.

After the meal, the gentlemen eschewed their port and joined the ladies in the drawing room.

"Shall we go?" Graham asked.

"Graham and I are going to take a walk," she announced to the room at large. Nobody seemed to pay them any attention. Graham was part of the family.

"You should get a cloak. It looks like it is going to snow," he said.

"Wonderful!" she exclaimed excitedly as they hurried into the entrance hall to don their coats, hats, and gloves.

They walked for a few minutes on the familiar path towards the woods. Their breath steamed in front of them and the cool, crisp air tingled on their cheeks. The scent of pine was heavy, just as it ought to be near to Christmas. Eugenia did not pester Graham for conversation; she knew he would talk if he needed to.

They passed Primrose Cottage and continued on until they reached the bridge over the river – the site of many adventurous escapades amongst the six of them. His family's property was just on the other side. It was a beautiful view down over the valley from there. The moon was bright and you could see the gables on the top of the Abbey.

Graham stopped and shoved his hands into his coat and looked off into the distance. Still Eugenia waited. She stepped up onto the bridge and walked to the center, leaning far enough over the railing to watch the water flowing beneath. It was something she could do for hours in the daylight. She loved to watch for fish and other animals that lived in their own world beneath the surface. Unfortunately, she could not see much at night, except for some ice forming around the edges. She exhaled and a cloud of steam misted the air then disappeared into the darkness. Was Graham going to speak? She looked over at him and he was watching her.

"I have been thinking a lot this week," he began.

It was all she had done as well. He joined her in leaning over the railing and watching the water below.

"At first, I thought, if you did not want me then I would have to let you go. Then, as I realized you were consuming my every thought, I decided that perhaps I would try to convince you." He shrugged a little and she felt it more than she saw it. "I had to do something or I would have run mad, so today, I decided I would shower you with gifts."

"That was not necessary," she said softly.

"But it is. I did not want you to think I took you for granted as a lady."

"I have never thought..."

He held up his hand. "I am not saying that I have mistreated you, but you need to understand that I think of you as more than a friend in order for this to succeed."

Perhaps he was right.

"So, I determined to court you properly. I went shopping today," he said, pride in his voice.

"Your gifts were perfect." She smiled, thinking of them. "I confess I was too miserable to fully enjoy them, however."

"And what made you miserable, if I might ask?" He turned his head enough that she could see the Knight eyebrow in elevation.

"I realized I had been a proper arse."

He chuckled at her gutter language.

"I did not know about your father. How could I have been so selfish?"

He reached over and took her hand. Even through gloves, she could feel the warmth.

"That is the other matter I wished to talk to you about. I mentioned that I spoke with my father before I arrived."

"I thought he was improving?"

"Be that as it may, there is no guarantee he will continue to do so.

He spoke of hoping to regain strength enough to greet my mother and sister. He spoke of wanting to see me wed and with children, and how that might not be possible. He spoke of perhaps going south to the warmer climes..." She could hear his voice becoming thick with emotion.

She squeezed his hand and gave him time to gather himself.

"It made me recognize that none of us are guaranteed time. I also realized that I want to fulfill at least one of his wishes."

She felt him move. "Graham?"

He still held her hand, but he had dropped to one knee before her. He took a deep breath and looked her in the eye. "I do not know how to say this, but you deserve a proper proposal. You know that I love you, and I realize you want more than you think I can give you. I am not certain what that other kind of love is, but I have been in an agony of despair, knowing you wanted me to stay away from you. I have thought of little else except how to win you. I have racked my brain for what gifts were special enough to send you so you would know that I appreciate you. In short, I have been consumed by you. Is that love as you wanted? Can you find it in you to return my affections and marry me?"

He slipped his free hand into his pocket and pulled out a betrothal ring. It was difficult to see it by the moonlight, but it sparkled nonetheless.

"Can it be true?" she whispered as she felt a tear roll down her cheek.

"I have never been more earnest in my life," he said. "But can I make you happy? I feel like a proper fool for not recognizing sooner that you are indeed the perfect mate for me."

She threw her arms around him – thank goodness he always seemed prepared for her sudden bursts of affection. "I cannot imagine being happy with anyone else," she confessed. "I do not know the exact moment my feelings changed, either, but I have also been miserable, thinking I might not be the best choice for you."

"My silly pet," he said as he kissed away the tears from her face and then kissed her with a passion she was only just beginning to recognize in herself.

He pulled back and drawing her to her feet, pulled off her left-hand glove. He slipped the ring onto her finger, making their betrothal feel real for the first time.

"Shall we tell the others? I do not wish my bride to freeze before I get her to the altar."

≫≫≪≪

WHEN GRAHAM ARRIVED home later that night, he was surprised to find his mother and sister had arrived and already retired. His father would be disappointed to know that he had missed their arrival, but hopefully the reunion the next day would be just as good. He could not regret spending the evening at The Grange, however, because all seemed to be well with Eugenia again. By the day of their wedding, she would—with God's grace—even be excited about it.

The next morning, after he had broken his fast, he sought out his mother and sister. They were both in the viscountess's sitting room, having chocolate and rolls. He supposed that was a French custom, but not a satisfying meal in his opinion.

"Graham!" his sister exclaimed. Jumping up, she hurled herself at him much in the way Eugenia did.

He chuckled. "Welcome home, Sister. I almost would not have recognized you. You have grown so much."

"I am old enough to make my début," she announced.

"Heaven help us," he said, meeting his mother's gaze. She was watching the exchange with a fond smile.

"And Mother..." He walked over and kissed her on the cheek. "It is wonderful to see you. Do you plan to stay long?"

"I suppose that depends on your father. Caroline's lungs are much improved, and I had thought perhaps we would stay for the next Season."

"I am glad to hear it, though Father might wish to spend the winter elsewhere."

"I have not yet seen him. I sent my maid to inquire if he is ready to receive."

"He is weak, but was in good spirits when I saw him last evening. He wanted to greet you himself."

She looked disappointed. "We were so anxious to be done with traveling that we decided not to make another overnight stop and thus arrived very late."

"I am also sorry I was not here to greet you, either. I dined at The Grange." He could not keep a smile from his face.

His mother was very perceptive. "Is there something you wish to tell me?"

"I am betrothed to Lady Eugenia."

She looked taken aback. "The little hoyden?"

"Mother!" Caroline scolded.

"It is the truth. She behaved like a boy, running wild all over the countryside, and no one to tell her nay."

That much was true, if through little fault of her own. "She is strong-willed, but not malicious. I invited her to call on you and I do hope you will give her a chance. She is now a grown woman, not a child." She was still inclined to be reckless, he reflected, but was certainly not wild. His mother made her sound like a feral cat.

His mother sighed. "Of course. If she is your choice, and makes you happy, then I will contrive to be kind and accepting. The connections certainly cannot be faulted."

"Thank you, Mother."

"I cannot wait to see her again. She was always very nice to me," Caroline added. His sister was turning into a beauty, his own coloring reflected in a feminine form. He vowed to himself that he would stand by her, no matter what, when it was time for her to navigate the dangerous waters of Society.

His mother's maid knocked on the door, remaining on the threshold. "His Lordship is ready to receive you, ma'am." She bobbed a curtsy to her mistress and then to Graham.

As his mother began to leave the room, she stopped before him. "Invite Lady Eugenia to tea. I shall be delighted to receive her."

Graham went downstairs to the study and penned a note to Eugenia. He certainly had not expected that reaction from his mother to the news of his betrothal. Had she not been urging him for long enough to marry and settle? There were certainly some things he would never understand about the female mind, but perhaps that was a good thing.

That afternoon, Eugenia arrived with the duchess. To him, she looked like a breath of fresh air. She was wearing a pale green velvet gown with a darker spencer and looked perfectly demure. She curtsied to his mother, who held out her hands and smiled at Eugenia.

"My dear, Graham's father and I are very pleased with the news."

"Thank you, my lady. I hope you do not mind that I brought with me my sister-in-law, Emma."

"Of course not. Your Grace, it is a pleasure to meet you."

Caroline suddenly became shy when she met the two ladies, and when they sat down, as tea was served, she scarcely spoke a word except for answers to questions.

"How old are you, Miss Tinsley? Do you intend to enjoy a London Season?" the duchess asked.

"I am to turn seventeen in the spring, Your Grace."

"We have been discussing a Season, although whether it will be this year or next is undecided," his mother answered. "It depends on my husband's health, of course."

"Eugenia and I would be happy to take her to Town and show her about if she wishes," said Graham.

The duchess almost choked on her tea, likely recalling with mirth Eugenia's antics in Town.

"You are the best of brothers!" Caroline said, giving him a bright smile.

"Of course she shall have a Season," a voice announced from the door.

"Father?" He looked up to see the viscount standing there on the arm of Martins.

"May I join you?"

Graham went over to assist, for his father was dressed and looking more whole than he had seen him in years.

"I can manage, thank you," he said, as he walked slowly to the chairs and made a bow to the ladies before taking a seat.

Graham made the introductions. "Father, this is Her Grace the Duchess of Knighton, and you remember Lady Eugenia, I trust?"

"Duchess," he inclined his head. "It is a pleasure." He turned to Lady Eugenia. "You have grown into a beautiful lady. May I say we are elated to hear you are to become our daughter?"

Eugenia blushed and it only heightened her beauty. "Thank you, my lord."

"When are the nuptials to be?" he asked pointedly.

Eugenia looked at Graham with panic in her eyes. He reached over and took her hand. "We have not yet decided, Father. We have just become engaged."

Graham felt as though all eyes were boring into him. He hoped it did not cause Eugenia to turn tail and run.

"Why wait?" his father asked. "Back in our day," he said, with a fond look to the viscountess, "the banns were read as soon as the announcement was made!"

"Christmas is soon, we may decide after the festivities, surely?"

"If it is all the same to you," his father said, "I would like to see you wed as soon as possible. You know my time may be short, and I am considering returning to France with your mother."

Graham was hoping to claim Eugenia soon as well, but he was not yet ready to push her that far.

He dared to glance at her, however, and was shocked when she opened her mouth and spoke. "I daresay that could be arranged, your lordship," she said. "I would prefer to marry here instead of in London."

"Excellent, my dear. You have made me most happy." His father accepted a cup of tea from his wife and Graham noticed how his hand shook as he lifted the cup to his mouth. What it must have taken, for him to come down and greet them!

His mother and the duchess began to talk of little George, and Graham took the opportunity to lean over and whisper to Eugenia. "Are you certain?"

"I am. And if we can make your father happy at the same time, then we should."

"I do love you, you know."

"Just promise me you will always keep that in mind," she said with a mischievous grin.

He caught his father smiling at them, though he was looking very tired.

"Should you discover if he wishes to return to bed?" Eugenia asked with endearing concern.

"Perhaps, but I do not wish to injure his pride."

"Then Emma and I will take our leave so he may have his dignity."

"Only if you promise to see me later."

"Try to keep me away," she retorted, daring him as she had since they had been playfellows.

Graham watched as the ladies took their leave, wondering what had come over Eugenia, but too pleased to question it.

# CHAPTER TWENTY-ONE

H ER FAMILY WAS overwhelming. Eugenia looked about at the family that had doubled in size and, by the looks of it, would be doubled again by next Christmas. This was saying quite a lot for someone who had always liked to be surrounded by jolliness, but these days her mind was very much on other things.

Her brothers and their wives chatted amiably, and she sat quietly listening, wondering if she would feel a part of it once she was wed— once Graham was there to share the experience. At the moment, she felt a bit like a fish gasping for air on land.

She stood up quickly. "I think I shall visit Granny."

"Give her our best wishes," Edmund called as she escaped from the drawing room, which was growing smaller by the minute. Hopefully, they did not realize she was trying to get away from all of them.

Once Cleo was happily grazing in the paddock after a brisk canter across the estate, Eugenia let herself into the Dower House again.

Her grandmother was napping in her favorite armchair by the window and Eugenia sat in the chair opposite it, content to wait until her grandmother awoke. There were so many memories in this house. Granny had been there to offer a kindly ear at first, after their parents died, but she had preferred town life and Eugenia had relished the times she had visited.

"How long have you been there, Genie?" the dowager asked.

"A while," she answered with a half-smile.

"You cannot take the bedlam, eh?"

"It is a bit much," Eugenia confessed, "even for me."

"'Tis is why I live here. My attics would be to let if I was there all the time. It is a very large house, but you must leave its walls truly to escape."

Eugenia chuckled.

Her grandmother's face grew abnormally solemn. "I must admit, I have never been very good with children. I should have returned from London and guided you more in the way of ladylike behavior."

"You would have resented me if you had done so. I may not be a conventional lady, but I have been happy." Granny was eccentric, which was acceptable if one was a duchess.

"Until now?" Her grandmother was perceptive.

"This Season was more difficult than the last, to be sure."

"But?"

"But... I want you to know that Mr. Tinsley and I are to have the banns read this Sunday."

Her grandmother cackled with glee. "I shall live to see you married yet!" Once she had ceased laughing, she looked sharply at Eugenia. "Why are you not happy?"

"I am happy. I suppose I am nervous."

"And you expect me to enlighten you on the ways of nature?"

She gave a swift nod.

"You are a country girl, go and spend some time with the animals."

Eugenia could feel her face burn with embarrassment. "That is it? That is your advice, to go and watch the animals mate?"

"It will give you the idea." Granny insouciantly waved her hand.

"That is horrific!" Eugenia exclaimed.

"You do have three new sisters you could ask. Heaven knows they are much more *au courant* on such matters than I."

"But they are married to my brothers!" Eugenia could not believe she was having to beg for information. She had felt if she could reassure herself, then she could ease her anxieties.

"I was married to your grandfather," her grandmother retorted.

"I was never acquainted with him! It is different, I assure you."

Granny looked up at the ceiling and leaned her head back in her chair, knocking her wig askew. "There is little advice I can offer you, other than to trust your husband. Things are very different now. My marriage was a business arrangement – the merging of dynasties. It seems all these marriages are for love these days and I am no authority on that."

Eugenia certainly had not expected that answer.

"Do not look so astonished, gel. Your grandfather and I were fond of each other, but I certainly had no say in the matter. The union was arranged when we were children."

Eugenia almost did not have a say. Ravenhill had taken that away from her, and she was grateful for Graham.

Her grandmother leaned forward with a naughty glint in her eye. "If I were to have Mr. Tinsley as a choice, I would be begging him to take me to Gretna Green!"

"Granny!" Eugenia chided as though scandalized, but her grandmother only laughed. "You must admit he is devilishly handsome, and charming to boot."

"I cannot argue with that," Eugenia replied. "He is almost too handsome. It is quite intimidating to think one's future husband is more beautiful than you."

"Oh, pish! You are one of the greatest beauties in society, Genie."

"I have never been called beautiful. Troublesome, wild, eccentric even, but not beautiful."

"I may be old, but I am not blind. It is just as well. You know Tinsley is marrying you for the right reasons—not for your fortune or connections, which are still good reasons, mind you."

"I suppose that is true." She had to fidget. It annoyed her grand-mother no end, but she could not be still.

"If no one called you a beauty, they are either blind or captivated by all your other qualities."

Eugenia snorted, then stilled. "What do I do about other women? I do not think I could bear to look the other way."

"You are afraid you will not be enough for him?" Her grandmother finally seemed to understand.

"Yes," she whispered.

"Then you must make it completely clear to him before you wed. Somehow I do not think he is the type to stray." She leaned forward, as though the room were full of people and she had a secret. "Remind him that you are a crack shot and know how to use a knife."

Eugenia laughed.

"And about the other matter," she added, "just ask him. He will be more than happy to instruct you, I assure you. My generation might not have had love-matches, but we were not prudish. If the animals can make sense of it then we can, too."

Perhaps it was as simple as that.

"Now, ring for some tea," her grandmother commanded, "and tell me what is going on up at the house. My nerves prefer hearing it at second-hand."

Eugenia pulled the bell-rope and then sat back down while they waited. "Rowley and Emma are busy with George, as usual. He is walking everywhere and speaking a few words."

"Humph. I suppose I should go have a look at that." Granny had closed her eyes while she was listening but one popped open as she made that pronouncement.

"Cecilia looks as though she might deliver here, instead of return-ing to Kent for that happy event."

"As large as a whale, is she?"

"She is, rather." Eugenia laughed. "And Edmund..." she began.

"I know all about Edmund. He visits every day. I think it is the vicar's nature to see if I am still breathing and pray for my soul."

"That is their calling," Eugenia muttered.

The butler entered with the tea and set the tray on the table before them. Eugenia prepared the tea the way she liked it and handed a cup to her grandmother. She took a sip and murmured appreciation. "You always make it better than anyone else."

"That is because it is how I like it myself."

"And what of Felix? You did not mention him." Her grandmother reverted to the previous topic.

"Rowley has just had a letter from him, but it was posted in July."

"And it is now December?" she asked as though she did not know.

"It is Christmas-tide, Granny. That is why we are all gathered here."

"I suppose I shall go to church on Sunday, then."

Now they had come full circle. "Yes, they will be reading the banns for Mr. Tinsley and I."

"Have I mentioned he is one of my favorites?"

"Once or twice," Eugenia agreed as she took one of the pieces of shortbread, still warm from the oven, and bit off a corner.

"What will the scandal sheets have to tattle about, with both of you off the market, I wonder?"

"Someone will come along and fill the void, I have no doubt."

"Perhaps," she agreed as her eyelids began to droop. Eugenia rose and took the teacup from her grandmother's hands as she fell asleep. She kissed her on the forehead and pulled the furry wool blanket already across the dowager's knees higher over her body. "Thank you, Granny," she whispered and let herself back out. She may not have received all of the answers she sought, but she did feel better. It was reassuring to hear that it was acceptable to ask her husband. Now, she had a wedding to plan and three weeks in which to do it. In some ways it seemed forever yet in others not nearly long enough. She was inordinately grateful to be marrying in Devonshire instead of in London. Would not the *ton* be surprised when they found out she and Graham had actually wed?

>>>><<<<

THE BANNS HAD been called and there was a general hum of excitement in the air as the village prepared for the big wedding. Neither Heath nor Edmund had married there, and Eugenia, though considered rather wild, was well beloved by all who lived thereabouts.

There was little needed that neither the Abbey nor The Grange could provide, but Eugenia was insistent on having the villagers do as much as possible. Graham had no doubt that she would be an excellent viscountess one day—hopefully a long way in the future. His father was slowly gaining strength and had decided to leave for France for his health after the wedding. He had asked Graham to take over the management of their properties. Caroline would stay behind. If his father was strong enough, his parents would return for Caroline's come-out Season. If not, Eugenia and the duchess would oversee her presentation.

But first of all, Christmas and then a wedding were to be enjoyed. Eugenia had asked him to join their family in gathering greenery for the day. Caroline had not been interested in any activity which involved being outdoors in the cold, so Graham went on his way alone to the Grange.

When he arrived, he was surprised to find that Felix had returned and with a Spanish wife.

As soon as he entered the house, Eugenia drew him aside. "Felix has just arrived and he is married!"

"That was unexpected," he said, pulling her into a small alcove and stealing a kiss. Her lips were soft and sweet, and he would be happy to stay there all day learning this part of his future wife.

"We should go," she murmured, having been thoroughly kissed. "We only have so much daylight in which to gather the greenery."

Graham smiled. Eugenia had always been eager about Christmas and her exuberance was infectious. He was more in the mood to steal her away to himself than join the large crowd of Knights—which was growing at an alarming rate—but for her he would do it.

Before he knew what she was about, she burst into the study without knocking, not intimidated at all by the masculine domain where her brothers had found sanctuary.

"Are you going to stay in here all day?" she asked. "Tinsley is here and we have greenery to gather!"

The brothers exchanged glances of fondness and exasperation, then with good-humored reluctance stood up to prepare themselves for the outdoors and to greet Graham.

"I had not realized how close to Christmas it was. One loses track of days on the ship," Felix said while gathering his coat and hat.

"And when newly wed," Heath retorted.

Felix came over and shook Graham's hand. "I hear congratulations are in order," Graham said. He and Felix had worked together on the Continent, and he had helped negotiate Felix's release from a French prison.

"Indeed. I still cannot quite believe I am married. You will fall soon enough," Felix teased before he left the room. Graham frowned. Apparently, Felix had not yet been informed. Perhaps Eugenia had not wished to steal the moment from Felix and his bride if they had recently arrived.

Once properly clad for the cold, the family gathered in the entrance hall.

It was not long before the brothers—Knighton included—began to race up the trees for the mistletoe. Normally, Eugenia joined in. "Is something the matter, pet?" he asked.

"I am practicing my ladylike restraint," she replied.

"Not on my account, I hope. I would find great amusement in watching you climb a tree in your skirts."

She punched him on the arm. "Once a rogue, always a rogue!"

"As long as I am yours and yours alone."

"Do you mean that?" She turned her large eyes to inspect his face.

"Of course, I mean it. How could you think I would want anyone else besides you? Simply because ours was not a traditional courtship, does not make it any less meaningful to me." He could see her visibly relax. "Is this what has been bothering you so?"

"It is part of it," she admitted.

He took her hand and led her away from the others. They appeared to be gathering enough mistletoe for all of Devonshire without their help. "What else is there? You have never been afraid to ask me anything before."

"But now what I wish to comprehend is about you and me," she said, waving her hand back and forth between them.

"Ah."

"I asked Granny to explain things to me, and she told me to go out to the pastures and watch."

Graham threw his head back and laughed.

"This is not funny!" Although she objected with some vehemence, she was fighting a grin.

"Oh, but it is. Your grandmother is beyond measure. What else did she say?"

"That I should ask you."

"Do not worry, pet. I will show you everything when the time comes. I beg of you not to ask me yet because we still have nearly a fortnight to wait."

She sighed with exasperation. "I hate being the only one ignorant on things that matter."

"Trust me, you will understand shortly." He tweaked her nose as she scowled at him. "Shall we re-join the others? I understand they are besotted, but eventually they will notice we are missing. Besides, I want a large piece of mistletoe with lots of berries on it."

She hit him in the arm. "As if you require mistletoe for kissing."

"I suppose I don't," he said, leaning down to take her lips. "Thank you for the reminder."

Shoving him away and tossing a pert look over her shoulder, she headed back to where the brothers were tossing down balls of mistletoe. She at once went over to speak with Felix's new wife, a Spanish beauty. In his considered opinion, though, Eugenia rivaled her in every way, except perhaps with the knowledge of her own attractiveness. It was hard to remind himself he had almost missed seeing her loveliness with eyes other than those of a friend.

He stood by the stand of trees, catching mistletoe as it fell, but he could not help but overhear Eugenia speaking to the Lady Catalina.

"I see you have also made a match," Lady Catalina said in a knowing voice.

"How did you know?" Eugenia asked.

"Perhaps because I am new and I see everyone with fresh eyes."

"I was waiting for the right time to tell Felix. He arrived unexpectedly, with you, and then I did not wish to take away from your celebration," Eugenia explained.

Lady Catalina waved her hand dramatically. "It is I who should be apologizing to you. My husband should not have surprised his family so."

"Nonsense! It is a wonderful surprise. We thought Felix would never marry."

"I hope you may love your Mr. Tinsley as much as I love your brother. I had never expected my marriage to be one of affection. Have you told him how you feel about him?"

Graham could not help but spy on the two ladies. Eugenia looked taken aback.

"It is written all over your face—on both of your faces, actually. I see how you look at each other."

"We care for each other, certainly. We have been friends and neighbors since my birth," Eugenia said. "I am sure you will hear, sooner or later, that he saved me from scandal."

"Ah, then he is handsome and honorable. You are most fortunate, but do not mistake that he has fallen on his sword for you."

Eugenia was watching Lady Catalina carefully.

"A man who is being forced to the altar does not look at his bride like Mr. Tinsley looks at you."

"How did you become so wise?" Eugenia asked.

Lady Catalina laughed. "Through the making of many mistakes. But I did not recognize love until I saw it in Felix's eyes. Your man looks at you in the same way."

Graham turned away before they saw him staring and eavesdropping.

Eugenia seemed to be struck speechless. Bravo, Lady Catalina! Perhaps his future bride would realize the truth from someone else's lips.

"Are we finished gathering these plants?" Lady Catalina asked.

"Oh, no. There is more!" Eugenia exclaimed, then proceeded to pronounce to the entire wood, "Now for the holly!" She began to lead them deeper into the wood.

With ten of them gathering, it did not take long to fill a second cart with holly and other green foliage. By the time they tramped back to the house, their cheeks were all bright red. The warmth inside the house was blissful, and the smell of spicy baking and wassail made every minute of being outside worth it.

Reluctantly, they shed their hats, coats, and gloves, and then they crowded around the fire.

Banks entered with a tray of warm gingerbread slices and Edmund instantly rubbed his hands together with glee.

Edmund handed one to Catalina. "Have you ever tried ginger-bread?" Edmund asked. "It is delicious."

"Now do you see what I mean?" Graham leaned over to murmur in Eugenia's ear.

"I suppose Cook does make Edmund's favorite goodies, but I do also enjoy gingerbread. Just as I like ices, he likes all biscuits."

"I suppose that is so, but it will not stop me from ensuring you always have what your heart desires."

# CHAPTER TWENTY-TWO

*D*ECISIONS, *DECISIONS.* EUGENIA was quite torn between wearing a dress she wanted to wear and what was considered proper. She had vacillated with her sisters-in-law the first time they had come to help her decide on a dress, and while she knew they had better taste, she could not help but reflect that it was her wedding day and she should be able to wear what she wanted. Yet, she had seen her sisters whispering, always stopping when she entered the room. There was definitely something going on.

It was difficult not to think about some of the mishaps which had occurred with her favorite bonnets, and part of her wondered if perhaps it was not nature's way of trying to give her hints. How often had she heard nature described as cruel? For Christmas, Graham had given her a replica of the fruit bowl bonnet, as he called it, and she had given him a new watch, on the back of which she had had the image of a monkey etched into the gold. The farther away from the incident she stood, the more humor she could see in it.

In the end, for her wedding, she decided to wear a gown of cerulean blue to match her eyes. It was difficult to find fault with that. She did not wish to compete with the greenery everything was festooned in for Christmas, and red was simply too bold—even for her—for a wedding.

Today was her final fitting, and then she hoped to find Graham a special gift for their wedding. He had sent more gifts to her, as if the posies and biscuits had not been pleasing enough. Every day since then, he had continued to send her flowers and treats, ranging from cakes and chocolates to more biscuits. Her lips twitched. At this rate, she would not fit into her gown, which was quite tasteful. She had not added any of the garish flounces or fripperies she had been so fond of her first Season. She was quite certain she chanted "less is more" in her sleep, from Emma saying it to her so many times.

When Eugenia slipped the gown on, it felt magical. The white gauze overdress had snowflakes embroidered all over it, with spangles at the center. She twirled around and laughed as her reflection sparkled.

"Now, if only it will snow for the wedding, it will be perfect!"

"What will you wear on your head, my lady?" the seamstress asked as she tucked and pinned the gown in a few places.

The question reminded Eugenia of a curiosity. Emma, Cecilia and Isabella had been dropping hints about how she should wear her hair, and asking if she had chosen a bonnet or wreath of flowers. It was all very odd, but she could not discern what lay behind their heightened interest.

"Something is afoot with my headdress." Eugenia turned to her maid, who was feigning ignorance. "Do you mean to tell me you are playing a part in my sisters' scheme?"

"Me, my lady? No, not at all. I was asked for a sample of the fabric, but I have seen or heard nothing."

"I will get to the bottom of it," Eugenia said with determination.

She did not miss the look that passed between the modiste and her maid. If she found out Stevens was conspiring with Emma and the others, Eugenia would have her head.

"There had better not be any unapproved changes to my gown," Eugenia warned without heat before they left.

"Where are we going, my lady?" Stevens asked.

"To call on the milliner. I wish to see my headdress."

"Oh, but my lady, please do not question everyone. There is a surprise."

"From whom?" Eugenia turned and eyed her long-time abigail.

"I can say no more. I am sworn to secrecy. Do not ask me, I beg. I will be in terrible trouble if I let the cat out of the bag."

"Very well. Go home, Stevens."

"But my lady!"

"If you wish to keep your position, you will leave me."

"But the duke will dismiss me on the instant," she protested.

"I will explain you were following my orders. I am most displeased with you."

The maid gave her a look of hurt, but turned on her heel and left in a huff. Eugenia was not worried about Stevens.

Once she saw the maid turn the corner down the street, she entered the hatmaker's.

"How may I help you, my lady?" Mrs. Smith asked when she saw Eugenia.

"I would like to order something for my wedding."

She saw the slight flicker of hesitation in the milliner's eyes. "Mrs. Sharpe said she had sent you some samples.

"Of course, my lady. What did you have in mind?"

Eugenia desperately wanted to know who had thought to circumvent her in what she wore. Most likely the culprit was one or more of her sisters, but they had seemed to give in about the gown. Part of her was tempted to order something outrageous; something more outrageous than anything she had ever worn before, but that was saying a lot. She actually did not know where to begin with designing bonnets. She simply knew when she saw one she liked. However, she had partially designed her dress, so why not her bonnet?

"I was thinking of something small. My gown is blue with embroidered white gauze and snowflakes," she said. "It sparkles in the light when I walk." she added, hoping to give the milliner some idea of what she wanted.

"Like an ice fairy?"

"I suppose so, but not too overdone."

"Of course not, my lady," the milliner replied, her solemn tone belied by the twinkle in her eye.

Eugenia left the milliner's, feeling not a little disappointed. Mrs. Smith had not only done just as Eugenia had asked, but she had not hinted at any possible surprises. What was happening and how could Eugenia discover it?

Really, she ought to wear the fruit bowl bonnet that Graham had given her for Christmas. It would serve everyone right and be exactly what they expected of her.

Eugenia left the milliner's establishment completely at a loss, but she did not know what else to do. She did not wish to return home yet, but there was little else she could do. When she went to fetch the carriage from the posting inn, Stevens was sitting on a bench, waiting for her.

"I should have expected you would be waiting here for me."

"Of course, my lady," she said, as though offended.

They called for the carriage and returned to The Grange. Eugenia waved Stevens ahead when they neared Primrose Cottage. "I wish to speak with my brother about the ceremony. I will expect you to wait on me in time to dress for dinner."

Stevens went on to the house, Eugenia preferring to walk.

"Eugenia!" Edmund greeted her in surprise as one of the servants let her into the house and Edmund's study. "What can I do for you?"

"I thought perhaps there might be some questions for the ceremony or...something."

"'Or something,'" Edmund repeated. "What is happening, Eugenia?"

"I have no idea! Someone is keeping secrets from me, and I will go mad if I do not find out what!"

"Who is keeping secrets from you?" He frowned and leaned against his desk.

"If I knew, I would ask him!"

"Start at the beginning."

"I do not know the beginning, but I fear my sisters are plotting something to do with my wedding gown or bonnets."

"Your wedding gown? Why ever would they do such a thing?"

She held up her hands. "All I know is that Stevens confessed there was a surprise, but I could discover nothing! The modiste pretended ignorance, as did the milliner."

"Have you seen your dress?"

"Well, yes. I have just had my final fitting."

"And what of your bonnet?"

"There was none. I asked her to make me one and she behaved as though everything were just as it should be."

"Then perhaps it is." He walked over and took her hands in his. "You are fretting needlessly, though it is quite normal. Most future brides are assailed by nerves."

She pursed her lips and furrowed her brow to consider the question. "No. I am quite sure something secretive is afoot. Has your wife said nothing?" At least Edmund was the one brother who would be completely honest with her. The others would not deliberately lie, but might bend the truth if they thought it necessary.

"Has she said anything about what?" Edmund asked.

Eugenia let out a squeal of frustration. "Not you as well? I am going mad." She paced a circle, then turned back to her brother. "Promise me, if you hear what they are about, you will not let them ruin what I have planned."

"Genie, do you truly think your sisters would ruin your wedding day?"

"Not on purpose," she admitted.

"Then do not fret."

She nibbled her bottom lip. "I expect you are right. Either way, I will be married at the end of it."

"Precisely," he said, pulling her into a hug.

"You would not lie to me?" She pulled back enough to eye him closely.

"I would not," he assured her.

"And there is nothing you need from me?"

"Nothing at all. The wedding ceremony has been the same for centuries."

She sighed and pulled away, turning round to look one last time to make sure he was not hiding a look or a smile, in the way siblings tended to do when they thought they had bested the other. There was absolutely nothing in his gaze or expression to indicate it. *Drat.*

⫸⫷

THE DAY OF the wedding dawned, as all good stories proclaimed. Graham felt like a giddy child, such was his excitement. It had taken the help of a duke and all the extended family to surprise Eugenia. She had become very suspicious—to the point she thought her sisters-in-law were going behind her back with regard her dress and headdress! He laughed. To an extent, they were, but not in the way she imagined. He could not wait to see what she had chosen to wear for their special day. Whatever it was, it would be perfect.

The only information he had gleaned from the modiste was that there were snowflakes and the color was blue. He had promptly ordered from her a waistcoat of the same fabric so that he would match his bride. Hopefully she would not feel betrayed by that.

He looked at his new pocket watch and chuckled again. He would forever treasure it, and perhaps hand it down to their eldest boy. It was half nine, so Eugenia's first gift of the day should be arriving. He had explored the family vaults, where he had found a diamond and sapphire tiara and matching necklace. These he had sent over for her to wear if she wished.

The ceremony was to be held that morning at the village church, conducted by Edmund. Hopefully, the other two surprises would follow without a hitch, but he was leaving early in order to see, despite the duchess having sent a message to assure him that all was well. His parents and sister would join them closer to the time, to save his father's strength.

It was an odd sensation when he entered the church to find it empty. He could not recall ever having done so. The nave was still decorated in the greenery from Christmas, with a few white ribbons along the ends of the pew, but the surprise was perfect. He had asked for spangled snowflakes to be hung from the rafters. Hopefully it was not sacrilege to do so, but Eugenia loved snow and Mother Nature had not seen fit to provide it. He looked up and smiled at the hundred white flakes, softly floating in the morning light, thankful Eugenia had agreed to be his bride.

He was not the most prayerful of man, but he thanked God for Eugenia and that his eyes had been opened before he had missed his chance.

"Welcome to our winter wonderland," Edmund said, approaching from the door behind the altar. "I am rather fond of it. Perhaps we may make it a tradition." He chuckled. "There are certainly worse things to do than marvel at God's creation."

Edmund would see it that way, Graham thought with amusement.

Soon, the villagers and invited guests began to fill the church. It was not large, but no one would want to miss the ceremony. When his family, and the rest of the Knight family, arrived and were shown to their pews at the front of the church, he nearly shouted with anticipation. The duchess gave him a nod before she sat down and he breathed a sigh of relief. The biggest surprise was yet to come.

Miss Hattie took her place at the organ and began to play some hymns. Edmund joined Graham near the altar; he was wearing his vestments and held the book of prayer in his hand. He watched the door at the rear of the aisle, willing it to open faster. Yet still it did not open.

The church bell rang, signaling the hour, and the congregation whispered a bit. Edmund indicated to Miss Hattie she should play another song. A bride being few minutes late was not so very unusual. Perhaps there had been a flounce torn that needed to be repaired, or a problem with the carriage or some such thing. Eugenia would not leave him at the altar. She would have sent a note or at the very least, Knighton would have—would he not?

Two more songs went by, and still Graham smiled. The murmurs and whispers became more prominent and he saw even the Knight and Tinsley clans begin to look worried.

Edmund leaned over. "She was happy when I left her this morning, just before I came to the church."

Graham gave a subtle acknowledgement of the words, although a sinking feeling was beginning in the pit of his stomach. Had he been so mistaken?

"Does Genie know the wedding is today?" the dowager asked too loudly when, at last, the doors at the back of the church were thrown open and the audience seemed to hold its breath, waiting to see if there was to be some announcement.

Instead, Eugenia appeared on the threshold, looking like a fairy princess, on the arms of her brother.

"Forgive me, there was a slight mishap with my bonnet." As she was not wearing a bonnet but instead the tiara he had sent, he could only begin to guess at what could have occurred. She smiled brightly, as though nothing had happened, and he no longer cared. The congregation seemed collectively to breathe a sigh of relief at the same time.

Edmund signaled to Hattie to play again. Knighton and Eugenia began their walk down the aisle. She looked up and saw the snowflakes and her expression of pure joy made everything worth it.

There was something magical about the occasion and he knew how lucky he was to be marrying for reasons beyond connections and fortune.

The duke placed Eugenia's hand in his and looked at Graham. "I could not be more pleased that you chose each other." Then he leaned over and kissed his sister on the cheek before taking his seat next to his duchess.

Graham squeezed Eugenia's hand as she stepped near him. "I am sorry."

"Everything is well?" he asked.

"You would not believe it if I told you. Thank you for the beautiful gifts."

"I wanted today to be perfect for you," he answered.

"Shall we begin?" Edmund asked, looking very amused.

"Oh, yes, of course!" Eugenia said, smiling brilliantly at her brother.

Graham heard the words which had been spoken for ages, and of course, they now held new meaning since their significance finally applied to him. He could not help but watch Eugenia in her bright blue gown that was covered in snowflakes and sparkled in the light from the windows and the candles around the chapel. He could not imagine any other lady of his acquaintance wearing such a garment, but for her, it was perfect. Her own light was shining brightly that day and it felt perfect when they both spoke their vows to love, honor, and cherish. He did not think that would be a hardship for either of them.

They partook of Holy Communion and Edmund prayed over them before they signed the register, then were pronounced man and wife.

Graham looked at Eugenia, who sparkled without the help of any jewelry, or her magnificent gown. This was right and felt blessed by God.

They passed back down the small aisle of the church, greeting everyone as they went. When they reached the outer door, he stole a quick kiss before wrapping her in a fur-lined cloak. They stepped outside and Eugenia gasped.

"It is snowing!" She turned her face up to catch some large flakes and laughed with joy. "Could anything have made this day more perfect?"

Graham could think of quite a few things, but he only smiled at his beautiful wife.

"Not that I did not love the snowflakes in the church and your waistcoat. I truly do not deserve you, but selfishly, I am glad you are shackled to me."

The carriage, which had been decorated with ribbons and flowers, pulled up in front of them and they walked towards it, being showered with seed from the villagers who had not been inside the church.

As they reached the carriage, they tossed coins back to the crowd, as was tradition, and waved as they climbed inside and pulled away.

He seated himself beside her as they drove back to The Grange for the wedding breakfast, and pulled her into his arms.

"Will you tell me now why you were late?" he asked while nuzzling her ear.

"It had to do with my headdress. I know that is difficult to imagine."

"You did not want to wear the parure I sent?"

"I did not have it at first. Barnes became distracted and forgot to send it up to my chambers."

It had not occurred to Graham that he should have delivered it himself to one of the brothers. "Go on."

"I had the milliner make me a pretty little head-piece of lace, spangles and blue ribbon. However, as Rowley and I were climbing into the coach, a bird flew overhead..."

Graham laughed. It could only happen to Eugenia. "Perhaps you should start a new trend, where ladies don't wear bonnets."

"Perhaps. Thankfully, the... excrement... was only on the head-piece, and Barnes remembered you had sent over the box of jewels. Stevens had not yet left for the church and was able to exchange the ruined headdress for your tiara."

Graham was shaking with laughter.

She hit him affectionately.

"You must admit your head-pieces are quite the disaster. I am only sorry I did not witness this one."

"There will be plenty of time for you to enjoy all my mishaps," she assured him, "but we have only a few minutes before we reach the house." Suggestively, she raised her eyebrows at him. She had never quite mastered the knack of raising a single eyebrow like the other Knights.

"Why, Mrs. Tinsley, are you suggesting I compromise you?"

"I am wholly, completely yours to do with as you wish."

"Then I am happy to oblige you, ma'am."

# EPILOGUE

E UGENIA FELT AS though she was floating on air. She had thought this day was going to be a disaster, but Graham had showered her with gifts, thus saving the infelicity of her bird encounter. Then he had decorated the church with snowflakes so she would have her wish and then they had stepped outside to be greeted by real snow. Even that was not the end of it. When they arrived at The Grange for the wedding breakfast, and entered the ballroom, the sight before her surpassed all expectation. Graham had ice sculptures of Tower animals placed around the room, and had somehow convinced Gunter's to come all the way to Devonshire to make ices.

"I cannot believe this!" she exclaimed. "It cannot be possible that one person could be so happy."

"That is all I had hoped for."

"Graham, I do not deserve you," she whispered, trying not to cry.

"Now, now, tears are not to be borne," he protested gently. "Not today."

"This is happiness, I assure you."

"I intend to make that condition my highest priority for the rest of our lives."

"You have certainly made a splendid beginning," she said as he led her to the display of ices and she chose the vanilla cream. "This one has always made me think of fresh snow." Her lips slid the taste of heaven from the dainty silver spoon and it melted on her tongue.

"I cannot take credit for the snow," he quipped.

Rowley entered the ballroom with Granny on his arm and led her to a chair. Eugenia turned to the waiter and asked for another serving. Before Graham could tease her, she spoke. "It is my wedding day. I shall have as many ices as I like, but Granny enjoys them as much, if not more, than I do."

She took the dish and spoon and sat next to the dowager.

That lady's eyes lit up when she saw what it was. "If I were a few years younger, I would have fought my granddaughter for you," she said, looking up at Graham, who had followed Eugenia over there. He bowed before her grandmother and kissed the back of her hand.

"I always did enjoy a proper rogue," she announced appreciatively.

"I hear they make excellent husbands," he said, eyeing Eugenia with a heated look.

Her grandmother cackled. "I hope you took my advice and spent some time at the farm," she whispered loudly to Eugenia. There was a sound of sputtering behind her as Graham almost choked on his spoonful of ice.

"Yes, Granny," she managed to say with a mostly straight face, though she was certain her eyes were laughing.

When she finished her ice, Graham took the dish from her hands and set it on a passing waiter's tray. "I beg your pardon, Your Grace," he said to the dowager, "but I do believe I would like to dance with my wife."

"I hope you have improved your steps, Genie," she said with a shooing motion.

Once they were out on the dance floor and Graham had pulled her into his arms, she allowed herself to laugh.

"Did you?" Graham asked.

"Did I what?" she asked innocently, though she had a sneaking suspicion she knew what he meant.

"Spend time at the farm," he said into her ear. She had no doubt that her face was bright red.

"I cannot believe she said that."

"Can you not?" He looked at her with disbelief. "It is precisely what I would have expected from her."

Eugenia chuckled. "She is precisely what I aspire to be in my old age."

"You have already made an excellent start," he said affectionately. "I only hope that you will simply be the viscountess and I the viscount in our old age. I want to experience it with you."

She looked up into his eyes, seeing the truth in those green depths and hoping she would never do anything to change that look.

"I love you, Eugenia," he said, more serious than she had ever seen him.

"I know," she replied, and she did. "I love you too, and not just in the brotherly way," she added for good measure.

He laughed and twirled her into a spin. It seemed impossible that she could be so happy. She saw her brothers join them, with their wives, on the dance floor and the five couples waltzed arm in arm with their loves. It was the dawn of a new day for the Knight family. Everything would be different now, but somehow it was as it ought to be. Rowley with Emma, Heath with Cecilia, Edmund with Isabella, Felix with Catalina and now she had Graham. Soon there would be many more Knight descendants, she thought to herself as she saw Granny holding George and looking at him in complete adoration.

"What are you thinking, pet?"

"I never knew this kind of happiness was possible."

"Sometimes it takes realizing what you have lost in order to value having a second chance."

"Are you referring to me?"

"To both of us, really, although I knew before you did, I think."

"I think not," she argued. "I did not believe you could truly be happy with me. I saw how the other ladies wanted you and wondered why you would choose me."

"I finally realized you believed that. 'Twas why I began sending you all those gifts. I was cognizant of your attractions a long time ago… in fact, at this very ball a couple of years ago," he said smugly.

"The night you first returned from Vienna?"

"The very one; and I was dismayed to know I wanted you."

She missed her footing in the dance, but scarcely noticed. "You never so much as hinted."

"Because we were more than just attraction."

"Yes." He was right. "Everything that has happened was for a reason—to bring us to this."

"Now, my love, everyone else may see your light shine like I do, but you are mine."

He spun her around again and she wanted to squeal to the world of her good fortune.

"Graham? I believe I am ready to visit the farm now."

He threw back his head and laughed.

# About the Author

Like many writers, Elizabeth Johns was first an avid reader, though she was a reluctant convert. It was Jane Austen's clever wit and unique turn of phrase that hooked Johns when she was "forced" to read Pride and Prejudice for a school assignment. She began writing when she ran out of her favorite author's books and decided to try her hand at crafting a Regency romance novel. Her journey into publishing began with the release of Surrender the Past, book one of the Loring-Abbott Series. Johns makes no pretensions to Austen's wit but hopes readers will perhaps laugh and find some enjoyment in her writing.

Johns attributes much of her inspiration to her mother, a former English teacher. During their last summer together, Johns would sit on the porch swing and read her stories to her mother, who encouraged her to continue writing. Busy with multiple careers, including a professional job in the medical field, author and mother of two children, Johns squeezes in time for reading whenever possible.

Made in the USA
Coppell, TX
07 April 2021